LINE OF DUTY

What Reviewers Say About VK Powell's Work

Second in Command

"I love the family at the centre of the Fairview Station series, and their various careers in and around law enforcement and other public service professions. …I greatly enjoyed the scenes involving the whole Carlyle family and was cheered to see various of the more peripheral members find their own place in the scheme of things."
—*The Good, the Bad and the Unread*

Incognito

"[F]ast paced, action packed and keeps you glued to the page."
—*Lesbian Reading Room*

"*Incognito* by V.K. Powell is the kind of intrigue/thriller novel that I enjoy. …If you enjoy a good mystery with interesting characters and a bit of romance, then try this book."—*Rainbow Reflections*

"Well written main characters with plenty of chemistry. A good supporting cast as well that provide some good laughs and emotional feels. A fun read with enough action and romance to keep you interested."—Kat Adams, Bookseller (QBD Books, Australia)

"The strongest part of the book was the interplay between leads. …Both women learned to keep people at arms' length, Frankie with her abilities to become almost anyone, and Evan with her almost obsessive need for rules and order. They clash, because Frankie's often mischievous behavior is so out of what Evan thinks she needs. But they are attracted to each other, and it does blow up their world view a bit."—Colleen Corgel, Librarian, Queens Borough Public Library

"If you're in the mood for a fast paced romantic intrigue novel with action, romance and humour, this might be one for you."—*C-Spot Reviews*

"[T]his book is exciting and fast-paced and the chemistry between the two main characters is great."—*Jude in the Stars*

Take Your Time

"The last book in the Pine Cone Romance series was excellent, and I reckon VK Powell wrote the perfect book to round up the series. …If these are the sex scenes VK Powell can write, then I have been missing out and I will definitely be checking out more because WOW! All in all…Fantastic! 5 stars"—*Les Reveur*

Captain's Choice

"VK Powell is the mistress of police romances and this one is another classic 'will she won't she' story of lost loves reunited by chance. Well written, lots of great sex and excellent sexual tension, great character building and use of the setting, this was a thoroughly enjoyable read."—*Lesbian Reading Room*

Deception

"In *Deception* VK Powell takes some difficult social issues and portrays them with intelligence and empathy. …Well-written, enjoyable storyline, excellent use of location to add colour to the background, and extremely well drawn characters. VK Powell has created a great sense of life on the streets in an excellent crime/mystery with a turbulent but charming romance."—*Lesbian Reading Room*

Side Effects

"[A] touching contemporary tale of two wounded souls hoping to find lasting love and redemption together. …Powell ably plots a plausible and suspenseful story, leading readers to fall in love with the characters she's created."—*Publishers Weekly*

About Face

"Powell excels at depicting complex, emotionally vulnerable characters who connect in a believable fashion and enjoy some genuinely hot erotic moments."—*Publishers Weekly*

Exit Wounds

"Powell's prose is no-nonsense and all business. It gets in and gets the job done, a few well-placed phrases sparkling in your memory and some trenchant observations about life in general and a cop's life in particular sticking to your psyche long after they've gone. After five books, Powell knows what her audience wants, and she delivers those goods with solid assurance. But be careful you don't get hooked. You only get six hits, then the supply's gone, and you'll be jonesin' for the next installment. It never pays to be at the mercy of a cop."—*Out in Print*

"Fascinating and complicated characters materialize, morph, and sometimes disappear testing the passionate yet nascent love of the book's focal pair. I was so totally glued to and amazed by the intricate layers that continued to materialize like an active volcano…dangerous and deadly until the last mystery is revealed. This book goes into my super special category. Please don't miss it."—*Rainbow Book Reviews*

Justifiable Risk

"This story takes some unusual twists and at one point, I was convinced that I knew 'who did it' only to find out that I was wrong. VK Powell knows crime drama, she kept me guessing until the end, and I was not disappointed at the outcome. And that's not to slight VK Powell's knack for romance. …Readers who appreciate mysteries with a touch of drama and intense erotic moments will enjoy *Justifiable Risk*."—*Queer Magazine*

"*Justifiable Risk* is an exciting, seat of your pants read. It also has some very hot sex scenes. Powell really shines, however, in showing the inner growth of Greer and Eva as they each deal with their personal issues. This is a very strong, multifaceted book. —*Just About Write*

Fever

"VK Powell has given her fans an exciting read. The plot of *Fever* is filled with twists, turns, and 'seat of your pants' danger…*Fever* gives readers both great characters and erotic scenes along with insight into life in the African bush."—*Just About Write*

Suspect Passions

"From the first chapter of *Suspect Passions* Powell builds erotic scenes which sear the page. She definitely takes her readers for a walk on the wild side! Her characters, however, are also women we care about. They are bright, witty, and strong. The combination of great sex and great characters make *Suspect Passions* a must read."—*Just About Write*

To Protect and Serve

"If you like cop novels, or even television cop shows with women as full partners with male officers…this is the book for you. It's got drama, excitement, conflict, and even some fairly hot lesbian sex. The writer is a retired cop, so she really writes from a place of authenticity. As a result, you have a realistic quality to the writing that puts me in mind of early Joseph Wambaugh."—Teresa DeCrescenzo, *Lesbian News*

"*To Protect and Serve* drew me in from the very first page with characters that captivated in their complexity. Powell writes with authority using the lingo and capturing the thoughts of the law enforcers who make the ultimate sacrifice in the fight against crime. What's more impressive is the command this debut author has of portraying a full gamut of emotion, from angst to elation, through dialogue and narrative. The images are vivid, the action is believable, and the police procedurals are authentic…VK Powell had me invested in the story of these women, heart, mind, body and soul. Along with danger and tension, Powell's well-developed erotic scenes sizzle and sate."—*Story Circle Book Reviews*

"*To Protect and Serve* drew me in from the very first page with characters that captivated in their complexity. Powell writes with authority using the lingo and capturing the thoughts of the law enforcers who make the ultimate sacrifice in the fight against crime."—*Just About Write*

Visit us at www.boldstrokesbooks.com

By the Author

To Protect and Serve

Suspect Passions

Fever

Justifiable Risk

Haunting Whispers

Exit Wounds

About Face

Side Effects

Deception

Lone Ranger

Take Your Time

Incognito

Fairview Station Series

Captain's Choice

Second in Command

Line of Duty

LINE OF DUTY

by

VK Powell

2019

LINE OF DUTY
© 2019 By VK Powell. All Rights Reserved.

ISBN 13: 978-1-63555-486-1

This Trade Paperback Original Is Published By
Bold Strokes Books, Inc.
P.O. Box 249
Valley Falls, NY 12185

First Edition: December 2019

Credits
Editor: Cindy Cresap
Production Design: Susan Ramundo
Cover Design By Sheri (hindsightgraphics@gmail.com)

Acknowledgments

First, to Len Barot, Sandy Lowe, and all the talented and insightful folks at Bold Strokes Books, thank you for allowing me to transform my law enforcement experiences into stories of survival, the struggle to balance love and livelihood, and the fight between good and evil. I am grateful for the opportunity and for the guidance you continually provide through each project.

Cindy Cresap, many thanks for your time and attention on this project. Your fresh perspective and insights were invaluable. The steady doses of humor didn't hurt either. Hopefully, I learn something new with each book.

To my beta readers—D. Jackson Leigh, Jenny Harmon, and Mary Margret Daughtridge—you guys are the best. This book is better for your efforts, and I am truly grateful.

And last, but never least, to all the readers who support and encourage my writing, thank you for buying my books, sending emails, giving shout-outs on social media, and showing up for events. Let's keep doing this.

CHAPTER ONE

Dylan Carlyle rubbed the conducting gel on the smooth face of the defibrillator paddles and waited for the words that would propel her to action. The brown-and-black checked curtains surrounding the ER treatment bay billowed with the team's swift movements and seemed to close around Dylan as she focused.

"Charged, Doctor," the nurse said.

"Everybody clear." She placed the paddles against the patient's chest, pressed the buttons to release the charge, and stepped back before checking the monitor. Nothing.

"Still flatlining."

"Charge to three hundred." She wasn't ready to let this soul slip away. Every patient whose eyes drained of life and clouded over represented a personal failure. She leaned close to the man's ear. "You will *not* die on my watch."

"Charged," the nurse called again.

"Clear." Dylan repeated the process and stepped away. Everyone automatically turned to the wall-mounted monitor and held a silent, collective breath.

"We've got sinus rhythm."

The monitor readings leveled, and Dylan flipped her stethoscope from around her neck and listened to the patient's heartbeat, finally convinced he'd stabilized. She breathed a grateful sigh and nodded to the others huddled around the gurney. "Good job, guys. Get the meds on board and monitor him closely. Let me know of any changes. I'll be on all night." She slid her stethoscope in her pocket and shucked off her green mask, matching gown, and gloves. Dylan pulled back the flimsy curtain that separated treatment areas and walked toward the semicircular nurses' station. "What's next?"

Holly Burns, charge nurse on night shift, gave her an appreciative nod as she approached. "Nice work in there, Doctor."

"Teamwork," Dylan replied.

"We're good for the moment." Holly's sharp focus put some folks off, but Dylan looked deeper into her friend's eyes and saw genuine concern.

"Anybody need relief?"

"I said, we're good." Holly checked her tablet and moved to Dylan's side of the station. "Come with me."

"Something urgent?" Dylan's adrenaline spiked as the possibilities flashed through her mind—gunshot wound, multiple-injury car accident, drug overdose. She hurried to keep up with Holly's longer strides and grinned at the way her pace made the Disney characters on her scrub bottoms dance.

"Yes, definitely urgent." Holly guided Dylan into a linen closet full of supplies, cleaning equipment, and staff coats hanging haphazardly on anything that supported their weight.

"Nurse Burns, I had no idea you were still interested." Dylan winked when the door closed behind them.

"Cut it out, Dylan. That ship sailed and eventually sank. Thank goodness we salvaged a friendship, but don't press your luck."

"That's one of the things I've always admired about you, Holly. No BS, straight to the point." Holly gave her a skeptical look, and Dylan added, "No, seriously." She held her arms out. "Bring it in." When they hugged, Holly relaxed. "You okay? You seem tense."

Holly squeezed her around the waist before stepping back. "Yeah, herding cats tonight. Must be a full moon. If it weren't for egotistical doctors, my job would actually be enjoyable."

"Ouch. You're the best ER nurse we've got, so don't let the bastards see you sweat. So…what's so important that you dragged me into the make-out closet in view of the staff? How can I help?"

"I'm glad you asked. As your friend, only I can say this to you, Dylan. You're tired and in danger of making mistakes. Go to the on-call room and get a few hours' sleep. I'll text you if anything breaks."

"But—"

"But nothing. It's my job to see the ER runs smoothly during my shift, and you're not only exhausted but you're boxing the interns and residents out of some great training opportunities. No arguments. Listen to your elder. Go."

"Come on, Holly. You know I hate being idle."

"Then act like a real doctor and find a nurse to grope." Holly grinned.

"You cured me of that." Holly had saved her in many ways—taught the junior doctor how to ingratiate herself with the nursing staff, pointed out shortcuts on the never-ending forms, showed her secret places to escape for a few minutes of alone time, and most importantly emphasized how not to become an arrogant know-it-all doctor. Dylan had also learned the pros and cons of sleeping with coworkers under Holly's gentle tutelage and decided against it.

"How about a nice police officer. They come and go through here like *The Bachelorette*. Surely one of them can rise to your high standards. Officer Masters just came in with an overdose. She's still in the building somewhere."

"And probably wrist deep in one of your nurses by now." The image of Finley Masters, who she knew only by sight and reputation, sauntering in earlier returned. She was arrogant, confident, and handsome wrapped in a black uniform, everything that sent Dylan running in the opposite direction.

Holly feigned shock. "Are you saying I don't run a tight ship, Dr. Carlyle?"

"Not at all. But in keeping with your nautical theme, Finley Masters could slide through the smallest crack in your tightly run ship and engage a nurse before you knew she was on board. You *have* heard the rumors?" Dylan leaned against a shelf stacked high with clean green scrubs.

"You know better than to listen to hospital gossip, Dylan. It's as reliable as a match in a windstorm. Besides, everybody has a private side. Doctors, nurses, and cops see the worst of humanity. Many of us end up together because we understand the need to compartmentalize our feelings and escape. I bet Officer Masters has a sensitive underbelly."

"Right, and I'm a brain surgeon. And just FYI, all that evil we see also makes us more susceptible to revolving door affairs and divorce. Jazz told me about the speech they give rookies the first week of the academy. 'Don't get divorced, married, engaged, or otherwise alter your status during this training process because your life is going to change drastically.' Really, Holly, who says that to new employees?"

"Well—"

"And *then* they teach them to be macho assholes who think they're God's gift to women, bulletproof, and can walk on water."

"You mean like doctors?" Holly raised her palms. "I give up. I just don't get your aversion to dating cops. You come from a family of police officers."

"And stop." Her tone was harsher than she'd intended, but Holly knew exactly why Dylan didn't date cops. Aside from the constant specter of death hovering on every call, they were notorious womanizers and cheats. Cops weren't unique in that respect, but they puffed their chests out farther and bragged about it more. Regardless, she wasn't interested. She just wanted to be the best doctor she could be and spend time with her family. End of story.

"You've just proven my point. You're never this negative and prickly unless you're tired, upset, or horny. Do you even remember the last time you had a date, much less sex? Just think about it." Holly separated the ear tubes of Dylan's stethoscope, placed the tips in her ears, and whispered into the diaphragm. "Go. Rest."

"Really cute," Dylan said and started to object again, but Holly raised her hand.

"I know you love your job, and you're good at it, but even super doctors need a break. Please, don't argue or you'll be having our pizza and movie nights alone forever."

"Fine. You know how to hurt a girl." Dylan couldn't imagine not having their bi-monthly snuggle-in-your-comfies-and-watch-chick-flick sessions. They were her only real social outlet since residency ended and her new job at Cone Hospital began. Serious dating, forget about it—no time, no interest, but more importantly, no prospects except an overabundance of cops and coworkers, both absolute no-nos, and in that order. She hadn't considered a fling. It wasn't really her style, but maybe a good old-fashioned sexcapade was exactly what she needed. "I'll be in the on-call room, sulking, if you want me."

Holly kissed Dylan on the cheek, opened the door, and waved her out. "See you later for breakfast."

Dylan pulled her phone from the pocket of her scrubs, tucked the earbuds in, and queued up a classical playlist to distract her from the hectic first half of her shift and being dismissed by Holly. Winding her way through the deserted beige hospital halls, Dylan waved her hands to the sensual textures of Debussy's "Clair de Lune," the ocean-like swells and tumbling waves of music that always brought lightheartedness. Part two of the song picked up tempo, and Dylan followed.

As the climactic moment of the piece peaked and then paused, Dylan pushed open the door of the on-call room and stopped at the sight of a bare ass pumping rhythmically against a woman bent over a chair. Uniform police pants pooled around the standing person's ankles, the shirt flapping open with every movement, and the nurse's navy skirt bunched around her waist. With each thrust, the pumper's muscles tightened, emphasizing a shapely backside. Light blond hair turned darker with sweat at the standing person's nape, and Dylan smelled their mingled sex. These two were brazen. They hadn't even locked the door.

She leaned against the doorjamb, pulled her earbuds out, and studied the scene. She wasn't a voyeur, but she could certainly appreciate a pleasing human form. Male or female pumper was unclear, but the butt cheeks were extremely smooth and hairless. Female then. But the force with which he/she pumped the nurse exhibited dominance and control. So, male. She hated to interrupt but decorum required it, and the male/female question had gotten the better of her. She cleared her throat.

The pumper finally glanced over her shoulder. Finley Masters. She raised her forefinger and gave a final powerful thrust that elicited a muffled scream from the other woman. Finley leaned over the moaning nurse and kissed her. "Thanks, babe. Better get dressed. We have company." She turned toward Dylan exposing her naked front with no hint of shyness. A silver chain with some type of medallion dangled between small breasts as she reached for her pants.

Every naked inch of Finley—broad shoulders, ripped abs, and a hollow that dipped to the triangle of dark blond hair between her legs—highlighted why nurses and doctors alike buzzed about her. She was certainly mouthwatering. Dylan flushed at the thought and forced it away. This type of unprofessional behavior gave cops and nurses a bad rap.

"Sorry about that." But the grin Finley gave Dylan said she wasn't really. She actually looked proud of being caught. "We'll be out of your way in a jiff." Finley turned back to her partner and spread her shirt to block Dylan's view while the nurse retrieved her panties and straightened her clothes.

Finley's chivalry was unexpected but didn't make up for her lack of propriety or professionalism. And Holly wondered why she didn't date cops. Decision confirmed, again. So why was she so warm and wobbly-legged? Maybe she did need a friend with benefits to occasionally take the edge off.

The nurse buttoned her white blouse and smoothed her skirt before turning toward Dylan. "I'm so sorry, Doctor. I'm not on shift yet, but please don't tell Holly about this or I'll be out of a job."

When she looked up, Dylan recognized the nurse as one of the more sociable of the staff, putting it kindly. "Anita, isn't that right?"

"Yes, ma'am, Anita Groome."

Dylan choked back a chuckle but kept her tone even. "Why don't you change and get on the floor. It's pretty busy tonight." Anita probably wasn't the first to be caught in a compromising position with Finley Masters.

"Thanks, Dylan," Anita said.

Dylan backed into the hallway and headed toward the locker room. She had no interest in being alone with Finley Masters, especially after seeing her naked. What could follow a show like that? So much for taking a nap. She needed a cold shower.

❖

Finley slung her gun belt over her shoulder, buttoned her shirt, and hurried after Dylan. "Wait. Please." How would she talk her way out of this? Her job was to clean up other people's messes, not create more. She tucked her shirt into her trousers and zipped them as she walked. "I'm Finley Masters." She offered her hand, the one she'd used on Anita. Dylan must've realized it too because she gave her an incredulous stare and shook her head. "We haven't met."

"I've seen you naked. Some would say that qualifies," Dylan said.

"Then shouldn't you reciprocate? I mean the introduction, not the naked part. You're the new ER doctor, right? Anita called you Dylan."

"I don't think we speak the same language."

"Wow, you don't even know me yet."

"If what I just saw is any indication, I know your type."

The comment hurt more than it should, but after what Dylan had seen, Finley couldn't blame her. *Damn, damnity damn.* She'd wanted to meet the new ER doc because she'd heard how gorgeous and feisty she was, but why did it happen when she had her fingers inside another woman? "Okay, well, that wasn't the way I'd hoped to introduce myself." Dylan finally stopped, and the gaze from her dark brown eyes burned a fiery path down Finley's body.

"The rumors finally got one thing right," Dylan said. "You're handsome in that wavy blond hair, blue eyes, and olive complexion clichéd type of way. Some of the nurses call you drool-worthy."

"And you, Doctor?" Finley clicked her utility belt around her waist without breaking eye contact with Dylan. "Do you think I'm drool-worthy?" Dylan's shapely lips curved into a partial smile, and Finley wanted to make it blossom.

"If you're into that." Finley's pulse quickened until Dylan added, "Which I'm not."

"That smarts." This was new territory for her, a woman immune to her charms. She nodded back the way they'd come. "You obviously don't think much of me right now, which I totally get, but please don't be too hard on Anita. It was my fault entirely, the on-call room…and everything else."

"Very decent of you, Officer. You could just blame your awesome charisma."

Were they flirting? Finley stood a little straighter. Felt like flirting with a twist. She hitched her thumbs in her utility belt and grinned. "I'm flattered you think so."

"Obviously my sarcasm was too subtle. I find you reckless and irresponsible. Charming, not so much. Irresistible, definitely not."

So, maybe not flirting but something about the way Dylan looked at her made Finley want to believe it could be. "Message received, loud and clear. I know it's not an excuse, but I'd just broken up a fight and brought in an overdose. Quite a night of ups and downs. I was a little keyed up. Doctors get that feeling too, right?"

"That's some schedule-one bullshit." Dylan shook her head. "I'm familiar with the effects of adrenaline on the body. The difference between us, Officer Masters, is I have self-respect and impulse control. The next time your libido kicks in, please take care of it outside the hospital. Our nurses' jobs don't include servicing the police force."

"Thanks for the advice." Finley licked her fingers, purposely the *same* fingers, and brushed them through her hair. Dylan's gaze never left her hand. Her pupils widened and her nostrils flared. Dylan might find her reckless and irresponsible, but she was also intrigued, which was a good thing because Finley definitely was. She struggled for something else to keep Dylan engaged, but she ducked into the locker rooms, and following her was another violation Finley probably shouldn't commit right now.

She drove home thinking about Dylan. Out of Finley's league, accomplished, and problematic. Dylan's semi-flirty banter, fearlessness, long chestnut hair, and gorgeous petite package titillated Finley but also spelled trouble. She should leave well enough alone and stick with what worked for her—being a good cop, making detective someday, and enjoying willing, uncomplicated partners. She'd seen what love and complex women did to a person and wanted no part of it.

She pulled in the driveway of her College Hills bungalow, glanced at the wide front porch, pulled her cell from her pocket, and hit speed dial. She couldn't deal with the memories this place held tonight. "Hey, Anita, interested in another round when you get off work?"

CHAPTER TWO

Finley woke the next morning in a pale pink bedroom with Anita's arms and legs draped across her. She tried to inch out of Anita's grasp, but she hugged harder. Finley gave her a quick kiss and then worked her way loose. As she stood, she thought about the new doctor she'd met last night, felt a tingle of arousal, and glanced over at Anita. Excitement changed to embarrassment and then shame. Not good to think about the next woman while she was still with the last. "Have to go. There's a kids' thing at the station. Can't be late."

"It's your day off and you hate kids."

"I don't hate them. I just never know what to do with them, except Robin."

"Who's Robin?" Anita asked sleepily.

"Never mind. I promised my lieutenant I'd help set up and take down the tents. Brownie points." She scooped her jeans and T-shirt off the floor on the way to the bathroom to brush her teeth. "Thanks for letting me drop by so late."

"Once more for the road? I never get enough of you, Fin." Anita grabbed for her as she came out of the bathroom and passed the bed, but Finley sidestepped.

She stopped at the bedroom door. She'd seen Anita three times this week and had a toothbrush in her bathroom, so a reminder couldn't hurt. "Babe, you know—"

"Yes, I know this is casual. At some point one of us is going to meet someone we really care about, but let's enjoy this while it lasts." She blew Finley an air kiss and rolled back over.

Finley checked her watch on the drive home, just enough time for a quick shower and to change into her uniform before heading to Fairview Station. When she pulled into the driveway of her gray bungalow, her Realtor was waiting out front. She'd completely forgotten Sharon's walk-through to give her an idea of a price range for the listing. "Good morning. Sorry I kept you waiting."

Sharon MacMillan, perfectly coiffed salt-and-pepper bob and blue eyes adorned with mascara and shadow, smiled her top-selling-agent smile. "I just pulled up, so your timing is perfect. Hope you don't mind the early morning appointment."

"Not at all. I was—"

"Working all night." She glanced at Finley's wrinkled clothes. "Anybody I know?" Sharon laughed. "My wife says we should buy this place for the sexual karma alone."

"In case you haven't noticed, fun doesn't happen here or hasn't in a long time."

Sharon placed a hand lightly on Finley's arm. "I'm sorry, Fin. Not enough coffee this morning. I know your dad passed recently. I didn't mean to bring up bad memories."

Her father's sad and lonely life had created the unpleasant memories that clung to the house long before his death. "No problem. Thanks for doing this for me. Shall we?" She waved Sharon toward the front porch and unlocked the door. "Why don't you look around while I change clothes. I've got work in about an hour."

While she showered, Finley wondered if she was doing the right thing. On the one hand, the house was paid for, but every room bled sadness and sucked the energy from her. She went to sleep with the echoes of her father's weeping, knowing she couldn't make it better. She woke to his heartfelt apologies, certain she'd never be enough to make up for his loss. Nothing about this house brought her peace or happiness so she stayed away working extra shifts and taking off-duty assignments, and she never brought women here.

She rejoined Sharon at the kitchen counter where she was flipping through paperwork and tapping on her tablet. "This is a great house, Fin. It appears structurally sound, the roof is good, and the HVAC is fairly new. The upgrades you've made to the kitchen and baths will also support a higher sale price." Sharon glanced toward her. "Are you sure about this?"

Finley nodded.

"It's only been six months since your dad passed. There's no rush as far as the sale goes. If you need more time to—"

"I don't. The house is in a good location and it's paid for, but the sooner it sells, the sooner I can find something that works for me. I've done the pros and cons, Sharon. I'm just tired of coming home to reruns of a childhood I'd rather forget."

"As long as you're sure, I'll stop trying to talk myself out of a commission." She turned her tablet toward Finley. "I'm thinking this range. You decide and let me know."

"Let's start at the high end."

"I like it. We get negotiating room at that price point. I have the contract, if you're ready to sign."

Finley slid Sharon's tablet toward her and stared at the blank line for her signature. It was a no-brainer—financial security or peace of mind.

"It's show ready," Sharon said. "All I have to do is open the door and let the clients walk through. Makes my job easy." She stood and gave Finley a quick kiss on the cheek. "Come by for dinner soon? We'd love to catch up. Casey and I live vicariously through your conquests of the Greensboro female population."

"And how is that gorgeous wife of yours? If she gets tired of you, send her my way."

"Down, girl. We're trying to get pregnant."

Finley flinched at the comment. Her playgirl persona worked so well that even her friends were sometimes wary of her intentions. "You know I'm kidding, right?"

"Of course. If I didn't, we wouldn't be friends." Sharon started toward the front door. "And I'm serious about dinner."

"Sounds great. Good luck with the pregnancy. Let me know when you get an offer on the house, any offer. I won't give the place away, but I'm a motivated seller. Thanks again."

"My pleasure, Fin. I'll put the sign up on my way out."

No matter how softly Finley closed the solid oak front door, she was always reminded of that hard slam years ago, the day her father broke and she stopped being a child. Had her parents ever been truly happy here? Could she be with someone she loved?

She leaned against the door, the rough grain uneven and biting, like her time here. She fingered the heavy silver chain around her neck, opened the platinum locket her father had left her, and stared at the laser photo of her parents inside. They smiled at each other like two people deeply in love. How much of their lives had been a lie? Had Finley somehow destroyed their happiness? She snapped the locket closed, grabbed her backpack, and headed to her Jeep.

She distracted herself from the hard questions as she drove by reliving last night—the softness of another woman, the smell and taste of her, the screams that Finley coaxed from her body—and breathed a little easier. The blessed diversion of sex, equaled only by the adrenaline-fueled challenges of the job. Work and easy liaisons kept her sane, not her home. All that remained there were ghosts and hard lessons.

❖

Dylan pulled earbuds from her nightstand and queued some soft jazz on her phone to wake up and ease her into the morning. Music was for her both sedative and stimulant. Although it didn't satisfy the physical needs of her body, it took her mind off of them temporarily. And she really needed a distraction after her restless sleep. She'd tossed all night with images of Finley Masters's naked body taunting her. Holly's advice and her own consideration of a fling hadn't helped either. If she was keeping it real, Finley was definitely a vivid-dreams woman, and Dylan was attracted to her physically, but not to her reckless, womanizing reputation.

Something else about her encounter with Finley intrigued Dylan as much as her physique. She'd seen discomfort in Finley's eyes when she'd requested Dylan go easy on Anita, almost like the asking was difficult. Or maybe Dylan had just imagined the whole thing. "Stop it. I refuse to think about that woman." She threw off the covers and started to get up, but jerked back. Her sister Bennett towered beside the bed, mouthing words she couldn't hear. Earbuds. She pulled them out. "Can you say heart attack?"

"I've been knocking. I could've been a burglar."

"Burglars don't knock. You're a police captain. You should know that."

Bennett swiped a hand through her short brown hair and then pointed at Dylan. "And I find you talking to yourself. I was about to call the psych ward. What woman?"

"Bad dream." She grabbed her favorite teal terrycloth robe and headed to the kitchen before Bennett saw her face and guessed she was holding back. "I need coffee."

Bennett's long strides caught up to her quickly. "You need to get dressed. We're late. Jazz and Emory are already at the station, and the rest of the family is waiting for us out front."

"Oh crap. I forgot. The children's festival. Some of the nurses are providing general health advice to parents. How could I forget?" The event was a big deal for the department, Fairview Station, and for Ben's and Jazz's careers. They needed to establish the flagship station as a go-to venue for community gatherings, and the festival was the premiere event. She'd promised to be there for moral support along with the rest of the family.

Bennett stopped her from reaching for a coffee cup and steered her toward the bathroom. "We'll have coffee at the station. Clothes. Now. And don't think I'll forget the woman part of this conversation."

"There is no woman and no conversation." While she pulled on jeans and a pale-yellow blouse, Dylan rehearsed explaining to the older, more experienced version of herself that she wasn't thinking about a woman she couldn't stop thinking about. The explanation was simple. Hormones. She hadn't had sex in months, so seeing two women together caused a chemical reaction in her body that needed attention. She brushed her hair, checked out her attire in the mirror, and then rushed past Bennett out the door.

G-ma, Mama, and Stephanie, Simon's wife, waited in front of the house in the Ma Rolls van, and Dylan headed over to speak with them, but Bennett nudged her from behind. Dylan barely had time to wave to Simon and the twins, Ryan and Riley, sitting in his white fire department vehicle, before Bennett tugged her to the passenger door of her police cruiser.

"Stop pushing." Dylan settled in and strapped the seat belt around her. "So, everything in place for the festival?"

"Fingers crossed. Jazz recruited volunteers to help set up this morning. She just texted. Folks are already arriving. If the weather holds, it'll be a great day."

"Our sister is nothing if not efficient. Is Shea coming with the Robinsons?" The ten-year-old child that Jazz had found wandering the downtown streets had won Jazz's heart; been fostered by Louis Robinson, the Fairview Station custodian; and become an extended part of the Carlyle clan.

"Of course. Louis came in early to get everything spotless and said Shea was up at daybreak, skipping around, asking a million questions. I can't wait to see her again. It's been a couple of months, but Jazz keeps me updated."

"She really bonded with that kid. Any trouble from Shea's father, Joshua Spencer?" Dylan had been young when the Carlyles adopted Jazz and couldn't imagine being without her biological family, but Jazz had turned out great and would help Shea through her transition.

"Nope. Hopefully, he's gone back to Atlanta to be with his brother, Jeremy, and other family. Not much left for him here with Shea being adopted soon. I hope he doesn't show up at the last minute and contest the adoption." Bennett cocked her head toward Dylan. "So, baby sister, back to this woman you're not going to think about."

Dylan pretended to pick something off the front of her blouse so Bennett couldn't read her. "Just a run-in at work last night. No big deal."

"Come on, Dylan. When I walked into the cottage this morning, your mind was in La-la Land. If your music didn't distract you, it's at least a medium deal."

Most of the time she loved that Bennett knew her so well. Being called Ben's mini-me was more often a blessing because she idolized her older sister, but sometimes the mind meld thing was too much. "I walked in on a police officer servicing one of our nurses in the on-call room during duty hours last night."

Bennett stiffened beside her. "One of mine?"

Uh-oh. She'd said the wrong thing. Bennett ran a tight station, and anything jeopardizing that professionalism was unacceptable to her. "I have no idea." She waved her hand in the air dismissively, the car suddenly seeming to close in around her. "That's not the point anyway."

"So, which one got under your skin? As if I have to ask. You've dated a few nurses and doctors in the past, but never a police officer. I'd take offense if I didn't understand you so well."

"It wasn't an attraction thing. At all." Bennett's eye roll told her she wasn't buying it. "Seriously, what self-respecting person engages in sex while they're supposed to be working in a space where they could easily be discovered? It felt...unseemly."

Bennett quirked her mouth into a sideways grin. "'Unseemly?' Who uses that word? Unless you're trying too hard to convince yourself you weren't attracted to this officer. Who is she? I assume it was a *she*?"

"Of course, it was a woman. You don't think I'd be—"

"Caught you."

Dylan blew out a long, frustrated breath. "And everybody wonders why I don't date cops. After living with them all my life, I should be used to the lack of privacy. I can't even *think* without being interrogated." Bennett tried to slide her arm around Dylan's shoulder. She pulled away. "Stop it. You tricked me with your cop-ish, voodoo mind games." She wiggled her fingers at Bennett. "So uncool."

"Is privacy really what you're upset about, kiddo? Something about this woman got to you." Bennett parked beside Jazz's police vehicle in the Fairview Station lot and turned to face Dylan. "Who is she?"

"Sorry, Ben, gotta bounce." Dylan opened the door and bolted.

"To be continued," Bennett called after her.

"Nope," Dylan mumbled as she sprinted toward the festival area. Finley Masters raised too many questions in Dylan's mind and aroused too many sensations in her body to be a safe topic of conversation with anyone.

The grassy picnic area behind the station was dotted with brightly colored tents, booths, and games, converting it into a kids' playground. From the size of the crowd, the event was going to be a big success. Dylan smiled at a face painter applying tiger stripes to a child's cheeks and at the joy in the girl's eyes.

"Hey, glad you made it," Kerstin said as she and Emory, wearing orange reflective traffic vests, walked toward Dylan, arms spread for a group hug. Her sisters chose perfect partners—Kerstin's creativity, idealism, and blond good looks suited Bennett's down-to-earth style perfectly; and Emory's compassion and nurturing nature, plus her auburn waves and gentle curves were everything Jazz said she wanted. Maybe one day Dylan would meet someone who felt just as right for her.

"Sorry. Long night in the ER. Ben dragged me out of bed." She pointed to the traffic vests. "Way to accessorize."

"Don't laugh," Emory said. "When Jazz sees you, you'll be sporting one too. They're actually helpful so parents and kids recognize us as staff if they have questions. My fiancé thinks of everything." She glanced across the yard and caught Jazz's gaze and a look of love passed between them.

Kerstin laughed. "Everything except a wedding date apparently. Ben set our date before she proposed. Cocky cop. We're all just eager for you to become an official part of the family."

"Don't blame Jazz," Emory said. "Once this event is over, we'll pick the date."

"Excellent." Dylan nodded toward the festival. "It looks like a good turnout. Hope the weather holds." She pointed toward a dark cloud in the east. "Fingers crossed that will pass. Keep your eye on the weather app. Guess I better report for duty and get my glamorous vest."

"We'll see you behind the magic tent. The three-legged sack races are about to begin." Emory squeezed her arm affectionately before she and Kerstin walked away.

"Be still my heart." Dylan turned toward where she'd seen Jazz and bumped into someone. "Sorr—" Her mouth stopped working when she looked up into Finley Masters's grinning face and blue eyes.

"I know you like me, but heart-stopping isn't good, Doc. Do you need CPR?"

"Uh..." She made herself breathe slowly and maintain eye contact. Finley's fitted uniform and mop of unruly hair reminded Dylan of a chocolate covered Dreamsicle. Why did this particular blonde look so damn good in black? Dylan's mind finally engaged. "If I do, there's a medical tent on site."

For once Finley didn't have a snappy comeback. She nervously hooked her thumbs in her utility belt, and Dylan glimpsed vulnerability she hadn't seen last night. Then Finley flashed a cocky smile. "Um, it's good to see you again, Dylan...under different circumstances."

Why did she have to say that? Visions of Finley naked from neck to ankles and pumping her perfect ass against Nurse Anita made Dylan flush. Her dreams last night hadn't done Finley justice. "What are you doing here?" Dylan lost concentration when Finley smiled revealing a scar in her chin beneath her plump bottom lip.

"Police function. Public relations. Sucking up to the bosses for career advancement. Take your pick. I volunteered weeks ago when Lieutenant Perry came to lineup asking for help. Why are you here?" For a second, Dylan thought Finley might be kidding, but before she could answer, Finley added, "Oh, right. You're a doctor. Medical tent."

"I'm not really here in an official capacity. I'm supporting my family." Why was she explaining herself to Finley?

A tall officer who'd been standing beside Finley with a young boy elbowed her in the ribs. "Dude, seriously? She's not just a doctor." He pointed to the station signboard near the side entrance. "This is Dylan Carlyle, baby sister to Bennett and Jazz, our bosses."

Finley's grin vanished and her face paled. "Oh shit..." She glanced at the boy. "I mean crap. You're one of *those* Carlyles?"

"Not the baby part but still the sister." Dylan started to fire off another snarky comment, but the surprised look on Finley's face stopped her. She really hadn't known who Dylan was.

The man beside Finley offered his hand. "Since my friend has temporarily lost her ability to speak, which doesn't happen often and for which I'm grateful, I'm Hank Hinson and this is my son, Robin." He ruffled the child's blond hair.

Dylan shook Hank's hand and fist-bumped Robin. "Nice to meet you both." She stooped to Robin's height. "How old are you?"

"Ten."

"I have a niece and nephew about your age. They're over at the basketball court, if you want to join them. You're going to have a great time." She stood again and addressed Hank, purposely avoiding Finley's stare. "I really have to go. Enjoy."

If Finley truly hadn't known who Dylan was, she was probably mortified about their first meeting. And the more time they spent dancing around each other like awkward teenagers, the greater chance Ben, Jazz, or another family member would notice and sniff out how they'd met, which could lead to discipline for Finley. Dylan wasn't interested in those two parts of her life colliding in that particular way.

As Dylan walked away, Finley raced to catch up and fell in step like she'd done at the hospital. "Could we talk...about what happened last night? I had no idea who you were. Really, no idea."

"There's nothing to discuss. I'd rather just forget it." She glanced around to make sure none of her family was close. This dyke drama would draw them like ants to a picnic. "Good-bye."

"But if my bosses find out—"

"What do you want, a blood oath?" Dylan walked faster. She understood Finley's anxiety, but someone would surely notice that they weren't complete strangers if they continued. "They won't hear it from me. I don't like keeping secrets from my family, but in this case, it wouldn't help either of us. Trust me on that."

"Thanks," Finley said. "I appreciate it."

"No problem." Dylan picked up her pace again to get away from Finley, and her heart rate climbed as well. "And stop doing that."

"Doing what?"

"Walking with me."

Finley grinned. "We just happen to be going in the same direction."

Dylan inhaled a deep breath before launching into another attempt to get rid of Finley but instead got a lungful of her sporty cologne. Damn. Dylan wanted to sprinkle Finley's fragrance in her bed and roll like a dog in her owner's scent. *What?* "Look, I really need to go. Good-bye, Officer Masters."

"Maybe I could treat you to a soda later, when things slow down."

"No thanks."

"You don't drink soda? How about cotton candy or a candy apple? We've got it all."

Oh yeah, Finley definitely had it all—fresh lines, the strut, confidence, and looks—but a perfect package sometimes masked an unwanted surprise. "I can't."

"Why not?" Finley asked. "I like you. And I think you like me too, maybe just a little."

Dylan stopped and faced Finley squarely, making eye contact. She didn't beat around the bush where feelings were concerned, hers or anyone else's. "Look, Finley, maybe I do like you just a little in spite of your arrogance. You have game—too practiced to be authentic—but still charming. But whatever you're hoping for here isn't happening. Don't waste your time."

"God, I love a woman who tells it like it is. Okay." She held her hands up and took a step back. "So long for now. I'll find you later." Finley gave her a slight bow and strutted off.

"Not if I can help it," Dylan mumbled under her breath and weaved her way through a crowd of people toward the race area. "Not a cop. Not *this* cop. Not even for a fling." She ruthlessly ignored the quickening of her pulse.

CHAPTER THREE

D amn, woman, you're playing with fire," Hank said as he and Robin caught up with Finley. "What's going on with you and Dylan?"

Finley squeezed Robin's shoulder and pointed to the basketball court behind the new station where kids were already playing. "Why don't you check your skills on the court?"

"So you can do more grown-up talk?"

"You know it, smart guy," Hank said. "We'll be watching, so do us proud."

Robin high-fived Finley and joined a group of kids engaged in a game.

When Robin was out of hearing range, Hank said, "Fucking around with the boss's sister is a really bad idea, Fin. If you screw up, you'll get a world of hurt from the captain and lieutenant, and you can kiss any promotion or transfer hopes good-bye."

Finley raised her hands. "Hold on. I didn't do anything."

"Right." Hank shook his head. "There was sex tension all over that little exchange just now. You forget who you're talking to, pal."

Hank had rescued her from one-nighters gone wrong on a few occasions and driven her home from a weekend getaway spoiled by her unwillingness to commit to her latest conquest. "It wasn't like that."

"So…" Hank cocked his head to one side. "What happened? Or if you don't want to talk, I'll leave you here with your dildo in your hand, join my son on the basketball court, and hope you don't dig yourself in any deeper."

"Okay. Hold up." Finley slid her hands in her pockets. "Dylan saw me hooking up with Anita in the doctor's on-call room last night. I...um...might've tried to hit on her, but I didn't know who she was at the time."

"You *might've*? Jeez, Fin, your life is a constant pussy prowl. I didn't get as much strange my entire life as you have in the past few years. So...you made a pass. And?"

"She shut me down. Nothing happened."

"Well, that's new. Maybe she's straight."

"I didn't get that vibe," Finley said.

"So why was she in such a hurry to get away from you?" Hank's stop-fucking-around stare from her field training days forced Finley to break eye contact. "Wait. Were you on duty? Fucking some nurse while you were working? And let me guess," his lips thinned in an expression between disgust and despair, "somewhere you weren't technically allowed to be."

Finley nodded.

"Did I teach you anything at all? You're determined to tank your career, and you're afraid Dylan will tell the brass. Is that why you're so hot to make nice with her?"

"No...not entirely. She promised she wouldn't say anything, but..."

He scowled at her. "But what?"

Finley shrugged. "I like her."

Hank slashed his hand through the air in a cutting motion. "As one of the most famous cops of all time said, 'Nip it. Nip it in the bud.'"

"Right, Barney Fife." Finley grinned at the reference to the hapless Mayberry deputy, then shook her head. "But what if she's the one?" She caught sight of Dylan across the fairground lining up for the three-legged sack race, tying her leg to another woman, and grinned. She'd been tracking Dylan since she arrived, noting how easily she spotted her in the crowd.

"Hey," Hank said. "Are you listening?"

"Yeah, sure."

"Just because a woman saw you naked and didn't jump your bones doesn't mean she's 'the one,' if there is such a thing." Hank guided Finley closer to the basketball court, cheered when Robin made a basket, and then turned his attention back to Finley. "Think very carefully before pursuing this woman and how it could impact your career. You want to make detective sooner rather than later. Having a fling with the boss's sister and tossing her aside can be a career-limiting move."

"Okay."

"I'm serious, Fin. That hunter between your legs will get you in serious trouble one day. Promise me."

"I promise," Finley said, but her heart wasn't in it. She'd never met a woman so immune to her game and who called her on it the way Dylan had. She was a puzzle Finley wanted to solve. If nothing else, she wanted to know more about her...and maybe bed her at least once. Her blood stirred at the thought.

"I'm not buying that piss-poor excuse of a promise, but there's nothing else I can do. It's on you now." Hank slapped her on the back and shoved her toward the court. "Let's get sweaty. It looks good for the police to engage with the community."

"Right, Coach." She and Hank went to opposite teams and blended easily into the game. She caught a pass from Robin, dribbled down court, and passed it back to him for the basket.

Finley glanced around the fairgrounds and spotted Dylan engaged in the sack race. When their eyes met, Dylan suddenly wobbled sideways and fell to the ground taking the other woman with her. Finley was so focused on Dylan that she missed an inbounds pass, but recovered, dribbled down court, and fired off a three-pointer. Swoosh. Take that, Dylan Carlyle.

If a single glance unraveled Finley so quickly, she couldn't imagine what having sex with Dylan would feel like. But damn it, she wanted to find out. She wouldn't allow any woman to throw her off her game plan, so the sooner she doused this fire, the sooner she'd return to her normal carefree life.

❖

"Why did you fall?" Kerstin demanded, brushing the dirt from her jeans. "We were at the front of the pack and then on the ground. Did I trip you or something?"

"I got distracted," Dylan said. "Sorry." *Distracted* didn't cover what she'd felt when Finley Masters caught her gaze and grinned. *Unhinged* fit. Time had slowed and everything around her faded until nothing else existed but her and Finley. Dylan rolled sideways on the ground and tried to get up, but the added weight made her feel like a toddler learning to walk. What was the universe playing at with this impossible attraction? Whatever it was, she refused to submit.

"Anybody I know?" Kerstin looked around the fairgrounds. "Are you seeing someone?"

"What? Seeing? No. I don't have time. I just ran into an annoying police officer I met yesterday. She doesn't seem the type to volunteer at a community function, yet here she is. Guess I was just shocked."

"I'd call going from a sprint to a face plant in seconds more than shocking. She definitely got your attention." Kerstin nudged her as they scrambled to right themselves with a leg hobbled to the other. "A police officer, huh?"

Dylan jerked loose the rope tying them together. "Don't you start too. I get enough grief from Bennett and Jazz about my aversion to dating their coworkers. They should do a happy dance that I steer clear of those whoremongers."

"That's a little harsh, isn't it?"

"This one reminds me of Bennett—"

"Watch it. You're talking about my wife," Kerstin said, her tone serious and protective.

"I meant when she was younger, before you came back into her life. She went wild after Papa died, and I think work and sex dulled the pain."

Kerstin guided Dylan away from the race area to a picnic table. "I know Ben had a life before me, and we've talked about it, but she's not that person anymore." She blew on her nails and brushed them against her T-shirt. "Took the right woman to help with the pain and show her how different life can be."

"Everyone isn't as patient as you, Kerstin, and not every savage beast can be calmed with love and kindness." What would it take to tame an edgy, dangerous woman like Finley? Would Dylan even be attracted to her if she changed? Why was she having a conversation with Kerstin about Finley while searching the grounds for her? And why was she thinking these insane questions? Admitting any interest at all should send her running in the opposite direction. So, why wasn't she?

"Dylan?"

"Huh?"

"I was just saying I think this officer might be more than annoying to you." When Dylan started to object, Kerstin raised her hands. "Just saying, you might want to consider it. I've never seen you so worked up about anybody, irritant or otherwise." She gave Dylan a hug and stood. "You want anything to eat or drink? I'm going to find my wife and give her a sloppy kiss."

"No thanks, Kerstin. I'll check in with G-ma and Mama at the Ma Rolls truck. Thanks for listening."

"Anytime. We're family." Kerstin waved at Bennett and then pointed at the sky. "We got lucky with the weather. Looks like the rain passed us by."

"Yeah, lucky." Dylan watched her petite sister-in-law practically skip across the yard toward Bennett, her blond curls bouncing with each step. She wanted a love like that one day. She hopped off the picnic table and saw Finley headed toward her. "Not now."

"Dylan, wait." Finley grabbed her hand, and Dylan stared down at their joined hands, irritated at Finley's invasion of her space— and her body's involuntary response. Finley followed her gaze and released Dylan's hand. "Sorry. I just wondered if we could talk."

"I'm going to help out at the food truck."

"Maybe later?" Finley asked.

"What do you want to talk about?"

Finley shuffled her feet and then looked at Dylan. "Maybe how we can't keep our eyes off each other."

Honesty. Unexpected, but Dylan appreciated that. "Yes, we do seem to track each other, don't we? And what does that mean to you exactly? Should we strip off our clothes and fuck right here?" The shock in Finley's eyes said Dylan had struck her mark. "You do prefer taboo settings, right? Or maybe you'd feel more comfortable in the station's linen closet or conference room?" Finley's expression shifted from shock to disbelief and then something akin to sadness. Dylan's stomach tightened. She'd only intended to push Finley away, but she'd gone too far.

"I'm sorry I've offended you. I realize my behavior at the hospital was reckless and irresponsible, not to mention unprofessional, but I'd hoped we could get past it. And since we're being totally honest, the idea of having sex with you works for me, or it did until about ten seconds ago. Now I'm having second thoughts."

"Too much?" Dylan infused the question with a hint of levity, trying to make up for her harsh outburst.

Finley held her thumb and forefinger slightly apart. "Little bit, yeah. I was going to add, sex with you appeals to me quite a lot, but I'm pretty sure you're not a one-and-done kind of woman. So, I'd be happy to start with a chat and see where it leads. How about you?"

"Actions speak louder than words, Finley, so no offense, but I'm going to decline your generous offer."

"They certainly do. And no offense taken. Don't worry, I won't bother you again."

When Finley walked away, Dylan felt the energy that had swelled between them lessen with every step Finley took. She blended into the crowd, and Dylan grabbed the picnic table for support.

Why had she been so brutally honest and cruel? She wasn't normally unkind, but she'd felt emotionally shaken, her defensive impulse to distance had kicked in, and she'd spoken without censoring. She should apologize, but Finley was nowhere in sight. What was it about Finley that made her question things she believed and thought she knew about herself?

CHAPTER FOUR

The crowd behind Fairview Station thinned as the afternoon air cooled, and Bennett called the festival to a close. A few police officers, most of the Carlyle family, the Robinsons, and ten-year-olds Shea and Robin pitched in, breaking down tents and clearing the grounds. Everyone agreed the event was a huge success, and Bennett promised a repeat next year. Dylan, G-ma, and Mama organized the food truck and ordered pizza for the remaining helpers.

Dylan glanced across the yard at Finley playing cornhole with Hank and Robin. The wholesome scene, contrasted to last night's erotic display, made Dylan smile. Throughout the day, she'd caught Finley staring, but Finley had been playing games with kids or talking with citizens and had kept her distance, for which Dylan was relieved. Mostly.

"Something you like, darling?" Mama asked from behind, placing her hand lightly on Dylan's shoulder.

"Occasionally, people surprise me, that's all."

"We should always give them room to do that, honey," G-ma said.

"I guess." While Dylan secured the upper cabinet doors in the food truck, she noticed a black SUV pull onto the lot. It was late for newcomers, but no one was turned away at these community gatherings.

Two men in dark hooded sweatshirts jumped out of the vehicle and ran toward the officers and civilians remaining on the fairgrounds, and one of them yelled, "Nobody takes my fucking daughter away from me. Shea, where are you?"

Adrenaline flooded Dylan's system, but she didn't feel the familiar hurry-and-save-a-life call to action. Instead, her gut tightened, she grew cold and sweaty simultaneously, and fought the urge to run. The fight-or-flight response. This was what her father and grandfather, and now her siblings, faced regularly. Fear momentarily paralyzed Dylan when one of the men pointed a sawed-off shotgun at Jazz and Emory. "Gun," she screamed, and then everything slowed.

Bennett and Kerstin were directly in the gunmen's line of fire, and Dylan yelled, "Run, Ben, run." Instead, Bennett shoved Kerstin to the ground, pulled her weapon as they fell, and draped herself over her. This couldn't be happening.

Jazz reached for her gun while shielding Emory and Shea behind her. Poor Shea. What kind of father brings a weapon to claim his child. Random thoughts raced through Dylan's mind while officers pulled their weapons and shouted for the gunmen to stop. Shots exploded like mini bombs. Bullets pinged off cars and blasted chunks of red brick from the side of the building. People dove for cover behind anything close or cowered on the ground and screamed for help and mercy.

Finley lunged toward Hank and Robin. More shots sounded and a spray of arterial blood arched through the air from one of them. The three of them struck the ground hard, and the grass under them turned crimson. Which one was hit?

Cops—her sisters—threw themselves in front of bullets to save loved ones and strangers. She had to do something. "Stay here," Dylan shouted to G-ma and Mama.

"Don't go out there, Dylan," Mama yelled, "They're still shooting."

"I have to. Don't come out until Ben or Jazz gives the all clear. And call ambulances, at least two." Dylan's insides jangled and her palms sweated while gunmen fired on her loved ones again. As she ran toward the wounded, Dylan searched for her family. Thank God Simon, Stephanie, and the twins had already left for Simon's shift at the fire department. Dylan glanced behind her. G-ma and Mama hurried from the van to help others. Stubborn Carlyle women. It wasn't their nature to remain idle in a crisis.

Dylan crouched low to the ground, moving cautiously toward the huddled group of people. The shooter who'd shouted for Shea fell near her, and blood oozed from his head and shoulder. He dropped the shotgun by his side. The other man kept firing and tried to drag his accomplice back to the SUV but finally gave up and jumped in the SUV alone.

The suspect's vehicle spun out of the lot, and Bennett rose, holstered her weapon, and helped Kerstin to her feet, pausing briefly to give her a grateful hug. She nodded to Dylan that they were okay and started shouting orders. "Check for wounded." As other officers ran from the station to assist, Bennett assigned duties. "If you fired your weapon, you're relieved. Form up by the picnic table."

Jazz sandwiched Shea between Emory and the Robinsons, knelt in front of her, and said, "You're going to be okay."

"My dad is hit," Shea said, her eyes wide with fear. "Don't let him die."

"We have a doctor and nurses on site. They'll take care of him." She turned to Louis and Denise Robinson. "Would you please take her inside?" She kissed Emory on the lips and said, "Do what you can to help. I have to go. Love you."

Then Jazz took charge of the scene, waving to the closest officers. "You two, secure the area." Her tone was calm and authoritative like a shooting at the station happened routinely, but she was trained for these things. Jazz pointed to two other officers. "Go after the suspect and put out an alert on the vehicle. His name is Jeremy Spencer from Atlanta. I met him when Shea went missing last year. The injured shooter," she nodded to her right, "is his younger brother, Joshua." The officers hurried to their vehicles, and Jazz called to Ben, "Get CSI rolling."

With the police in charge of the scene, chaos quickly shifted to a semblance of order, and people stood, found friends and family, and made sure they were okay. Dylan did a final scan to confirm her relatives were safe. G-ma and Mama comforted people and escorted them into the substation where they'd be interviewed. Her sisters assumed their professional roles—Ben administrative, Jazz operational—as if they'd practiced often. Time for her to do the same.

Dylan choked down the bitter taste of fear and shifted into work mode. She stopped at the first victim she encountered, Shea's father. Gunshot wound to the head and shoulder, unconscious but breathing. Before she could assess his injuries further, someone shouted for her.

"Dylan, over here." Finley crouched over Hank, her hands over a spurting injury to his thigh, and Robin sobbing beside her.

She glanced back and forth between the victims. Triage required that she determine the priority of patient treatment based on the severity of their condition. This one was unresponsive, and the officer was bleeding out. Two nurses who'd been working the event ran toward Dylan. She spoke to the first to arrive. "Check his vitals," and then to the other, "Come with me."

She rushed to Finley's side and knelt. "We've got this." Finley stared at her, but didn't move, and Dylan recognized the look in her eyes. She needed to be useful. "Give me his belt and keep his head down." Finley's hands and shirt dripped blood. Then Dylan asked the question that wouldn't wait. "Are you hurt?"

Finley shook her head.

She released a long breath and addressed the nurse. "Elevate his legs, use the belt as a tourniquet, and hold pressure over the wound." She gave her orders aloud, more as a checklist than because the nurse needed instructions. "I've done a primary sweep, and he doesn't appear to be injured anywhere else." She glanced at Robin, bloodied too, his eyes red from crying. "You okay, Robin?"

"Y…yes." His voice quivered as another round of sobs took over.

"Are you hurt anywhere?"

Robin shook his head and pointed at the officer on the ground. "My dad."

"I know, sweetie. I know and I'm going to take good care of him." Dylan's heart twisted in sympathy, and she glanced from

Robin to Shea and shivered. No child should see a parent injured and bleeding or shooting into a crowd of people. She caught sight of Emory's auburn hair in a small group, made eye contact with her, and nodded toward Robin. She rushed over, dropped the station's first aid kit at Dylan's feet, and reached for the boy's hand, but he clung to Finley.

"It's okay, Robin," Finley said. "Both of us have to be brave. Go with the lady while I ride with your dad to the hospital. I'll call your mom, okay? You're going to be fine, buddy. I promise." Robin nodded, and Finley hugged him before guiding him toward Emory.

"Thank you," Dylan said to Finley, taking a second to make eye contact and stress her sincerity.

Mama ran toward Dylan gesturing toward her cell. "EMT."

Everything was happening at once, just like in the ER, and Dylan fell into the familiar rhythm. This was her scene now. She tucked the phone between her ear and shoulder. "This is Dr. Carlyle. I have a forty-ish male, GSW to right thigh, femoral bleed, controlled with pressure and tourniquet. Significant blood loss, semiconscious, unobstructed breathing, pulse thin and thready."

She started to get up but looked at Finley and stopped. Her face was twisted in a mask of uncertainty and fear, and Dylan wanted to reassure her. "You did a good job protecting Robin. I'm sure Hank is grateful."

Finley shook her head. "I just wasn't quick enough to help Hank."

The scornful tone of Finley's voice and anguished look in her eyes made Dylan's heart ache. She'd seen that look from survivors before but had no time to further console Finley. "You did your best. Are you sure you're not hurt?" Dylan stood.

"Yeah. Where are you going?"

"There's another victim."

"I don't care about that fucking guy. This is my friend, a fellow officer, and in case you didn't notice, a father."

"I've done all I can for him. The nurse will hold pressure until EMS arrives." Dylan tried to be reassuring because Finley needed it, but her response sounded curt and she didn't have time to check her bedside manner.

"What the hell does that mean? You're just going to leave him to—"

"Easy, Fin." Bennett said in her commander's voice as she squatted beside Finley. "Dylan needs to take care of everyone." She nodded for Dylan to attend to the downed shooter, and Dylan had never been prouder of her big sister. "Did you fire your weapon, Fin?"

"No, ma'am," Finley replied.

"Good. Would you go with Hank to the hospital and keep us posted on his condition?"

"Yes, ma'am," Finley said.

Dylan returned to the injured shooter and leaned over him, rubbed her knuckles in the center of his chest to check for pain response, and relayed to the EMTs. "I also have a thirty-ish male, GSW to the head, pupils reactive but unresponsive to pain. Possible drugs on board based on erratic behavior prior to incident. Second GSW to shoulder, appears to be a through and through." She packed a bandage over the shoulder wound and directed the nurse to secure it. "Controlled with pressure."

"Thanks, Dr. Carlyle. ETA one minute."

Dylan handed the phone back to Mama as the ambulance screamed onto the lot. Nothing more she could do now. No one else appeared injured, but they would all certainly be traumatized. As the EMTs got to work, the Carlyles briefly huddled together.

"Is everyone okay?" Mama asked, her brown eyes visually checking each of them as only a mother could. They all nodded and clung to one another for a few seconds, needing the comfort and reassurance that their family was still intact.

"P.S. Dr. Carlyle should not be rushing into a bullet storm," Bennett said.

"Right," Jazz agreed, scrubbing her fingers through her close-cropped hair. "Your job starts when the bullets stop."

"No idea where to start unpacking everything those comments bring up," Dylan said.

Mama squeezed her arm. "Later, honey. Love you all. I know you have jobs to do, so just be careful. Brunch tomorrow, no matter what."

Dylan met the gazes of every family member relaying how much she loved and appreciated them before waving over the two nurses who'd assisted her. "Are you both good to help out a little longer?" They nodded, and Dylan pointed toward the station. "Clear it with the officer in charge of witnesses and then check that everyone is okay, no shock or minor injuries. Ask only medically necessary questions, nothing about the incident." She'd learned in her first year of internship to keep her medicine separate from her family's police work. The practice prevented legal entanglements on both sides and kept the peace at home.

As she started inside, one of the EMTs called, "Dr. Carlyle, would you ride with us? This is my first week, and I could use a second pair of eyes and hands. This guy's pulse just bottomed out and his breathing is extremely shallow."

"Sure." She started toward the second ambulance, but Finley, who was running alongside Hank's stretcher, hooked Dylan's arm and pulled her toward the other ambulance.

"Come with us. Hank needs your help...*I* need you."

Finley's eyes showed panic and the same discomfort Dylan had noticed last night when she'd asked for Dylan's assistance. Hank was important to Finley, and Dylan wanted to say yes, but the rules of triage were clear and existed for a reason. Dylan's duty to her patients had to come first. She clasped Finley's hand and answered with all the confidence and concern she could muster. "Hank will be okay. I have to go with the other victim." The look Finley gave her said she'd committed an unforgivable sin.

❖

Finley climbed into the first ambulance and called back to Dylan, her throat tight with fear and anger. "Can you *at least* make sure Robin is okay until I make other arrangements? His mom is visiting her mother in California."

"Of course. And, Finley, I'm sorry—"

"Don't worry. I've got this." Finley shrugged away when Dylan reached out. She took care of herself and everyone else, but she'd made the mistake of asking Dylan for help. That wouldn't happen again. She prayed Hank wouldn't need it on the ride to the hospital. She settled in beside him, and the driver sped away with lights and sirens rolling.

"Here, clean yourself up." The EMT absently passed her hand sanitizer and wipes while monitoring Hank's condition. "Don't want to scare the nurses."

Finley's arms were sticky with blood up to her elbows, her uniform soaked. The whole box of wipes wouldn't clean up the mess, but she focused on the deliberate, mundane task as the adrenaline ebbed and her pulse slowed. She'd been blindsided, laughing and joking with Hank and Robin one second, in a shit storm the next. She'd violated a basic police rule—always be aware of your surroundings—and Hank paid the price.

The bad guys had surprised them, and everyone was lucky more people weren't injured or killed. She'd responded quickly when someone shouted *gun*, but she was already seconds behind the shooters. She hadn't even gotten off a round because other officers and civilians stood between her and the suspects. She shuddered. If she lost her best friend, made Becky a widow and Robin fatherless, she'd never forgive herself.

The ambulance slammed to a stop in the ER bay, and Finley bailed out with the EMT and ran beside the stretcher into the ER. Hank was pale, his eyes closed. She leaned down and whispered, "You're going to be fine. You have to be."

"Give us room, Officer." A doctor elbowed her aside. "We'll take it from here."

"But I need—" What did she need? To be with Hank in case he…she couldn't even think the die word.

"Fin." Nurse Anita, her friend with benefits, put a hand on her arm, but Finley resisted.

"I want to be in there with him, in case he needs me."

"Finley, there's nothing you can do." Anita eased her toward a consult room and closed the door. "Are you hurt? You're covered in blood."

Finley shook her head.

"Look at me, Fin. Your friend is going to be okay. You got him here in time."

She protected people and kept them safe, but she'd failed, and Hank was paying for it. The adrenaline effects faded, and Finley slumped in a chair, feeling jittery. When it mattered most, when it was personal, she'd let Hank down. The thought that he might die or be permanently handicapped terrified her.

"Is there anything I can get you, babe?" Anita asked. "I really need to get back out there."

Anita stroked her arm, but Finley stared straight ahead, refusing comfort. "Just let me know how he's doing."

When Anita left, Finley wrapped her arms around herself and rocked while the scene and her failure played over and over in her head. "Be aware of your surroundings. Expect the unexpected. Ever vigilant. Never lose focus. Always watch the hands." She'd failed Hank, Becky, Robin, her bosses, and her fellow officers. She stifled a sob, and her father's voice sounded in her head. *"Get off your ass and do something."*

CHAPTER FIVE

Dylan followed the stretcher carrying the shooter into the ER and ahead, saw Finley trail behind the EMTs with Hank. Finley's body practically pulsed with the combination of fear, anger, and adrenaline that were keeping her going, but Dylan could tell she was headed for a crash.

"Unconscious GSW?" An older doctor Dylan recognized from her residency came toward her. "Any change in his condition?"

"Yes and no." She gave him a quick rundown. "Do you want me to assist?"

"Type and cross times two," he yelled to a nurse. "I'll take it from here, Dylan, but if you would, run interference with the police. One of theirs is injured, and you know cops."

"Not really," she muttered. She'd lived with cops all her life but never understood why they jumped in front of guns and knives to protect strangers without regard for their own safety or the consequences to their families. "I'll do my best." When it came to protecting their own, cops were dogmatic, and Dylan wasn't anxious to stick her head further into their business, especially when she was still so unsettled.

She walked toward the consulting room where she'd seen Anita take Finley but instead veered toward the locker room. Her workplace felt different when people she knew were patients. She needed a few minutes to wrap her mind around the difference and clean up before facing them again. Consoling families and friends never got easier, and they certainly didn't need to see her covered in their loved one's blood. She peeled off her blood-spattered blouse and tossed it in the hazardous materials trash bin. She knew several ways to remove blood from clothing, but she'd never be able to wear the blouse again. She showered quickly and put on a fresh pair of scrubs. Before heading back to the ER, she stopped at the desk to check on both patients.

In the few minutes she'd been away, the ER waiting area and adjoining consult rooms had filled with police officers, plainclothes and uniform. She recognized uniforms of the Greensboro, High Point, Winston-Salem, and Burlington departments, along with members of the SBI, FBI, and sheriff's department. They huddled in small groups, some paired off talking quietly in corners, and others stood alone. She felt their fear and helplessness like another presence in the crowded space.

Dylan spotted Bennett's tall frame in the center of a group of officers, waved to get her attention, and nodded toward the consulting room she'd seen Finley enter earlier. When Bennett joined her, Dylan pushed on the door, but officers were packed inside so tightly, it wouldn't open. She placed both hands against the door to try again, but Bennett shook her head.

"Will you wait a minute, please?"

"Why?"

Bennett stepped in front of Dylan so she'd have to look at her. "I need to know my baby sister is okay." When Dylan didn't answer immediately, Bennett asked, "Are you...okay? I know this is hard and I'm sorry they sent you to deal with us. Cops are a handful at the best of times."

"Don't I know it." Dylan suppressed her case of nerves and bad memories. "I'm fine, Ben. I went into medicine to help people who've suffered and lost, the way we have."

"Just remember I'm here if you need me."

Big sister to the rescue. As much as Dylan argued for her independence and wanted to take Jazz's turn in the cottage out back for some separation, family was her strength and foundation. "Thanks, but I'm okay." The tangles in her stomach released a little at the concerned look in Bennett's eyes. "How are things at the station?"

"Shea is pretty torn up. Poor kid blames herself for the whole thing. Robin is worried about his dad. Emory is distracting them with games and story time."

"Hopefully, Emory can help them understand." Dylan took a deep breath and nodded toward the door. "Let's do this." She saw Bennett stand a little taller and shift from big sister to police captain mode.

Bennett shouldered her way into the room and waved for silence. "Guys, we've located the suspect vehicle abandoned at Four Seasons Mall. CSI is processing it now. The other shooter is still at large and could've stolen another vehicle or be on foot in the area. Stay sharp when you get back in the field and keep your cool. We'll catch this guy, but we need to do it by the numbers." After a round of muted agreement from the troops, Bennett motioned to Dylan. "Dr. Carlyle can give us an update on Hank."

She swallowed hard. Everyone looked at her like she had a magic pellet to make this all go away. If only. "Officer Hinson suffered a gunshot that nicked his right femoral artery. Fortunately, we got him here in time. He's going to surgery shortly and will be in recovery after. His prognosis is good, barring unforeseen complications, but it'll be a while before he can have visitors."

The officers fired questions, but Bennett shook her head. "That's all we know right now, guys. Give us the room. If you're on duty, get back to it. I'll update Communications Center when I have something new. If you're here for support, keep the hallway clear so the staff can do their jobs."

The officers filed out, leaving Dylan, Bennett, and Finley Masters. Finley stood alone in the center of the room—pale, blue eyes wide, gaze locked on the floor, and sweating in her black uniform pants and sleeveless T-shirt—a total contrast to her usual cocky arrogance. The vulnerable sight tugged at Dylan's heart, bringing out the nurturer in her. Finley's bloodied uniform shirt and utility belt rested in a heap on the floor beside a chair. Dylan guided Finley toward the chair, concerned she might be in shock. "How do you feel?"

"Fine." Finley shrugged her off. "I'm not the one with the problem."

"You're sweating and—"

"The room was packed with cops and hot as hell. Of course, I'm sweating," she snapped, sharp and loud.

"Steady, Fin," Bennett said. "Dylan is just trying to help."

"Like she did in the field leaving Hank to bleed out?" Finley glared at her, and Dylan felt her fear and frustration like a wall between them.

She tamped down the urge to defend her actions and motioned for Finley to take a seat beside her on the sofa. She was hurting, and Dylan wanted to comfort her. "You're upset about Hank, and I'm so sorry he was hurt. One day when things aren't so chaotic, if you want, I'll explain triage, but right now, let's focus on what's going on with you."

Dylan reached for Finley's hand and again she pulled away. "I need to make sure you're okay..." Stubborn cops. Never admitted they needed anything or anyone. She tried another tack. "If you don't get medical clearance, you can't go back to work." She glanced to Bennett for support.

"You've been through a lot tonight, Fin. Let Dylan check you out."

Finley finally sat, and Dylan pressed her fingers against the pulse point at her wrist. Strong and regular. Good. Her skin was warm and dry to the touch. She cupped Finley's chin and forced eye contact. Energy vibrated between them, and Dylan gulped for air. "I'm going to check your pupillary response."

"Is that really necessary?"

"You hit the ground pretty hard. I'm being cautious." Finley stared at her, and Dylan momentarily lost concentration and focused on the silver necklace around Finley's neck instead. Dog-tag shaped locket with a tree engraved on the front. Was there a picture inside? She took another breath, regained her composure, and pulled the penlight from her scrubs pocket. She flashed it in Finley's eyes, satisfied with their response. "You seem okay." But Finley still looked shaken, and Dylan didn't want to leave her. "Hank was lucky you were there."

Finley scoffed and scooted away from her on the sofa. "Right, because I kept him from getting shot? Kept Robin from a life of nightmares? Or because I caught the suspects?"

Dylan flinched at the anger and hurt in Finley's voice but kept her tone even, reassuring. "Because you pushed him and Robin out of the line of fire. His injury could've been worse or Robin could've been hurt. And you immediately applied pressure and helped us stabilize Hank."

"I did?" Finley's shoulders visibly relaxed. "I did." She sounded almost wistful as she glanced at Dylan. "You did too. Sorry for earlier."

"No problem. It was chaotic. Is his family here yet?"

Finley jumped up. "Oh, God, I forgot. Becky."

"I called her," Bennett said. Dylan had almost forgotten her sister was in the room, watching quietly close by. "Becky is in California with her mother, and they're catching the next available flight. She asked if you'd take Robin overnight since Hank doesn't have any immediate family."

"Yeah, sure. He's been to my place. It's familiar."

Bennett turned to Dylan. "And the suspect? What's his condition?"

"Gunshot wounds to the shoulder and head. The one to the shoulder isn't problematic. The fact that he's still unconscious is. He's in X-ray to determine the path of the bullet to the head and see if there are any bone or bullet fragments in the skull we need to be concerned about. We'll have to wait and see." She stood and touched Bennett's arm, needing to feel the physical connection to family.

"Are you heading home now?" Bennett asked Dylan.

"I don't feel comfortable leaving yet." She glanced toward Finley and then realized Bennett would attach significance to that look, but she wasn't sticking around because of Finley. "I won't be much longer...unlike you, Captain. I'm sure you have details to attend to before you call it a day. I'll keep you posted on the officer's condition." She kissed Bennett's cheek and looked at Finley one last time. "Let me know if you or Hank's family needs anything."

❖

Finley waited until Dylan left before addressing Captain Carlyle. "Ma'am, I'm sorry for giving her a hard time. It's just—"

"Been an emotional day. I hope you don't have any hard feelings toward Dylan about how she handled the shooting victims earlier. She's a good doctor, just doing her job. Was that the cause of the tension between you?"

Finley couldn't tell the captain about her first encounter with Dylan so she skirted the question. "I was off base tonight. I'll apologize again next time I see her." Bennett Carlyle and Jazz Perry were revered, practically legends at Fairview Station, and they'd probably hate the idea of her even thinking about their sister.

"You're a cop. None of us likes hospitals or feeling helpless. I sometimes wonder whether we're born with those feelings or if they become ingrained through the job." She studied Finley for several seconds before adding, "Are you all right being our liaison with Hank's family or would you prefer I assign someone else?"

"I'm good, but I'd like…" Finley forced her shoulders back and met Bennett's gaze, her brown eyes so much like Dylan's that Finley did a double take. She'd been short and rude to Dylan, so Bennett might not be receptive to her request, but Finley had to try. "Captain, I'd like to be on the team investigating the shooting."

"I appreciate the offer, but you know how this works, Fin. CID handles the criminal case, and IA conducts the officer involved shootings. It's protocol."

"But I didn't fire my weapon." Finley wiped her sweaty face on the tail of her T-shirt.

"It's not a good idea," Bennett said. "You're close friends with Hank and his family. He was your training coach, for God's sake. That's a bond that lasts forever."

Securing a position on the team was a tough sell, but she gave it everything she had. "Aren't we all family? Detectives are seldom on scene at the time of an offense, but they're still invested in catching the suspect. We're all willing to do whatever it takes. I have to do this, boss. I owe it to Hank. I can be objective, just like any other officer working the case."

Bennett shook her head. "The CID sergeant assigns detectives to his cases. If he asks for patrol assistance, I'll consider putting your name forward. You'll be busy with Hank and the family for a while. It's handholding, not the fieldwork you want—"

"But it's important they know we're here for them. I get that, ma'am, and I won't let them or you down." Whether she was part of the investigation or not, she'd find a way to contribute, but she still wanted just a hint of legitimacy for her efforts. "You won't mind if I ask some questions, check with informants, that kind of stuff, right?"

"I expect that from everyone." Bennett's phone pinged and she glanced down. "Emory and Jazz are bringing Robin over." Finley stared at her boots, and Bennett added, "Don't blame yourself for any of this, Fin. You did all you could, more than most. Take a break and get something to eat and drink before you come back. Robin will need your strength." When Finley started to object, she added, "That's an order."

"Yes, ma'am." Finley retrieved her shirt and utility belt from the floor, threw them over her shoulder, and left the consulting room. She headed mechanically toward the canteen, more concerned about Hank's condition than eating. As soon as she was sure Hank was okay and Robin had his mother back, she needed to find the second suspect. At the end of the hallway, she turned toward the canteen, but a muffled cry drew her in the opposite direction.

She stopped near the doorway of another consulting room and peered inside. Dylan was slumped forward in a chair with her hands clasped between her knees. Her long chestnut hair hung around her pale face like a veil.

"Mind if I join you?" Dylan didn't respond. Didn't seem to notice her. After the way she'd behaved earlier, she should probably keep walking, but she'd promised to apologize, again. "Dylan?"

"Yeah?" She didn't look up.

"Dylan, are you okay?"

"Of course."

When Dylan finally looked at Finley, her eyes were dark with the kind of pain that came from the soul. She'd seen it in her father.

Finley was no good with emotions because she couldn't fix them. She should leave, but instead she sat down across from Dylan. "You're not okay. Should I get Ben?"

"No, she's got enough on her hands. I'll be fine. Just leave me alone."

"I can't." Finley placed her hands cautiously over Dylan's, expecting her to pull away. When she didn't, Finley felt surprisingly calm and concerned—not at all the customary arousal of touching a beautiful woman.

"There's nothing you can do. Please, go be with your coworkers. They need you."

"Dylan, let me—"

"What's going on?" A tall nurse with short curly red hair stood at the door, her gaze honed in on their joined hands. "Dylan, are you all right?"

Finley released her grasp and stood. "She's upset."

"I've got this, Officer. Thanks."

Finley started to leave but stopped in the doorway and watched as Dylan ran into the nurse's arms. The trust and comfort they shared was obvious. When the nurse hugged Dylan, Finley wished it could've been her.

"I can only imagine the memories this shooting has dredged up for you," the nurse said.

"They're never far from the surface, but today I saw firsthand what my sisters face and what it must've been like for…" She glanced toward Finley and stopped.

"I'm sorry," Finley said. "I didn't mean to eavesdrop. Are you sure I can't help?"

"You'll only make things worse," the nurse said as she closed the door in Finley's face.

CHAPTER SIX

Finley stopped by McDonald's for Robin's favorite fish sandwich before arriving at her house just after midnight. He'd fallen asleep on the sofa, refusing to be alone in a bedroom. She glanced down at his ten-year-old frame dwarfed under the heavy black-and-white Sherpa blanket, relieved his face was finally free of worry and fear. Could she have done something more? She didn't know about parenting, but everybody needed food, sleep, and a safe place. She prayed it was enough.

She tucked the blanket tighter around Robin and pulled up the BOLO for the second shooter, Jeremy Spencer, on her phone. The resemblance to his brother, Josh, Shea's father, was obvious. She'd never forget either of them—the curve of their noses, the high foreheads, black hair, and the hate in their eyes as they'd fired bullets into the crowd and her best friend. She tiptoed into the kitchen and dialed her cell. "What's going on out there, Sarge?" she whispered.

"Nothing new on the other suspect yet, Fin."

"I should be searching with you guys, but—"

"You're doing Hank more of a service by taking care of his boy. You'll be back with us soon enough. I'll keep you updated. Get some rest while you can."

Finley hung up and paced the living room, circling in front of the fireplace, through the open kitchen and dining room and back, glancing at Robin with each pass. His sandy blond hair stuck out from under the cover, and he looked peaceful snuggled in the blanket. She was anything but. Being here set her teeth on edge. Too many bad memories threatening to overwhelm—mother slamming out the front door for the last time; father in the worn brown recliner in the corner drowning his pain in a bottle of booze; and her, huddled in her bedroom trying to muffle his agonized sobs.

She forced herself to think about something else. Dylan. Why had she been so upset about the station shooting? She'd probably seen more injured people than Finley ever would, but she'd been physically and emotionally shaken. The redheaded nurse who held and comforted her obviously knew the reason. Maybe one day Finley would have a chance to ask Dylan.

"Forget about Dylan." Dylan Carlyle, of the police-royalty Carlyles, would never be interested in her, especially not after how they'd met.

Then full awareness hit her—*those* Carlyles. The Carlyle building was named for Dylan's grandfather and father, Garrett and Bryce Carlyle, who had both been killed in the line of duty. Every year during National Police Week, Finley heard their names. When she visited the station's community room, she saw the plaques dedicated to them. No wonder Dylan had been upset. She must think Finley horribly dense and insensitive. And she'd be right. Emotional situations were messy, defied logic and easy solutions. Finley avoided them whenever possible.

Robin tossed fitfully in his sleep, and Finley eased onto the end of the sofa and lifted his feet onto her lap. "You're all right, buddy. I've got you." She rubbed his legs gently until he quieted and then rested her head back against the sofa and closed her eyes.

❖

Dylan cranked Abba's "*Dancing Queen*" up on her iPhone and twirled around the cottage while she dressed the next morning, hoping it would improve her mood. The extreme highs and lows, followed by melancholy, of the attack at Fairview Station had robbed her of sleep. She felt sluggish and distracted as she thought about her siblings. Her sisters and brother had chosen challenging and dangerous jobs, just like her father and grandfather. Maybe the whole family were adrenaline junkies. She got her rush after the carnage, piecing people back together, but it still provided the need for immediate, focused effort.

"Dylan, honey?" G-ma's voice barely pierced the music through her earbuds.

She tapped her phone and everything went eerily quiet. "Yes?"

"May I come in?" G-ma stood tentatively in the doorway, dressed in a pair of coveralls with butterfly designs, and her gray windblown hair stuck out at odd angles.

"G-ma, you never have to ask." She stepped into her grandmother's arms and held on. "How did you know I needed to see you right now?"

G-ma returned the hug and guided her to the sofa. "Because I know my girls. Music therapy isn't working this morning, is it?" She eased Dylan back to arm's length and made eye contact, and Dylan shook her head. "So, how're you holding up?"

Dylan's eyes filled with tears at the concern in G-ma's voice and she let them fall. She couldn't hide anything from G-ma anyway. "Yesterday was too close to home. I saw firsthand what my siblings face on the job, and it rattled me. I'm sure everybody feels the same, maybe for different reasons, but the whole family was in danger this time. We could've been wiped out, along with everyone else there, if those guys were better shots and had automatic weapons."

"And?" G-ma probed deeper.

"It reminded us all of things we'd rather forget. G-pa killed by a gunman when a domestic went horribly wrong, and Papa ambushed by an armed burglar." She brushed her cheeks and sniffed back another burst of tears.

"Yes, police officers and firefighters have dangerous jobs, but public service is what we do. And we *always* get through the challenges, good and bad. We're Carlyles." G-ma glanced around the room, her green eyes searching for the same thing every time she visited—her son's Lucite encased police badge.

"I haven't unpacked it since I moved into the cottage, but I want to display it in my home, someday."

"When you're ready, honey."

"It's been eighteen years since Papa died, G-ma. Will I ever be ready? He was my father." She sucked in a sharp breath as the selfishness of her grief registered. "And your son. I'm sorry, G-ma. I can't imagine what it's like for you, losing your husband and only son."

G-ma kissed her cheek. "It's hard on the whole family, honey. This thing at the station has rattled us all, but we'll be okay as long as we have each other. Do you want to spend a couple of nights at the house with us? Your mama and I love girls' nights."

"I'll think about it. I'm off today, but when I start back to work, I'll be fine. Not so much time to think. Ben and Jazz have already texted, and Mama came by earlier. Everybody's looking after me, as usual." She loved that her family was so protective, most of the time, but she'd asked for the cottage out back so she could take care of herself and establish more independence, while weaning off slowly. She still needed her family and would never break from them completely.

G-ma stood and hugged Dylan again. "If you need to talk, you know where we are. I love you, baby. See you at brunch."

"I'm going in to check on Hank, the injured officer, but I'll be back." Tears stung Dylan's eyes again as G-ma headed for the door. "Thanks, G-ma. I love you."

Dylan dressed in a pair of jeans and a blue checked blouse and drove to the hospital. On the way, she wondered if a few nights with her mother and grandmother might be exactly what she needed. She parked and headed for Hank Hinson's room so she could update Ben and Jazz, the second reason for their early texts.

Two officers were posted across from each other in the hallway of the ICU floor, one to monitor people going in Hank's room and as a sign of respect, and another across the hall to keep the suspect in his room since he was technically under arrest. She stopped by the nurses' station and got updates on both patients before heading to Hank's room first. According to the overnight staff, surgery to mend Hank's femoral artery had been successful, he'd rested during the night, and was progressing well. Dylan peeped into the dimly lit room, and Hank's eyes were closed, so she tiptoed in for a visual check and to listen to his breathing and check the monitors for herself. She sent a quick text to her sisters and started across the hall.

When she entered the shooter's room, the privacy curtain was drawn and she heard angry whispering. "Where is your damn brother, Spencer? Tell me."

Dylan pulled back the curtain, and Finley Masters straightened beside the bed. The curtain stirred the air around them, and Dylan caught a whiff of Finley's tantalizing cologne and pulled it deeply into her lungs. Finley's jeans and flannel shirt looked fresh, but her eyes were bloodshot and shuttered as she clutched the bedrail. "What are you doing?"

"Trying to get information."

"You shouldn't be here." The neurologist had induced a coma to facilitate healing, and Spencer needed rest to recover. "You can't question him, even if you were on the case, which I'm pretty sure you're not, at least not officially."

Finley moved closer. "What's with you? Yesterday you chose to help this would-be cop killer over one of our own, and today you won't let me do my job."

Dylan waved toward the unconscious man on the bed. "Hello. He's in a coma." Cops were relentless predators when one of their own was hurt, stopping at nothing until they caught the suspects. But they also made mistakes from being tired, pushing too hard, and bypassing laws and protocols in the name of closure and not-so-subtle revenge for a fellow officer.

Finley looked between Dylan and Spencer, her brows crunching closer together. "I thought he was sleeping or medicated. But I'm not really trying to interview him, just find out where his brother is. I couldn't take a formal statement in his current condition anyway. It would be illegal and never hold up in court. A coma, huh?"

"Slowing brain function allows time to heal, reduces swelling, and lowers but doesn't cut off blood flow to damaged areas." Dylan nodded toward the door. "You're not allowed in here, and questioning is totally off limits until his condition improves. Understood?" They stepped outside, and Dylan glared at the officer guarding the door. "No other visitors, police or otherwise, unless cleared by his doctor." The officer nodded sheepishly at Dylan. "Sorry, ma'am." "My fault entirely," Finley said with a heavy sigh. She looked like she was about to collapse.

Dylan steered her to a chair near the nurses' station and squatted beside her. "Did you get any sleep last night?"

"Not much. Robin had nightmares and woke up a lot. He needs his mother, or somebody better at parenting than I am. The wildfires in California delayed Becky's flight, so who knows when she'll get here." Finley swept a hand through her blond hair and then tugged on the chain at her neck.

"And you want to go back to work and search for the other suspect," Dylan said.

"Yeah, I want to be out there. Hank was my training coach and now he's my best friend. I have to catch this guy, but my primary responsibility right now is to his son."

Dylan felt a wave of admiration for Finley. She was desperate for the hunt, but she put loyalty and duty to family first, an endearing quality Dylan hadn't expected. "Good for you. And where is Robin now?"

"Asleep in the waiting room at the end of the hall. He wanted to be near his dad. A nice older lady waiting for her husband to come out of surgery is watching him while I—"

"Yeah, I got that part. If his mother doesn't make it home tonight, let him sleep in his own bed, if you have access. It might help."

"Good idea. Thanks." Finley lowered her head but looked up at Dylan through thick lashes. "I really want to interview this guy. When he wakes up, maybe you could let me know?"

"That's not my call, Finley. I'm not his doctor. And you're not on the case, are you?" Police procedure didn't allow best friends to investigate each other's cases, nevertheless they still worked them— just without authorization. Dylan was certain Finley wouldn't stop.

"Not officially, but the captain said I could ask questions and nose around. We both want the same thing, Dylan, to do our jobs, be the best. Am I right?"

"Is that a trick question? My job requires that I consider the patient's health first and foremost, even if justice takes a back seat." Finley wouldn't trick her into giving an inch so she could take a mile. Other officers had tried to play her, but she knew their tricks.

Dylan wondered if Finley was mounting another argument as she rubbed the back of her neck and stretched her shoulders, but Dylan spoke first. "Why don't you go home and rest? You look exhausted."

"I won't rest until Becky gets here. I need to explain what happened and make sure she and Robin are okay. Maybe after… after we catch the other guy."

"Fine, then we better get some coffee in you if you insist on staying upright."

Before Finley could respond, Robin ran down the hallway yelling. "Daddy. Daddy."

Finley jumped up and sprinted toward him, falling to her knees and sliding to a stop in front of him. "What's wrong, buddy? Are you okay?"

"I dreamed…my…daddy was…dead. Is he dead, Fin?" Robin asked through tears. He wiped his eyes on the sleeve of the Carolina sweatshirt he'd worn yesterday.

"No, pal. He's just sleeping."

Dylan watched the exchange with awe and disbelief. Was this the same woman who'd been so casual about having sex in an on-call room two days ago? The same woman who'd put herself in harm's way for her friend and his son? Beneath her cavalier persona and bravado, Finley Masters actually cared. Her concern for Robin was palpable, and it stole Dylan's breath.

"Are you sure?" Robin sucked back a sniffle.

"Totally, dude. I looked in on him a few minutes ago." Finley's voice dropped to a gentle whisper and she slowly rubbed Robin's back.

"Can I see him?"

When Finley glanced up at her, Dylan offered them her hands. "Why don't we check on your dad, Robin?" Both of them squeezed Dylan's hands as they walked, and her heart ached for their pain.

Finley could be frustrating and reckless, but right now she and Robin were like lost children who needed comfort and reassurance, and Dylan couldn't deny them.

She reluctantly released Finley's hand, pushed open the door, and waved them both inside Hank's room. The dim light meant to facilitate sleep made Hank's color seem too pale and unhealthy, so Dylan upped the level as Finley and Robin got closer to the bed.

Robin sniffled. "He looks…so white. Like a ghost."

Finley knelt beside Robin, took his hand, and placed it on top of Hank's. "He lost a lot of blood, but he's still very much alive and warm. Feel."

"Yeah," Robin said uncertainly. "But what are all those tubes and wires for?"

To the ten-year-old, the ICU probably seemed like a terrifying place. Dylan stepped closer to the bed. "These," she pointed to the tubes from the IV bag, "are replacing the fluids your father lost so he can get stronger. The wires are connected to a heart monitor. If anything is off, a very loud alarm will sound, and the nurse will be here immediately to check on him. All this stuff just looks scary, but it's really helping him. He's doing very well, Robin."

"Okay. Can I kiss him?"

"Of course, you can, buddy," Finley said. She picked Robin up under the arms and held him closer to Hank so he could kiss his father's cheek.

"I love you, Daddy," Robin whispered.

Dylan moved toward the door to give Robin and Finley privacy and lowered the lights again. While she waited, she made a split-second decision, and when they joined her, she asked, "Do you guys want to come to brunch with me?" Finley studied her hard for several seconds, as if trying to decide if she was serious.

"I'm not sure that's a good idea," Finley said. "Isn't Sunday mealtime like a big deal at your house? I'd hate to intrude."

"So, you've heard about the famous Carlyle family brunches." She grinned and stooped to Robin's level. "You met my niece and nephew at the fair yesterday. Remember? They have a cool gaming system."

Robin's eyes brightened and he pulled on Finley's arm. "Can we, Fin? Please?"

Finley glanced between the two of them. Was she just worried about imposing on a family tradition? No doubt Robin would have fun and be distracted from the trauma of yesterday for a while, but what about Finley? Was she thinking the same thing Dylan was—how she'd explain bringing Finley home for brunch? Would the family assume she and Finley were an item?

"I'm not very good with families," Finley finally admitted.

"We don't bite…not on the first visit anyway." Why was she trying so hard to convince Finley to do something Dylan wasn't sure she wanted either? She'd made a totally spontaneous, emotional decision, and her family would attach meaning to it. Was she ready for questions about Finley's presence on top of everything else they'd be dissecting at brunch?

Robin jerked on Finley's shirttail. "Can we please go?"

Finley nodded and looked at Dylan. "If you're sure."

Dylan wasn't, but she said, "See you both at eleven thirty."

CHAPTER SEVEN

Finley parked her old red Jeep in front of the two-story Carlyle home and took in the welcoming wraparound porch with cushioned rockers and the colorful pansies and ornamental cabbages in the yard. She imagined the Carlyle clan sitting on the porch sipping beverages, watching the kids play, and sharing their days, just like a real family should. She couldn't remember a time when her family had sat on their porch for any reason. And if it weren't for landscapers, her lawn would be overrun with weeds and not a plant in sight. "I can't believe I'm doing this."

"Doing what?" Robin asked.

"Coming here. What was I thinking?" She turned in her seat to look at him and chuckled at how his mouth twisted and his nose crinkled in an inquisitive expression.

"Uh-oh. You've got that you-better-behave look."

Finley ruffled his sandy hair. "And you're just too smart for your own good sometimes. We both need to be on our best behavior because Bennett and Jazz are your dad's and my bosses. I think you'll be fine. Not so sure about me though. I'm not good with families...or behaving sometimes."

"You're good with my family."

"Yeah, but..." She couldn't explain to a ten-year-old that all families weren't like his or how dysfunctional hers had been. He didn't need to know, and she didn't need to remember. "Your family is special."

"Obvi." He pointed to himself.

"Good point. Come on, rock star. Let's eat so you can play longer."

She rang the doorbell and brushed the sleeve of her soft plaid flannel shirt. She should've worn something less woodsy and stopped by Hank's to get Robin some clean clothes. Serious parenting fail. She was about to turn around when Dylan opened the door.

"You made it. Welcome." She stepped aside and waved them in.

But Finley couldn't move. She stared at Dylan's parted lips, her smile, and her chestnut ponytail wrapped into a loose knot atop her head. Her mind flashed to their first meeting—Dylan leaning in the doorway, feet crossed at the ankles, watching her having sex with another woman—so attractive that Finley had totally lost concentration. Dylan was more beautiful now, her cheeks flushed and her steady gaze pulling Finley in.

Robin pushed her from behind. "Hello. The lady said welcome."

The strawberry-blond Carlyle twins rushed to the door and saved Finley from offering an embarrassing excuse.

"Hey," Ryan said to Robin. "Riley and I are playing Dragon's Crown on our PlayStation. Dragons, sorcerers, treasure. It's got everything. Wanna join?"

"Yeah."

"The three Rs together again," Riley said. "We whipped serious butt in basketball yesterday."

Finley caught Robin's arm before he shot after the twins. "Remember your manners. Say hello to the family first and don't forget to wash your hands before you eat."

"Guys, introduce Robin to everyone," Dylan said. "Finley and I will be there in a sec." The kids dashed toward the back of the house, and Dylan turned to her again. "I need a favor."

"Anything...I mean sure." Either she was in serious danger of being irrevocably attracted to Dylan or she was more nervous than she thought.

"This invitation, actually any invitation to Sunday brunch, is a big deal to our family. I asked you because—"

"It would be good for Robin to be around other kids, have some play time, and distract him from what happened and his dad's condition." The considerate gesture was just so Dylan. Finley had experienced her nurturing side at the hospital last night and with Robin earlier today. Dylan's compassion and caring made her an excellent doctor and a very appealing woman; the kind of woman who'd be an excellent partner and loving mother, exactly the kind of woman Finley should avoid.

"Yes. I just didn't want you to think..." Dylan flushed a light shade of pink. "My family tends to jump to conclusions when we bring someone to Sunday brunch, so don't be put off if they ask questions. We talk about everything. If you feel uncomfortable at any time, you can say so...or leave if you prefer."

Finley tried for what she hoped was a cocky smile but felt a pang of disappointment. "I get that it's not about me." Had she wanted the invitation to mean more? How could it? "Would you prefer arrogant or flirtatious?" Detachment was her trademark, but it felt forced and shallow under the circumstances. Damn it, she wanted the Carlyles, and especially Dylan, to like her.

"Just be yourself, Finley. My family is pretty good at figuring out the truth anyway."

Dylan clasped Finley's hand and drew her toward the kitchen. The way her smaller hand curled into Finley's and the silkiness of her skin sparked a longing for something Finley couldn't name. Before they entered the eating area, Finley stopped her. "In case I forget to say this later, thank you for the invitation, for both of us."

Dylan stared at her a few seconds longer, took a deep breath, and preceded her into the room. "Everyone, this is Finley Masters, an officer at Fairview Station." She launched into introductions as she pointed around the large refectory table. "At the head of the table, Norma Carlyle, affectionately known as G-ma, and to her right is my mother, Gayle, aka Mama."

"Ma'ams, thank you for having me." Finley nodded toward Norma. Her overalls, covered with bright balloon designs, and red T-shirt added a touch of lightheartedness to a room filled with serious faces directed at her. Finley suppressed an urge to laugh.

"Oh my, you're a handsome one," G-ma said. "I can see why Dylan brought you home."

Gayle brushed a hand through her loose curls, and Finley saw where Dylan, Bennett, and Simon got their rich brown hair color. "Norma, don't start," Gayle said, waving her down like a dog whisperer soothing an overzealous puppy.

Dylan pretended not to hear or ignored the exchange. "You already know Ben and Kerstin," she said.

"Welcome, Fin," Bennett said in her captain's voice.

Bennett and Jazz looked less imposing in casual clothes, but today their eyelids drooped and shoulders sagged, like they were near exhaustion. Finley hadn't heard anything about the search for the second shooter today and had to ask, "Anything new in the case?" Bennett shook her head, and Dylan directed her attention to the opposite end of the table.

"And you've probably seen my brother around. This is Simon, the firefighter."

"The city's newest battalion chief, if memory serves." Finley shook hands with Simon. "We've rolled on some fire calls together."

"How's it going?" Simon grinned, flicked the collar of his plaid shirt, and then nodded at Bennett and Jazz. "Glad you got the dress code memo."

"Comfort first, dude."

Dylan pointed to the woman next to Simon. "This is Stephanie, Simon's better half, and the new owner of Ma Rolls food truck. You've already met their kids, Riley and Ryan."

"Nice to meet you, Stephanie," Finley said. "I see where your twins get their gorgeous reddish-blond hair. Definitely not the Carlyle side of the family."

Stephanie smiled appreciatively and her freckled face flushed.

Dylan guided Finley around the table. "And this lovely creature is Emory Blake, Jazz's fiancée."

Dylan wasn't kidding. Emory's auburn hair, twisted in a French braid down her back, sparkling green eyes, and full figure made her hard to forget. "I've seen you around the hospital. You a doctor too?"

"Social worker," Emory said.

"You were at the station yesterday. Thanks for what you did for Robin," Finley said.

"Just glad I could help. He and Shea will need to talk to someone about what happened, but they're young and resilient."

"Let's save that discussion until after we eat," G-ma said and motioned toward the adjoining room. "Since the kids are happier in front of that machine in the den, I'll let them eat in there just this once." She hollered over her shoulder, "Come and get it, kids. The rest of you unload." She pointed to the sideboard. "Phones in the basket."

Everybody complied, and then Bennett and Jazz played block the food from Ryan and Riley as they dodged between them snagging bacon and biscuits. Robin stuck close to Finley and behaved like a perfect little gentleman. Though she had no part in his upbringing, Finley couldn't have been prouder.

"Seriously, guys," Simon said, "if you don't stop playing, we'll never eat."

While the children filled their plates and disappeared again, the rest of the family took their places around the table. Mama waved to an empty chair between Emory and Stephanie. "Finley, you can sit there. Neither my daughter-in-law nor soon-to-be bite."

When Finley settled and looked up, she found herself across from Captain Carlyle. Damn her luck. Which was worse, staring at the woman she wanted to sleep with or her sister who could probably read that desire on her face? Finley started to reach for the bacon but caught Dylan's eye and got a slight head shake.

Everyone focused on G-ma, the shot-calling matriarch. From the few interactions she'd seen, Finley deduced the role dynamics around the table. They deferred to gray-haired Norma, not from some outdated sense of duty, but because of deep love and devotion to her and their traditions. Gayle served as second-chair, the conductor, and smoother of rough patches. Simon, de facto patriarch, herded the unruly pack. Bennett and Jazz played equal parts jester and fierce protector, while their accomplished wives nurtured, guided, and supported with equal vigor. Dylan acted as the heart of the family, full of raw emotion, honesty, and compassion. No wonder everyone wanted to protect her. Finley wanted the same—wanted and didn't want. She'd never fit in here.

G-ma lifted the bacon tray, took a few slices, and passed the plate right, which seemed to be the go signal. Everybody grabbed, their spoons and forks clattering against the dishes. After several minutes, the room quieted while everyone ate. Finley glanced toward Dylan, but she hunched over her plate as if her food might try to escape. When Finley looked up again, Bennett stared at her, brows knitted, eyes searching. Was she the reason everyone was so quiet?

"So, where did you meet my baby sister, Finley?" Bennett crossed her arms over her chest as Finley had seen her do often when addressing lineups. Her tone was full of protectiveness and a hint of warning.

Finley swallowed hard and searched for an answer that wasn't a total lie, wouldn't make her sound exactly the way she'd behaved that night, and wouldn't result in discipline.

"At the hospital, where do you think?" Dylan said without looking up. "Cops, doctors, nurses, patients, and visitors, you meet the whole community eventually."

"Sooo, you two aren't dat—"

"No, Kerstin, we're not dating," Dylan snapped. "I simply asked Finley and Robin to join us because I thought they could use a hot meal and a distraction for an hour or so."

Finley glanced around the table, and everybody was staring at Dylan, who still hadn't looked up from her plate. Bennett nodded with a satisfied grin, and the rest of the family kept eating. Finley had a feeling she was missing something. This family talked about things. Novel approach. Love bound them to each other like invisible strings, a connection that both comforted and saddened Finley for her loss.

"Well…" G-ma placed her fork across her plate and released a deep sigh. "In case you're wondering, Finley, we're not usually so touchy or so quiet. My husband, Garrett, and I started these brunches years ago to keep in touch with each other and our children when he worked shifts as a patrol officer. These times are usually filled with good food, sharing our weekly news, and lots of laughter." She took another deep breath. "But the shooting dug up painful memories and put everyone on edge."

Dylan finally looked up and dropped her fork, the sound reverberating in the silence. "Do we have to—"

"Yes, darling." Mama cupped her hand. "We need to talk about what happened. Our family faces things and deals with them."

"In front of strangers?" Dylan motioned toward Finley. "No offense."

Finley wiped her mouth. "None taken." Family drama was the last thing she wanted. She'd had enough of that to last a lifetime. And she wasn't anxious to expose her emotional discomfort and clumsiness to the entire Carlyle clan at once.

"And you, young lady," G-ma said nodding toward Finley. "Your friend was shot, nearly killed, and his son watched the whole thing. That leaves a mark."

Finley's throat tightened. "Yes...ma'am." The words barely squeaked out past a jumble of unexpected and unwanted emotions.

"Norma, really?" Mama asked.

G-ma shrugged. "Since when isn't honesty welcome at our table?"

"We usually wait until our guests have eaten to begin the inquisition," Mama said.

Dylan shook her head. "We might have to do this, G-ma, but Finley doesn't."

"And you, my precious baby girl." Mama took Dylan's hands in hers. "You ran into a gunfight. I thought you were the only child I wouldn't have to worry about getting killed on the job." She made eye contact with Bennett, Jazz, and Simon and gave each a weak smile. "What were you thinking?"

Dylan stared at her mother, and Finley felt exactly what she saw reflected in Dylan's brown eyes—fear, anger, and sadness. "She had to help," Finley said. "Isn't that what we all do, in the line of duty?" She understood the all-consuming need to do something in times of crisis. It defined her, and doing was better than feeling any day.

Tears pooled in Dylan's eyes, and she swiped them away before giving Finley a hard head shake as if to say, don't be nice to me right now.

Finley wanted to draw attention away from Dylan, but everything inside her resisted exposing herself any further. She didn't share her feelings, especially with strangers. She cleared her throat. "If you'll excuse me, I'll check on Robin." She stood and started toward the den.

"Sorry if we made you uncomfortable, Finley," Mama said and then turned to Dylan. "I love you, darling, so please don't ever take that kind of risk again."

Dylan pushed her chair back from the table and stood slowly, and Finley waited for what came next. "Seriously? G-pa and Papa died in the line of duty. Ben and Jazz face the same dangers every day, and Simon runs into burning buildings. But I'm supposed to stand by and watch people die when I could be useful? If you know me at all, you know that's not me." She threw her napkin on the table. "I can't do this right now." She headed toward the front door.

"Honey, wait," G-ma said, but when Dylan didn't stop, she called after her, "Remember the fundraiser next weekend. We need to discuss the arrangements. It's all hands on deck."

Finley started after Dylan, but Mama waved her off. "She needs to process. Let her go."

For some reason, that was the last thing Finley wanted to do.

❖

Dylan fast-walked down Elm Street, her boots tapping angrily against naked concrete or crunching dried, fallen leaves with each step. Her family was unbelievably insensitive sometimes, or maybe she was too sensitive. She yanked the hairpin from her topknot letting her hair fall and enjoying the way it whipped around her face in the cool breeze. It symbolized freedom and separation from the heavy mood at home. She usually looked forward to family brunches and found them restorative, but Finley staring at her across the table like she understood had proved too personal and intimate on top of the recent shooting. What did Finley know about losing someone or a need to serve so deep it felt like hunger?

Dylan passed through the arched stacked-rock pillars marking the entrance to Green Hill Cemetery on Wharton Street and continued to the circular family plot where G-pa and Papa were buried. A few months earlier, the family celebrated her father's birthday here with their annual picnic, but today she needed to be alone and think.

She brushed a pile of dried leaves away from the headstone, sat on the corner, and lowered her head in her hands. "Why am I such a mess, Papa? I've put police officers back together after shootings, knifings, fights, and car accidents. Why is this one different?" She closed her eyes to an image of Finley kneeling in front of Robin. "No, it's *not* about her."

Talking with Papa made things easier when she was a child, but since that horrible night the police chief and chaplain knocked on their door to deliver the news, Papa's comments had been internal. She still imagined them as clearly as if he sat next to her, his rich baritone voice always kind.

"*You experienced the danger your sisters face.*"

"I preferred to imagine their jobs like on TV where everything turns out right, but I saw happiness turn to tragedy in a second. It scared me, Papa."

"*I know, and you did what had to be done, just like they do every day. What else? Are you close to the injured officer?*"

"Not really. He's one of Bennett's and Jazz's...and he has a child..."

"*And...*"

Even in death, Papa forced her to face her feelings and the truth. He'd inherited G-ma's candor gene and been the perfect complement to Mama's tact and diplomacy. "I've seen a different side of Finley since the shooting, but it doesn't change my decision about dating cops. I can't lose someone else I care about. It's easier to be alone."

"*But is easy enough, my girl?*" Warmth spread through Dylan and tears spilled down her cheeks. Papa was still with her. He'd always called her *my girl*, though he'd had three.

"It has to be enough." Dylan heard the crunch of dead leaves and looked up as Bennett sauntered toward her. "Should've known they'd send you."

Bennett casually stretched her long jeans-clad legs out on the raised platform beside Dylan and leaned back against the headstone. "Nobody sent me. I knew you'd be here and wanted to check on you. Papa not giving you the answers you want?"

"God, you're so much like him—"

"And you." Bennett grinned and gave her a wink.

"It's totally annoying because I get away with nothing, not even my own thoughts." Dylan blew out a long breath.

Bennett's grin vanished and hurt clouded her brown eyes. "I'll leave you to it then."

She started to get up, but Dylan grabbed the tail of her flannel shirt and pulled her back down. "I'm sorry, Ben. I don't mean to take my frustrations out on you." They were quiet for a few minutes, Dylan staring at Papa's headstone, and Bennett retying her hiking boot laces with mock concentration.

"So, what's really going on? You've patched up injured cops before. Watching it happen in real time?" Bennett clasped one of Dylan's hands and made her look at her.

She nodded. "Seeing my family in the line of fire sucked, big time. And you, Jazz, and…Finley acting bulletproof didn't help." Her gut twisted with the memory. "Two children's lives changed forever because of what happened. Papa's death resurrected. If you need more reasons why I'm upset, I can go on."

"Would you bite my head off if I offered an additional possibility?" Bennett asked.

"Can I stop you?"

"Probably not. Somebody needs to say it aloud, and since Papa can't and you won't…" Dylan looked away, but Bennett waited until she made eye contact again before continuing. "Maybe something, or someone, is waking you up inside—"

"Stop." Dylan buried her face in her hands again. "I can't."

"Finley Masters is a cop's cop who works and plays hard. She has a reputation with women, and from what I've heard, had a difficult family life. She is *not* the kind of woman I'd choose for my baby sister, but you two sparred and pranced around each other like cats in heat at the fair. And when you weren't together, you were tracking each other." Dylan cocked her head and started to speak, but Bennett continued, "I'm a trained observer."

"I don't pran—"

"I'm not saying you should marry or even seriously date her, but if you're interested, maybe you should check it out. And if you're not, find someone else. Anyone else who appeals."

"I won't mention to G-ma or Mama that you advised me to have a fling with a notorious womanizer. That *is* what you're suggesting, right?"

"You haven't been attracted to anyone in a long time, Dylan. It's not healthy for someone as young and vibrant as you to be alone. I want you to be happy."

"Dating Finley Masters won't make me happy. Total nightmare. Maybe I *should* start seriously looking for someone to date who isn't a cop or in any way related to my job." Dylan shook her head so hard she felt dizzy like she'd done as a kid when she didn't want to hear or accept the truth. "The only thing worse than worrying about my family every day they go to work is having my lover climb out of bed and strap on a gun. I can't and I won't. End of subject."

CHAPTER EIGHT

F inley woke the next day in the pink bedroom again with Anita sleeping beside her. The details of why she'd come here again were fuzzy. She searched her memory and replayed the previous afternoon and evening. Becky Hinson and her mother arrived from California and went directly to the hospital to check on Hank. Afterward, they picked up Robin and left Finley at home alone with her memories. She grabbed the vodka bottle—her father's crutch of choice—and downed part of it before running to Anita for hers. But she'd choked, halfheartedly having sex with Anita while remembering how much she'd enjoyed holding Dylan's hand yesterday before brunch.

She glanced at the bedside clock. "Shit, I'm going to be late my first day back." Anita didn't budge, for which Finley was grateful. She grabbed her clothes, deciding to shower and change at the station. On the way in, she called the hospital to check on Hank, and thirty minutes later, slid into a chair in the lineup room.

"Welcome back, Fin," the sergeant said. "What's the latest on Hank?"

"The nurse said he slept well last night and ate some solid food this morning. He might be going home soon. Becky and her mother finally got here after the wildfire delays in Cali, so Robin is back with her."

"Excellent. Let us know if we can help at all." The rest of the guys offered their support before the sergeant gave out assignments. "Evening shift is busy, as you know, but stay sharp. The second shooter is still at large. He came to our house and hit one of our guys. Let's find him. Dismissed."

Finley strapped her leather carry bag that held personal equipment across her body, picked up the department-issued gear bag containing her gas mask, helmet, citation book, and other forms, and followed her squad out the back door of the station to the police parking lot. She popped the trunk of her squad car and inventoried the equipment—spare tire, fire extinguisher, yellow crime scene tape, flares, and orange safety cones. She flipped open the tachograph mounted in the trunk to record speed and times the vehicle was in motion and stationary and slid the round record disk into place. Next, she opened the back door of the squad car and tipped the seat up, checking underneath for evidence, weapons, or other contraband left by prisoners and not removed by the previous shift officer. All clear and good to go.

Finley checked on duty with her call sign and badge number before heading for the Daytime Resource Center on East Washington Street. Her number one informant, Badger, a former soldier now homeless, usually hung out there until closing time every day. She teased him that he had a serious crush on the director, Adena Weber, which he never denied.

Adena, tall with auburn hair and a gorgeous body, was walking toward her car with Badger tagging behind and his arms full of papers when Finley pulled into the lot. He glanced around furtively as if looking for something or someone. Badger didn't appear dangerous, but Finley knew his wiry frame was all muscle because he prided himself on staying in shape.

Finley watched from her car while Adena took the papers from Badger, climbed in her car, and waved as she pulled out of the lot.

"You know she's gay, right?" Finley said to Badger watching him stare after Adena.

He kicked the tires of Finley's car and shrugged. "Does that mean I can't like a person?" He wiped a hand over his tanned face as if the gesture would erase some of the heavy wrinkles from sun and exposure. He kept scanning the area around the DRC, and Finley suddenly got it.

"You're looking out for her."

Badger tipped his head slightly. "That drug ring operating out of the DRC freaked Miss Adena out. She asked if I'd stick around during the day until they closed. And if I get myself straight, she might make it a permanent paying gig. Bouncer lite."

"That would be great, Badger. You're a good man."

"Once a soldier...or a cop...never changes, right? We know which rocks to look under for the vermin." He tugged a toboggan from his back pocket and pulled it down over his ears. "What's up with you?"

"Same ole, same ole. Get in. We'll do a drive-thru somewhere. What're you in the mood for?" Finley shifted her briefcase into the trunk while Badger settled in the passenger seat beside her. Being caged in the back didn't agree with his PTSD.

"Taco Bell?"

"Works for me." She checked out on the radio so she wouldn't get a call while they talked and then drove toward Summit Avenue. "So, how you been doing?"

"Not bad. Miss Adena found these jeans for me." He rolled up one leg and pointed. "Flannel lined. They'll come in good this winter if I'm still on the street."

"Nice. Have you seen that therapist anymore?"

He nodded.

"Taking your meds?" She didn't probe too deeply because Badger didn't like to talk about Afghanistan. He was too young to be so messed up, but with Adena's help, maybe he'd get back on his feet.

"The DRC staff gets my med refills." Finley pulled up to the order window, glanced his way, and he said, "I'll have two Burrito Supremes and a large Pepsi."

She doubled the drinks, paid and collected their order, and then drove to Third Street behind Fairview Station and parked. Badger didn't really like being seen as an informant under his current circumstances, so she kept it simple for him.

He took a big bite of the burrito, chewed a bit, and said, "Sorry about the guy who got shot. Friend of yours?"

The familiar ache tightened Finley's chest, and she took a moment to recover. "My best friend. That's why I need your help, Badger. He has a wife and kid, and he almost died. The second shooter is from Atlanta and ditched his SUV at Four Seasons Mall." She pulled up the BOLO on the computer mounted in the floor between them and swiveled it so he could get a look. Can you ask around?"

Badger studied the photo and stroked the stubble on his chin. "I've seen him."

Finley felt a prickle of anticipation. "When? Where?"

"I left the DRC walking toward the depot late yesterday. I check on the place after they close on the weekends, you know, for something to do. This guy was standing near the train overpass looking toward the center chomping on his cigarette butt like he was pissed."

"Are you sure it's the same guy?"

Badger nodded several times. "We made eye contact. I might be fucked up from the war, but I'm still good with faces. It's him." He took another bite of his burrito and washed it down with Pepsi.

"Did you see him today?"

"No, but I wasn't outside much because of the rain. I'll let you know if I do."

"You still got your cell phone and my number?"

Badger nodded again, finished his food, grabbed his drink, and reached for the door handle. "Thanks for this. I'll walk back."

Before he left, Finley pulled a twenty from her wallet and offered it to him.

"I'm good. You've done enough."

She tucked the bill in his shirt pocket. "Just in case." Too many good people like Badger ended up homeless because of bad circumstances, bad choices, or bad luck. Her father could've been one of them if their house hadn't been paid for when her mother left.

She shook off the thought and drove toward the DRC to check it out before dark. If Jeremy Spencer had been there before, he might go back, but why? Jeremy and Josh had a couple of family members in town, along with Josh's ex-girlfriend, but officers had them staked out. Jeremy wouldn't go there for help. And he'd abandoned his vehicle, so he was either walking or using cabs, buses, rentals, or Uber, all risky since the police were monitoring those as well. He hadn't bought a bus, train, or plane ticket, at least not under his own name. Maybe he was looking for clothes to alter his appearance or some assistance from the DRC to get back to Atlanta.

Finley parked in the DRC lot, tucked her Maglite under her arm, and walked to the overpass. Near the edge of the sidewalk, she spotted several cigarette butts and a crushed patch of vegetation as if someone had stood there for a while. She squatted for a closer look. Newport menthols. The cigarette butts had been chewed until the white filter frayed and stuck out of the brown tipping paper like bushy hair from a toboggan.

She flipped on her Maglite as the sky grew darker and followed a trail of butts and trampled grass up the side of the embankment to an abandoned building with a shipping container in front. She tried the front door. Locked. Metal grating covered the windows, and the garage doors along the front hadn't been raised recently as evidenced by families of spiders occupying the corners. Next, she inspected the padlocks on the container and saw no signs of tampering.

Finley made her way around the building, flashed her light along the side, and jumped back. "Shit." A huge white face with a black mask and green lips glared at her. "Dumb ass," she mumbled to herself. The garage door and entire side of the building had been tagged with colorful graffiti. She grinned at the flowers, strangely shaped creatures, and symbols but had no idea what they meant. Shining her flashlight on the ground again, she followed the now sparse trail of cigarette butts toward a stack of railroad ties beside the railroad tracks.

She stopped near the corner of the building and listened. Voices from restaurants and bars across the tracks on Elm Street, cars traveling along Washington Street below, and the distant horn of an approaching train echoed on the cool night air. Then to her right, she heard rustling, a furtive movement, and strained to pinpoint the exact location, but the train's horn grew louder and masked the sound. She crouched and edged closer to the stack of railroad ties, the only place for someone to hide.

She was about to turn her Maglite on when the train rounded the corner and its headlight blinded her. She blinked several times. A flash of something to her left. A creature, the shadow of a tree limb, or a person? She spun and ran toward the movement and felt a sharp pain in her shins. Was she hit? She lost her grip on her flashlight and grabbed for it as she fell. Her head struck the ground and then nothing.

CHAPTER NINE

The overdose in treatment four is puking her guts up and wishing she'd never seen a bottle of Tylenol. She'll be pooping tiny charcoal pellets later. What's next?" Dylan rested her elbows on the nurses' station and gave Holly a wink. "Send me in, Coach."

Holly pulled at a short strand of red hair that refused to lay flat beside her ear and checked her tablet. "I've got a Braxton Hicks in two who insists she's going to drop that baby any minute. Irregular contractions that don't get any closer, stop when she walks, and only in the abdominal area. Want to try convincing her she's not really in labor?"

Dylan shook her head. "Hard pass. I'll grab a coffee. Want one?" Holly nodded, and Dylan started toward the elevator until a commotion from the front of the ER drew her attention. Finley Masters stood at the check-in desk in uniform with her bare feet bloody, boots in her hand, and a goose egg sized knot on her forehead. Dylan's heartbeat throbbed in her throat and her mouth dried.

"Want me to have one of the residents take it?" Holly asked, giving her a strange look.

The fact that she hesitated before answering annoyed Dylan. "Please." She wasn't over how Finley had kindly taken up for her and sympathized with her at brunch yesterday, or Bennett's suggestion that maybe she should do—what with Finley—or someone. She pushed the elevator button twice and prayed the car would hurry.

"Dylan." Finley hobbled toward her. "Will you tell the sergeant I don't need to see a doctor?" She gestured at one of the men beside her.

The hematoma over Finley's left eye was dark purple, and Dylan couldn't help shifting into doctor mode. She checked Finley's pupils and glanced at her carotid pulse. "Let one of the residents check you out just to be sure, since you're here." Finley's face paled and she swallowed hard, glancing at the men beside her. She was afraid and afraid for them to see.

"Could you do it? I mean, I only skinned my shins on a couple of railroad spikes and bumped my head when I fell. No big deal." Finley's blue eyes drilled into hers, pleading.

She should say no and walk away, but the last two times Finley had asked for help, Dylan had refused and Finley shut down. For some reason, she didn't want that to happen again. "Okay." She guided Finley toward an open treatment area and nodded for Holly to send the other officers back to the waiting area. "Have a seat on the gurney and look at me." She pulled on gloves and flashed the penlight from her pocket in Finley's eyes, satisfied with their response to stimulus. "Does your head hurt?"

"No."

"Did you lose consciousness?"

"Yeah. When I woke up, the sergeant and a couple of the other guys were standing over me. But I feel fine in the head." She lifted her feet and raised her uniform pants legs. Blood-soaked bandages barely clung to both shins.

"What the hell is that?" Dylan asked.

"QuikClot. I tried to convince the sarge I could stop the bleeding and keep going, but it didn't work."

"You carry QuikClot in your equipment bag?" She shivered at the thought of Finley or one of her sisters trying to stop themselves from bleeding out on the street.

"On my utility belt. And Narcan. You never know when a victim might need help before EMS arrives. Besides, when you've been in as many scrapes as I have, you learn to take care of yourself. And it won't do any good if it's in my bag in the car." She nodded toward the boots she'd brought in with her. "I took those off so the blood wouldn't ruin them. You couldn't tell it by looking, but those steel-toed puppies are expensive, probably as much as a pair of your girly heels. You do wear heels, right? If I'm—"

"Finley, stop the nervous chatter."

"I'm not nervous." Her eyes widened, and she looked everywhere else in the room except at Dylan or her injuries. "I just don't like hospitals much or feeling…"

Dylan rolled Finley's pants legs higher, picked an edge of the dressing between her thumb and forefinger, and slowly peeled it away from the cut. "Don't like feeling what? Helpless, needy?" Every cop she treated believed he should be invincible, immune to injury and pain. But Finley seemed scared or at the least tormented. Did something else contribute to her dislike of hospitals and feeling powerless?

"Any of that." Finley flinched when Dylan eased the bandage back. "And I don't need…to be here, but the sergeant insisted."

"Maybe you're right, but let's make sure." The quiver in Finley's voice softened Dylan's resolve to remain professional and she tried to distract her with one of the things cops loved to talk about, their work. "Tell me what happened while I clean this and take a closer look."

"I was checking the DRC after an informant said he'd seen our second shooter hanging around. I thought I saw someone move in the shadows and ran toward him. When I woke up, we couldn't find any trace of another person. I apparently bumped into a railroad tie with two spikes sticking up. Not too smooth."

Dylan stood at the foot of the bed and rubbed her hands up the sides of Finley's bare legs checking for fractures and sensitivity. Her muscles were tight and skin hot with no other signs of injury. Dylan released a breath and slowed her movements. Her stomach clenched, and her nipples hardened with arousal as she slipped from being a doctor checking a patient to a woman caressing another. That never happened to her on duty. Finley shuddered, and Dylan jerked her hands away. "Did I hurt you?"

"N…no."

"What then?" Dylan summoned her professional persona and repeated the exam, certain Finley was being macho.

Finley's gaze rested on Dylan's hands as she moved up and down her legs from knees to ankles. "Your touch is so gentle. It's—"

"Focus, Masters," Dylan said, trying not to think about what Finley had said or how touching Finley felt personal to her as well. She cleared her throat. Damn it. *She* needed to focus. "Were the spikes rusty?"

"I didn't check, but I imagine so. Those ties have been there for ages."

"You'll need a tetanus shot, if you haven't had one in the past ten years."

"I'm sure I have. I spend way more time here than I'd like." Finley glanced down at her injuries and then quickly away. "Will I need stitches?"

"Maybe a couple. Shins are a little bony for staples, and I don't think Steri-Strips will work in your case."

"Why? They're quicker, don't hurt as bad, and I like both of those things, a lot."

Finley acted like a kid anxious to play in the sandbox again, but her game involved danger and life-threatening situations. No matter how much Dylan disliked the thought of Finley in harm's way, it was none of her business. "Will you stay off your feet for a couple of days so you don't risk reopening the wounds?"

Finley shook her head. "I have to get this guy before he finds a way to skip town."

"Stitches it is then. And you should probably have someone check on you during the night. You were unconscious, so there could be complications from the bump on your head. Maybe Anita could help." Why did she say that? It was definitely not her concern who Finley spent time with or why. She stood and pulled back the curtain.

"Where are you going?"

Finley reached for her, but Dylan sidestepped. She couldn't bear Finley's imploring look any longer or seeing her in pain. "I'll have a resident get you stitched up and out of here as quickly as possible."

Finley scooted to the edge of the bed and was about to jump off.

"Stay right there." Dylan said. "We don't need your blood all over the ER."

"But I thought you'd..." Finley clutched the locket around her neck and swallowed several times. "I wanted you...never mind."

Finley asked for her help, and Dylan had wanted to comply so badly it scared her. Instead she said, "Our residents are perfectly capable of closing a laceration, and they need the practice." She rushed toward the elevator, calling over her shoulder. "Resident and suture tray to treatment five. I'll be in the canteen if you need me." Disliking arrogant, reckless Finley was easy, but this vulnerable one aroused something in Dylan she didn't want to acknowledge.

❖

The flimsy gray-green curtain fanned in the breeze behind Dylan as she rushed from the treatment area, and Finley stared open-mouthed. What had she done that sent Dylan hurrying from the room this time? It was becoming a habit. And why did she keep asking, *asking* Dylan to help her? She didn't need people and she certainly didn't ask for help, except when Dylan was around apparently. Before she could examine the questions further, a peppy man holding a medical supply tray like a waiter offering filet mignon threw back the curtain.

"Okay, Officer, let's get you stitched up and back on the job."

"That's the best news I've heard all night." Finley lay back on the gurney, focused on the glaring light the young resident now trained on her legs, and tried not to think about what he was doing.

"You'll feel a little stick and some tingling while I numb the area."

Needles. She remembered being with Hank the past couple of days, the constant presence of nurses and doctors with needles, and then further back to her father's bedside. She trembled.

"Did I hurt you?"

"No, I'm fine." She closed her eyes and recalled Dylan touching her legs earlier. Finley had been excited, no doubt, but also comforted, a soothing feeling more intimately stirring than physically arousing.

"Okay, I think we're good." The man glanced at Finley as if expecting praise for his stitching efforts, but Finley didn't even look at his work.

"Thanks. Can I go now?"

"Sure. Here are the care instructions for your injuries. Dr. Carlyle recommends you not be alone tonight because of the blow to your head. Otherwise, you're free to go."

Finley took the offered paper and gingerly stood, thankful that the pain from earlier was gone. After putting her boots back on, she found the sergeant and her other squad member still waiting in the lobby. "Is my patrol car here?"

"No, because you're going home." Her sergeant gave her a pointed stare. "I'll give you a ride, and don't come in tomorrow unless you're one hundred percent."

"But, Sarge."

"Don't 'but, Sarge' me. While you check out, I'm going to see Hank. You'll probably want to do the same. I bet he's going stir-crazy up there with nothing to do."

"Roger that." Finley completed the paperwork to check out and when she finished, the redhead who'd comforted Dylan two days ago was staring at her with a look she couldn't decipher. She glanced at the nurse's name badge. "Holly, is Dr. Carlyle around?"

"I think she went to the canteen, but I wouldn't bother her if I were you."

"Thanks for the warning and no disrespect, but you're not me." Holly obviously knew Dylan better, but Finley couldn't leave without seeing her. After upsetting her at the Carlyle brunch yesterday and again today, she needed to explain, but what or how she wasn't sure. Emotional situations and explanations weren't her strength.

Finley stood outside the canteen, scanned the room, and located Dylan near the back at a small aluminum table overlooking an interior courtyard. She caged a beige paper coffee cup in her hands and stared out the window, her face drawn and pensive. Finley hesitated, second-guessing her intrusion, and then walked toward her. "Mind if I join you?"

"Can I stop you?" Dylan's voice was low, almost pained.

"Yes, but I wish you wouldn't." Finley waited, clutching the back of a chair. "I wanted to apologize and thank you."

When Dylan finally looked up, her brown eyes were filled with agony and tears until she blinked them away like drizzle on a windshield. She nodded toward a seat.

Finley eased the chair out, afraid if she made a loud noise Dylan might come to her senses and send her away. "I wanted to apologize for yesterday at your family's brunch. It was nice...but I obviously upset you. And I'm sorry for walking out." She shook her head. "Not what I wanted to say first. I should've remembered that your grandfather and father were killed in the line of duty. Sometimes I'm not really sensitive, not even close. I'm just no good at...this."

"What exactly is this?"

Finley fidgeted with her necklace and forced eye contact with Dylan. "Talking about stuff, sharing, especially feelings. But it's not something I've consciously worked on either. I'm from a family of emotional morons, or so my father said." Dylan shifted in her chair to face her, and Finley savored the minor victory. She had Dylan's full attention, and the connection made her want to try harder to explain herself. "I can't get away with diversions around you though. Not sure why." Finley raked her fingers through her hair. *Where did that come from?*

"I like talking about things. Guess that's in my blood," Dylan said. "So, tell me about you and Hank. How did you get so close?"

"He was my training coach for eighteen weeks after recruit school." Her voice sounded foreign, too timid and needy, but she continued. "That bonds you for life. He and I paced while Robin was being born. He stood with me at my father's funeral. And I couldn't keep him safe."

"But you helped keep him alive and possibly saved his son's life. You stepped up in a big way. And what you did for his son after the shooting means more than you know. Nothing is more important than family." Dylan gave her a smile that lit up her eyes. "Why were you so uncomfortable Sunday, if you can tell me? I know my family can be full-on."

"You're all so close and you talk about everything. I didn't grow up like that, which is probably why this is so hard for me. I felt like an outsider, not because anyone made me feel unwelcome but because of who I am. And, let's face it, there's about a million of you." She poked at Dylan's hand playfully.

"How did your father die?"

Finley withdrew her hand. She didn't want to talk about her father, but she'd opened the door, and if she slammed it shut now, they might never have another real conversation. Was that even what she wanted—this intimate back and forth exchange? She swallowed hard. "He drank himself to death."

"I'm sorry, Fin."

It was the first time Dylan had called her Fin, and it felt like she was talking to an old friend who understood. But Dylan wasn't a friend, just a gorgeous, accomplished woman with a perfect family that Finley didn't fit into. She must seem like such a loser to Dylan. Tears threatened, and her father's voice sounded in her mind. *"Do something."* She shoved her chair back as she stood and said, "I'm sorry I disturbed you. I wanted to apologize."

"Fin, wait."

But she was already halfway across the room. She needed to go before she came totally unglued in front of Dylan. Finley took the stairs to the ICU, wincing with each step but determined to keep going in spite of her injured shins. She inched the door of Hank's private room open and peered around the corner to make sure he was alone.

"Are you going to skulk in the shadows or come in?"

Finley dragged one of the cushioned green hospital chairs to his beside and flopped down. "I can tell you're feeling better. You're already busting my balls."

Hank chuckled and nodded toward her feet. "Why are you hobbling?"

"Tangled with some railroad spikes and lost. Just a couple of stitches in each shin. The meds haven't completely worn off yet, so it doesn't hurt much right now."

He shook his head. "You can't stay out of trouble without me."

"Fortunately, you're being sprung soon, so there's that."

"Yeah, but I won't be back on the job for a while. You've got to take it easy. We can't both be riding a bed or recliner while this other guy is still loose."

Finley felt a pang of guilt. She should've already figured out how to locate the suspect.

"And don't beat yourself up for any of this. It's not on you, Fin." He studied her for a few seconds. "So, what else is bothering you? Woman trouble?"

"What? No way." But she'd answered too quickly and with too much feeling.

"Who is she?"

Hank didn't need to worry about her problems right now. "No one." Nothing had ever been further from the truth. Dylan Carlyle was far from no one, but Finley wasn't certain why she felt that way or how to explain it to Hank. He'd warned her away from Dylan once already.

She stood. "The drugs are making you sappy. Get some sleep. I'll check by again tomorrow." He started to say something, but she held up her hand, unsure she could take another serious conversation right now. She waved good-bye, closed the door, and stepped across the hall to the officer standing guard at Spencer's room. "Is he still out?"

"Yeah."

"Have you heard anything? Any chance he's faking?" Finley asked.

"Nothing new. I don't think he's faking though. He's definitely in a coma."

"Damn it." She cursed under her breath and pulled a business card from her pocket. "Give me a call when he starts to come around. Just me. Pass it along to your relief. Okay? I'll owe you."

The officer hesitated before he accepted the card, tapped her number into his mobile, and handed it back to her. "I'd like patrol to catch this guy. Detectives get all the glory."

"Thanks, man." She texted her sergeant that she was staying with Hank, went to the canteen for a coffee, and snuck back into Hank's room. He was already asleep, so she stretched out in the chair beside his bed. She'd rather be awake here with a man she admired and cared about than at home remembering the one she'd lost long ago.

CHAPTER TEN

A fter her shift in the ER ended the next morning, Dylan stopped by the ICU to check on the Fairview Station patients as she referred to them. Neither was technically her patient, but she'd treated them first and would always remember them because of how their worlds had collided. Besides, Ben and Jazz would expect updates on the officer.

When she entered Josh Spencer's room, he lay under white sheets tucked neatly that showed no signs of recent movement. His condition hadn't changed either, still comatose. Did he, as Finley suspected, know where his brother was and if so, would he help police find him? And what would become of his daughter, Shea, who'd seen her father shot and shooting at others? Finley's father had slowly killed himself with alcohol. Both situations left lasting marks on a child's life. She wanted to know more about Finley's childhood and her mother, but she'd looked ready to break last night before hurrying from the canteen.

Dylan finished reading the overnight notes on Spencer's chart and walked across the hall to Hank Hinson's room. She opened the door and stopped. Finley was slouched in one of the uncomfortable hospital chairs at Hank's bedside, still wearing the bloody-legged uniform she'd worn yesterday. Her chin rested on her chest, and she breathed heavily. In the relaxed posture of sleep, Finley's features were softer, unguarded, and almost innocent. Dylan had seen a different side of Finley during and after the shooting—unselfish, loyal, kind, compassionate, and a bit afraid. This was the side Finley shielded behind her tough cop exterior, and the one that interested Dylan.

Hank mumbled in his sleep, and Finley jerked awake and rose to his side, flinching as she stood. "You're okay, pal. I'm right here."

"He's probably dreaming," Dylan said, moving from the shadowed corner into the light.

Finley whirled around. "How long have you been here?" She brushed a hand through her blond hair and wiped her chin.

"Long enough to see you drooling in your sleep. Very attractive." Dylan was pleased the kidding eased the tight lines around Finley's mouth. She nodded toward Hank. "He's going home today. Maybe you want to change clothes and come back later. The discharge paperwork won't clear until at least eleven. You have time."

Finley nodded. "If you're leaving, I'll walk out with you."

Dylan turned and led the way to the elevator. "Hank will be fine if he takes it easy and follows doctor's orders. Would you consider doing the same and give your shins a chance to heal before going back to work, Fin?"

"I'm fine."

"Of course, you are." She'd fought this battle with her sisters too many times and lost to think she'd have any luck with Finley. When the elevator door opened and they crossed to the walkway leading to the parking deck, Dylan pointed. "I'm up there. I'll see you around."

Finley followed. "Me too." When they reached her level, she unlocked the door of an older model red Jeep parked next to Dylan and climbed in. "Thanks for looking out for Hank." She turned the ignition, and Dylan heard a clicking noise.

"You could trade this antique and get a Subaru like a good lesbian," Dylan joked.

Finley nodded toward Dylan's bright yellow VW bug. "If that's yours, you're not a good lesbian either."

"I used to be, but I lapsed. My camping days are over, and I'm partial to yellow."

Finley tried to start the Jeep again. More clicking. "Damn."

"Problem?"

"I was going to get the battery and starter checked, but things happened." Finley got out of the Jeep, waved, and started walking. "See you."

"What are you doing?"

"Going home."

"Don't be silly. I'll give you a ride. Get in the car, Masters."

"You don't even know where I live," Finley said.

"Can't be that far if you were going to hoof it. Besides, I can't let an injured person walk home." Dylan unlocked the doors of her bug and got behind the wheel. When Finley settled beside her, she headed for the exit. "Where to?"

"College Hills."

"That's pretty far from Cone Hospital." But she appreciated that Finley hadn't taken her assistance for granted. "Have you lived there long?"

"Family home. It's for sale if you know anyone who might be interested." Finley stared out the window, her face blank.

Obviously a sore subject. Maybe Finley thought she'd revealed too much last night. Dylan preferred the more approachable, vulnerable Finley Masters, but to get her back, Dylan would have to open up as well. *But she's a cop.* Dylan brushed aside the warning. This was just a conversation, not a lifetime commitment.

"I understand family homes, full of memories, dreams, and ghosts. The house my grandparents and parents lived in and reared their children is still our family home. It's the place my grandmother and mother lived when their husbands died. All the children were born and two of them married there. Simon, Stephanie, and the twins, and now Bennett and Kerstin live in homes in the same neighborhood, and Jazz and Emory have made an offer on a house across the park from Bennett. Fisher Park is gradually becoming Carlyleville."

"That's quite a legacy. It was obvious at brunch that you're very close," Finley said wistfully.

"A blessing and a curse. Sometimes I feel not even my thoughts are private."

"But you still live at home?"

"Sort of. The carriage house out back." Dylan glanced at Finley who now stared at her with interest. "Don't get me wrong, I love my family. They're my lifeline. I just need a bit of space, a place where I'm not constantly reminded that I'm the baby. The overprotectiveness is suffocating at times. My grandmother lost her husband and son, my mother's husband, in the line of duty. I have two alpha cop sisters, and a macho brother who tries to ride herd over a family of strong, independent women. Imagine being the youngest child in *that* family and not carrying a gun."

"I see your problem." Finley was quiet for a few minutes before adding, "I like my neighborhood, set between Greensboro College and UNC-G. It's lively and has a nice mix of historic and new builds, residential and commercial, and it's also close to downtown. I've walked home more than once after a pub crawl at Hamburger Square."

Dylan noted that none of Finley's descriptions offered anything personal like her own oversharing comments about family and feelings.

Finley rubbed her hands down her uniform pants, and Dylan felt her stiffen beside her. "Still, overprotectiveness is better than none. At least you know your family cares." She pointed for Dylan to make a turn.

"What about your family? Any siblings?"

Finley reached for the door handle. "Just stop here at the curb."

Dylan pulled over in front of a pale gray single-story bungalow with white columns across the wide front porch and a swing to one side. "This is beautiful. Why would you sell?" Finley gave her a hard stare. "Sorry…memories. I get it. I didn't mean to make you uncomfortable."

"I'm good. Thanks for the ride." Finley got out but ducked her head back inside. "Hey, I was wondering…would you maybe want to go…with me…to see *Hamilton* in Durham?"

"What?" Her pulse trebled, but was *Hamilton* or Finley asking her out the cause? Was this like a date? If so, she had to say no, but it was *Hamilton*. "Really?"

Finley started to close the car door. "You can think about it and—"

"Wait. You can't just lob that out there and walk away. How did you score tickets to the hottest show in the country? I've been trying for months, but they're sold out."

For the first time since they left the hospital, Finley's face transformed into her trademark cocky grin, the adorable scar under her lip deepening like a dimple. "I know people in high places."

"Seriously, Masters, spill."

"Hank and Becky were going. She gave me the tickets, said I'd earned them. You helped when he got shot too, so I thought you might like it. I'm not really a musical fan and I feel bad about enjoying them when they can't. And there's the whole crowd thing. On second thought, maybe I'll sell them."

"Now you're just messing with me. I'd love to go. I mean…I'll help shoulder your guilt. When is it?"

"Tomorrow night. I know that's short notice, but—"

"I'll make it happen if I have to bribe somebody to fill in for me…as long as it's not…a date because I don't date cops. And you let me pay for my ticket."

"I didn't pay, so why should you? And definitely not a date. I just don't want to go alone, and it seems a crime to leave a seat vacant when people would almost sacrifice a limb for a ticket. If you don't want to go because people might get the wrong idea, fine. I'll ask Anita."

"Stop. I'm in," Dylan said.

"Okay then. I'll pick you up at the carriage house at five tomorrow afternoon. The show starts at eight, but traffic will probably be crazy and we have VIP seats." Finley's smug smile grew before she closed the door and walked away.

Dylan didn't think about her motivation for accepting the offer so quickly—*Hamilton*, Finley, or keeping her away from Anita—what difference did it make? She was going to freaking *Hamilton*…

with Finley Masters. Nerves bunched in her stomach as she drove home. She took a deep breath and let it out slowly. Totally all about the play.

❖

Finley made a show of reaching for her house keys, but when Dylan's car disappeared on Spring Garden Street, she plopped into the swing on the porch, in no hurry to go inside. She'd spent many nights out here, snuggled under a blanket, head between two pillows, hiding from the stench of alcohol and her father's weepy stories about how much he loved her mother. If he'd loved her so much, why had she left? She hadn't even sent a card when he died. Maybe their love had been one-sided. Same story replayed ad nauseam through time. But Finley wasn't going to be a victim. She'd seen the pain love caused and was just fine playing the field, playing it safe.

She forced herself to focus on something more pleasant. She'd asked Dylan Carlyle on a faux date. But they'd agreed it wasn't a date. They were going on an outing. Whatever, she felt totally amped that she'd had the courage to ask, and completely shocked when Dylan said yes.

But what next? She couldn't slip into the carriage house a couple of times a month for a quickie with the protective Carlyles nearby, even if Dylan wanted her to.

Something about her usual game plan seemed off. She'd seen Dylan's professional side at work, laughed with her about Subarus, experienced her connection to family at brunch, and heard the love in her voice when she talked about them, but something about their interactions bothered Finley. Simple. Dylan wasn't fling material. Plus, she was too close to her livelihood to fool around with. If her sisters found out—she didn't want to consider the repercussions.

The rising sun peeped through the trees across the street, reminding her to take things one day at a time. She and Dylan would go to the play and then return to their normal lives. They were simply too different to have anything more, even a fling. With a heaviness she hadn't felt before, Finley rose and entered her empty house. She had more immediate things to worry about than a date that wasn't and a woman she'd never have—showering, getting back to the hospital for Hank's discharge, finding a mechanic who made house calls, evening shift, and finding the second shooter.

CHAPTER ELEVEN

Finley waved to Robin and Becky standing in the front yard of Hank's house and backed her patrol car out of the driveway. Her partner was safely home, surrounded by family, cops, and more comfort food than a small army could handle. He was in for a long recuperation period, but at least he was alive.

She steered her cruiser toward the parking deck at Cone Hospital where she was meeting Phil to look at her dead Jeep. When she pulled in, he was already under the hood, hands dirty, and a happy grin on his face. "Damn, you don't waste time, buddy."

"I love being a backyard mechanic. If it paid better, I'd quit the force and do it full time."

"So, what's the prognosis?"

"Dead battery. Patsy is bringing a replacement. I'm just unhooking the old one."

"Your wife helps you on road calls?"

"She loves it. Gives her something to do while the kids are in school and it gives us more time together."

Finley gave him a skeptical look. "Seriously?"

"Between shifts, bomb squad call outs, and extra duty, we don't get a lot of quality time at night, so this works for us. You should try settling down, Fin. Not as bad as you think."

"Yeah, right." Patsy rolled up in their old SUV, and Finley ran to help. "I've got it, Patsy." Finley gave Patsy a quick hug and took the battery to Phil. "I should probably get going. I'm still checked out of service at Hank's. I'll pick the Jeep up after my shift."

Phil stopped work long enough to give his wife an affectionate hug and a quick kiss before saying, "We can drop it off at Fairview Station on our way home. It's not out of our way."

"That would be great. Thanks. What do I owe you?"

"Just for the battery and maybe twenty. Does that sound okay?"

"Does that sound okay? You're seriously underselling your worth, dude. You're an excellent mechanic *and* you make service calls. Way better than AAA." She handed him the money and added an extra twenty. They had four kids, so it would be put to good use.

She watched them hug again as she pulled out of the lot. Would she ever find a woman she wanted to settle down with and one she missed enough to plan extra time together? With her background and track record, it seemed unlikely. Her cell rang, and she pulled it from the clip on the dash. "Masters."

"It's Badger. That guy you were looking for is back at the DRC."

Finley's pulse raced and she whipped the cruiser around in the street. "Hold on." She keyed the mike. "Car 1212."

"Go ahead, 1212."

"I've received info the Fairview Station shooting suspect is at the DRC. Dispatch a unit to East Market Street near the railroad overpass, one to Lyndon Street on the west side, another to Murrow Boulevard on the east, and I'll approach from the front." She waited until the other units had been dispatched and continued. "Give us an operational frequency, have the other cars switch over, and stand by for further." She returned to her cell. "You still with me, Badger?"

"Yeah. You better hurry. He's headed for the front door."

"What's he wearing?"

"Blue jeans, a green Army fatigue jacket, and a red toboggan. I'll follow him out...and see if he gets...in a vehicle."

Badger breathed hard, and Finley followed his pounding footsteps as if she was running beside him. "Just get a description of the car, Badger. Don't try to stop him." She keyed the mike again. "All units, I have an informant on site, and the suspect is heading to the DRC parking lot." She relayed the clothing description. "He might have a vehicle. Will advise shortly." She floored the gas pedal and flinched when her stitched shin ached in response. She was still too far away to help Badger if he got in trouble or to spot the vehicle if the suspect had one.

"Damn, he's fast," Badger said. "He's pulling out of the lot in a beige Camry, heading east. I'm not close enough to get the tag. Sorry, Fin."

"It's okay. Thanks for your help." She hung up and spoke into the mike. "The suspect is in a beige Camry headed east on Washington Street. No tag available. Unit on East Market, head toward Pastor Anderson Drive. I'll take East Washington." The problem was Spencer had three possible escape routes from Washington Street, including doubling back into downtown.

Her sergeant came over the frequency, "Fin, I'm moving more units in to lock down the area. Let us know if you see the vehicle."

She gripped the wheel tighter and whizzed past the DRC, sliding sideways into the right turn following East Washington. She slammed on brakes after the railroad overpass and glanced to the right down Medley Street. No sign of the car. He'd have more options and a greater chance of escape going forward, and he'd know that since he grew up in Greensboro. She scanned the area but had no idea which path he'd taken. Damn. She pounded the seat beside her. "I've got nothing," she said. Gunning the gas again, she steered straight toward Dudley Street, but when she got to the intersection, if he'd come this way, he was long gone. "No sign of the vehicle."

After an hour of officers searching the area and stopping any vehicle close to beige, the sergeant cleared the units for calls. Energy drained from Finley, and she felt helpless and angry. She'd blown two opportunities to stop the suspect, once at the original scene and again today. What kind of cop and friend was she?

❖

Dylan's earbuds blared eighties dance tunes while she switched from her blouse and jeans to scrubs in the hospital locker room. The changing ritual delineated her personal life from the often horrific professional one, and the music amped her up for night shift. Someone tapped her shoulder as she pulled her scrub top on, and she turned, tucking her phone and earbuds into her pocket.

"How's it going?" Holly asked. "I tried to catch you this morning in the parking lot, but you were too far ahead. And you were walking with a cop. Was that—"

"Yes." She forced her breath out normally because the mention of Finley sent her pulse and temperature skyrocketing. Hoping no one had seen them together in the parking lot of the biggest gossip center in town had been futile, and denying or avoiding now was wasting time. Holly would get the truth out of her anyway. "It was Finley Masters, but don't get any ideas."

"And wasn't she in your little yellow bug when you left?"

"Yes."

Holly backed her against a locker and placed her hands on either side. "Dylan Carlyle, if you don't tell me what happened, I'll be forced to make up my own version and spread it around the ER like warm butter on hot toast. By the end of the shift, you'll be having sex with her." She pulled back and stared down at Dylan. "Are you? Having sex with her?"

Dylan slipped under her arms and spun away. "Of course not. Don't be ridiculous."

"And why not?" Holly wiggled her eyebrows. "I damn sure would be if she'd stand next to me for a few seconds."

Dylan mentally erased the bad visual. "Uh-uh. She was sleeping in the officer's room this morning, and we walked to the parking lot together because we were both leaving. Nothing else. And then her car wouldn't start. And she'd just had her shins stitched after running into rusty railroad spikes. I couldn't let her walk to College Hills injured. Could I?" She was rambling and offering too much information. Nerves.

Holly grinned. "Of course not. You're so kind." She edged closer, her green eyes twinkling with mischief. "So, what's she like? What did you talk about?"

"Nothing really."

"You drove all the way to College Hills without speaking a word?"

She'd done most of the talking, and Finley's revelation about her father had occurred last night, not on the drive home. But sharing anything Finley said with Holly felt like a breach of confidence because Finley was so private. Dylan had to say something or Holly wouldn't let it rest. Before she could think it through properly, she blurted, "She asked me to go to *Hamilton* with her tomorrow night."

Holly's mouth fell open, closed, and then opened again before she said, "And you refused."

Dylan's face heated and she turned back toward her locker to keep Holly from seeing her guilty expression. She took deep breaths, grabbed her stethoscope, and slowly looped it around her neck, buying time before facing Holly again. She shook her head.

"You said *yes*? Seriously?" She took Dylan's hands and guided her to the bench in front of the lockers. "Tell me."

"It's *Hamilton*, Lin-Manuel Miranda's baby. Tickets are gold." Holly kept staring, and Dylan had to be honest. She relaxed her shoulders and said aloud what she'd only thought and tried to deny before. "And I've gotten a glimpse behind her macho butch facade. She might have a few redeeming qualities. I said might. We'll see. But we're just going to a play, and I made it clear it wasn't a date. She understands."

Holly leaned forward and hugged her. "I'm not sure I do, but just FYI, sex doesn't have to include dating. I'm happy for you."

"There's nothing to get excited about. It's just—"

Holly's phone beeped and she glanced down. "Multiple MVAs inbound. We better get going." She stood. "I'll see you on the floor."

"And don't spread a word of this to anyone," Dylan shouted as Holly disappeared behind the row of lockers. Holly didn't need reminding, but Dylan felt better saying the words aloud. She checked her scrubs, retrieved her tablet, and joined the fray. At least work would distract her from Finley Masters and everybody's advice that she take her on. Maybe she would. The thought of sex with Finley excited her, so actually having sex with her was bound to be at least decent.

CHAPTER TWELVE

Dylan rolled another pair of clingy leggings off and tossed them on the discard pile on her bed. The stack of clothes that hadn't made the cut for *Hamilton* teetered near the topple point, and she was no closer to choosing an outfit. This wasn't a date, but the reminder didn't make her choice any easier.

"Hey, you in there?" Bennett's voice sounded at the front door along with her usual triple-tap knock.

"Go away." She didn't want Bennett anywhere near her right now. She'd draw the wrong conclusion from Dylan's indecisiveness. "I'm busy. Come back tomorrow."

"No can do. Mama sent tomato soup and a grilled cheese sandwich since you missed breakfast and lunch." Bennett opened the door, set something down on the counter, and her voice grew louder as she moved closer to the bedroom.

"Don't come in here. I'll be out in a minute." But she and Bennett were too much alike, and the warning cued her big sister that something interesting was happening.

She nudged the door open and leaned against the frame. "Wow. Moving? Purging? I haven't seen your room this messy since..." She snapped her fingers and grinned. "Since your first date with that jock in high school, the one who took you to prom." She glanced from Dylan to the discarded clothes. "Oh my God, you've got a date."

"No, I do not. I'm going to see *Hamilton*."

"Uh-huh. With whom?"

"That's not important." She couldn't look at Bennett because she read her like the clichéd open book.

"Apparently, it's very important or you wouldn't be drowning in rejected outfits and flitting around like a teenager."

Dylan ducked into her closet to hide the flush of heat burning her face and slid her little black dress from the hanger. "Seriously, Ben. I'm not even sure what flitting is, but I'm not doing it. My outfit is important because *Hamilton* is a big deal. The play won eleven Tony Awards, including best musical. Lin-Manuel Miranda is a theatrical god. He's won a Pulitzer, MacArthur Fellowship, and Grammys. I could see anyone there, so attire is critical."

"Because you're trying out for a part, you want to impress society's elite, or because of your date?"

She slipped the dress over her head and turned for Bennett to zip it. "Again, no date."

"Then tell me who you're going with or I'll stake out the cottage and wait for her to pick you up."

Dylan flipped a leather, short-waisted jacket off the rack and dug the matching calf-length boots from a pile on the closet floor. "I'm thinking the dress, but tone down the formal with these." She held the items up for Bennett's approval.

"Damn. That's hot. Not something I should say about my sister. I meant the outfit. Who is she, Dylan? You're killing me. And your avoidance just fuels the fire. Don't make me guess."

"You'd never—"

"Finley Masters."

Dylan's jaw tightened, and Bennett added, "Nailed it."

"I'm going to kill Holly Burns. She swore."

Bennett reached for her, but Dylan rolled out of her grasp. "Don't be upset with her. The canary feathers were practically sticking out of her mouth, and she folds like a cheap chair under my considerable charms. She never actually said anything, but I could tell when I got it right."

Dylan laughed. "She does find you irresistible for some reason, but still...And it's *not* a date. Finley had a free ticket, and I'd go with anyone to see *Hamilton*, so don't give me grief."

This time when Bennett moved to hug her, Dylan didn't resist. "I'm not, really. I couldn't be happier that you're going out. I'm just surprised it's with her." She kissed Dylan's forehead. "Please be careful. Fin's a great cop, but she's got a reputation, and I don't want you to get hurt."

"Aren't you the one who suggested I give her a shot, big sister?"

"My protection gene is kicking in, and I'm reconsidering."

"Don't worry. I know what she's like. I've seen her in action." Dylan broke their embrace and busied herself with the discarded clothes on her bed so Bennett wouldn't see the look on her face. She'd slipped up, and if Ben put two and two together, she'd know exactly what Dylan meant.

"Dylan." She didn't move. "Dylan Carlyle, look at me."

She slowly turned to face Bennett. "What? I promise I'll be careful."

"Finley was the officer you saw servicing one of the nurses. While she was on duty. In the on-call room." Dylan didn't answer, and Bennett continued. "I knew she was a player, but that is totally unacceptable. I have to—"

"You have to do nothing. Promise me. After almost a week, if you say something now, she'll know I told you. I got the point across, and since she knows we're related now, I doubt she'll be so careless again."

"Not the point. She violated the code of professional conduct, and I can't let that stand."

Dylan grabbed Bennett's arms and rose on her tiptoes so they were closer to eye contact. "Can you please stop thinking like a police captain for one minute and just be my big sister?" She sounded urgent, almost pleading, but she wasn't just protecting Finley. She hadn't reported Anita either.

"You like her." Dylan shook her head, but Bennett held her gaze. "You don't want to, but you do. I know you, baby girl, and if this is important to you, I won't say anything."

Dylan sighed. "Thanks. I'm not sure what I feel, so don't jump to conclusions. I don't plan to. Now help me clean up this mess so I can eat my soup and sandwich and finish getting dressed." Bennett handed her clothes, and she hung them back in the closet, wondering if she'd been honest with Bennett and herself.

❖

Finley paced her living room in a black sports bra and glanced at the vintage Omega Constellation watch she'd spruced up with a red leather band. Was it still working? The hands had hardly moved since she last checked, but it seemed like forever ago. She hadn't slept the night before because she'd let Jeremy Spencer get away again. And now, she was skittish like her outing with Dylan was her first date ever. "Snap out of it," she said aloud, hoping the verbal slap would help. Ten more minutes before her designated dressing time.

She paced through the living room and kitchen again and then stomped into the bedroom. Close enough. Refusing to overthink the evening or her outfit, she grabbed a pair of black jeans and slid into them. Silk briefs. She liked the way they hugged her legs and sent a charge through her when she snugged them against her crotch. White shirt? No harm in playing to her strengths, date or not. Black made her blond hair pop. She exchanged the shirts, stepped into black boots, and scanned herself in the full-length mirror on the back of the door. Her red watchband added an unexpected dash of color. Almost perfect.

At the front door, she grabbed her gray leather coat and glanced back inside. She hadn't thought about being in the house alone today or about its sad memories. Interesting, but she'd been preoccupied about going out tonight. Somehow thoughts of Dylan had temporarily masked the bad in the house and made it tolerable again. Her cell rang, and she answered without looking at the caller ID.

"Fin, it's Anita. Are we still on for tonight?"

"Huh?" Her gut tightened. Had she made a date with Anita and forgotten about it when Dylan accepted her invitation? She reviewed their last hookup. Nothing. "We didn't make plans. Did we?"

Anita paused before answering. "Not specifically, but we usually get together for some midweek stress relief." Her tone was low and teasing.

They did have a fluid arrangement to meet for sex at least once a week, usually Wednesday. The thought brought Finley up short because it suddenly felt like a habit, an obligation she no longer wanted to honor. "I can't tonight."

"Why? Are you…" Her words trailed off. Perhaps she remembered their agreement about no questions or commitments. "Okay, sure. No problem. Call me when you're free."

"Will do. Thanks, babe." She slid the phone back in her pocket, feeling almost as cheap as the night Dylan caught her having sex with Anita. What would Dylan think about their arrangement? It was none of her business. She probably had flings too. Nobody really dated these days anyway. They just hung out with friends and hooked up until they found the right fit. But as she drove, she had trouble imagining sex with Dylan as casual.

Finley cruised by the Carlyle home and breathed a sigh of relief when none of the family was on the wide front porch or in the yard. She wasn't ready for the Carlyles to know she was sniffing around Dylan or for their questions about her intentions when she wasn't sure of the answers. She turned onto the side street and stopped in front of the cozy cottage that looked like a miniature version of the big house. She cut the ignition, grabbed the door handle, and forced her thudding heart to calm. Why was she nervous or excited…or was it both? She grabbed her crotch. "And you behave tonight. Dylan isn't our usual type and she's *not* for you."

She plopped a piece of peppermint gum in her mouth to help with the dryness, opened the car door, and started toward the cottage, but the lights went off inside so she leaned against the side of the Jeep and waited. She wanted to see Dylan's outfit while her expression was partially concealed by shadows from the sun setting behind her. And she wanted to watch Dylan walk down the sidewalk, to her.

When Dylan closed the door and turned, Finley stopped in mid-chew and swallowed hard. "Damn." She should've given more thought to her clothes choice.

Dylan smiled. "You approve?"

"Totally. You look unbelievable." Her heart raced again, and arousal thrummed between her legs. She was in so much trouble.

CHAPTER THIRTEEN

Dylan walked down the sidewalk toward Finley, trying not to stare, but she failed. Her ash blond hair shone in the waning sunlight, a beacon atop an outfit of black. She leaned casually against the side of the red Jeep with her ankles crossed and a gray leather coat hanging open just above her knees. Definitely drool-worthy. Dylan walked slower to give her heart time to calm and for a flush of heat to pass. She had the same reaction every time she saw Finley.

When Finley looked up, her eyes widened and her lips parted. Slowly, she scanned Dylan. Twice. The smile on Finley's face told Dylan she'd chosen the right outfit. Finley shot her cuffs, something Dylan usually found arrogant and showy, but Finley looked nervous and sexy as hell. The flash of red at Finley's left wrist hinted at a secret as elusive as the woman herself.

She offered Dylan her arm. "May I?"

Without answering, Dylan looped her hand over Finley's arm and followed her to the passenger door. Her chivalry felt a bit like a date, but Dylan rationalized that good manners were never a bad thing. She took her seat, licked her lips, and whispered, "Thank you."

Finley passed in front of the Jeep, and Dylan studied the set of her shoulders, her confident posture and relaxed stride. Was she as calm and controlled as she looked or was it her cop persona? At the driver's door, Finley shrugged out of her coat and tossed it in the back seat before climbing in beside her.

Dylan swore the temperature in the car rose several degrees. Her palms were sweaty and she felt jittery. Nerves maybe. Or excitement. Finley was definitely attractive and sexy, but she wasn't the woman for Dylan. *At least not in the long-term.* The thought brought her up short. Was she seriously rethinking her once steadfast rule? Finley was like a mirage in the desert—hypnotic and compelling—but Dylan hoped she wasn't that thirsty. She could control her physical attraction with good old common sense. She hoped.

Finley pulled away from the curb, and Dylan said, "You look handsome." Understatement. The skinny jeans and shirt looked tailored to fit Finley, and Dylan's body hummed with arousal from just looking at her. "Very handsome."

"Thanks." Finley grinned and steered the vehicle onto the major artery that would take them through town to the interstate.

"What's the story with your watch? It looks old and well-loved."

"One of three possessions that I value. My paternal grandfather bought it in Germany during the war, left it to my dad, and he passed it along. It was made in Switzerland. Self-winding and never loses time. It's the only thing my father ever owned outright, except for the house." Finley stretched her arm across the console to give Dylan a closer look.

"Very nice, and the red band?"

"My addition. A little flash to go with the traditional."

"Traditions and reminders of our history can be good." Dylan fingered the intricate feathered dream catcher dangling from the rearview mirror. "And this?"

Finley shook her head. "You don't miss much, do you?" She didn't wait for an answer but went on, "You're right. That's also a possession I value. It was my mother's." Finley's tone lowered and became more wistful. "She was part native American."

"That explains your terrific cheekbones." Dylan nudged Finley with her elbow. She liked that Finley treasured things from her past. It gave her a deeper look into the woman behind the badge and made her feel closer to her. "And the third thing?"

Finley tugged the silver chain over her head and handed it to Dylan.

She turned on the dome light and fingered the intricate figure of a tree on the front before flipping it open. A smiling couple, and Dylan could tell they loved each other. "Your parents?"

Finley nodded. "He gave that to me after she left, but I'd rather not talk about that right now." Dylan handed the necklace back, and Finley held it in the palm of her hand for several seconds before slipping it back over her head.

Finley shifted uncomfortably and stared straight ahead, so Dylan changed the subject. "Why did we leave so early? The play doesn't start until eight."

"We have VIP tickets, which means special parking at the front and drinks in the VIP lounge before the show."

"Shut up." Dylan turned sideways to look at Finley. She liked the view and it made conversation easier when she could read her reactions. "You're not kidding, are you?"

"Nope. And…if you're interested, our seats are fourth row center."

Dylan bounced in her seat. "No freaking way? I would've been happy with the nosebleed section. This is too much. How will I ever repay you?"

Finley grinned and even in the low light, Dylan saw her eyes spark mischievously. "Well…"

"No. We're not doing *that*." Even if she had been thinking about it recently.

"What?" Finley seemed genuinely shocked. "No, no. I wasn't talking about sex. Really." Her face flushed, and she shot her cuff again. "I mean that would be awesome, and I wouldn't turn it down, like ever, but I didn't mean that."

Dylan liked Finley a little off her game, nervous, vulnerable, and showing more of her true self. Dylan took pity on her. "What then?"

"I was hoping you'd give me a heads up when Josh Spencer comes out of his coma. We're not having any luck tracking down his brother, and I'm hoping he will give us a lead in return for some consideration at his trial."

"Oh, I see." She couldn't resist teasing Finley. "This invitation is a bribe for first access to Spencer. Are you bucking for detective or something?"

"Yeah, I'd like to make detective, and helping clear this case couldn't hurt."

"Thank you for being honest. I'm not sure I'll be around when Spencer wakes up because I'm not his doctor, but if I am, I'll let you know. We're required to notify the department, and you're with the department, so I wouldn't technically be violating any rules."

"I appreciate it." Finley maneuvered into traffic on I-40. "Can I ask you a personal question?"

Dylan nodded.

"Does anyone in your family know about our da—outing?"

So, Dylan wasn't the only one feeling the dating vibe. "Ben guessed." She kept the rest of their conversation to herself.

Finley shook her head. "Damn. I bet that went well." When Dylan didn't reply, she didn't push. "Tell me about growing up in the Carlyle clan, other than being the baby girl."

Dylan laughed to cover a surge of joy followed closely by pain. "A lot of talk about periods, training bras, makeup, and fashion with three girls, two of whom couldn't care less. Ben and Jazz wanted to play sports and do anything Simon did. My parents were probably relieved when they could give the dating-girls speech to their three oldest. I sometimes wonder if they hoped I'd be different."

"It is interesting that all three girls are lesbians. Was Simon okay with that?" She waved her hand in the air. "Not that he'd be all manly weird about it. I could just see a problem if two of you wanted to date the same woman."

Dylan laughed again. "Simon was totally cool. He thought it made him more popular, sort of a novelty. But he, Ben, and Jazz did all go for the same type. Femmes."

"And you?" Finley passed a few cars before looking at her.

"If you're fishing, you're totally my type, at least physically. I prefer butch-lite or androgynous, and you're all that. Just being honest." Sometimes she should keep her mouth shut, but if she

wanted another real conversation, she'd have to lead the way. "So...
tell me about your family. You've mentioned your father's problem."
Finley reached behind the seat, jerked a Kleenex from the box,
and spat her gum into it. She slowly rolled the tissue over and over
and placed it in the console cup holder. Dylan thought she wasn't
going to respond, but Finley cleared her throat and finally said, "He
was an alcoholic. I'd call that a problem."

Dylan placed her hand on Finley's arm and felt the muscle
tighten under her grip. "You don't have to talk about it if you don't
want to. I'd just like to know more about you."

Finley nodded. "Guess it's fair. He was a postal worker with
a decent salary, paying for our home, and then..." She cleared her
throat several times. "I'm sorry. When I talk about him, I feel like
I'm being dragged back into that dark place all over again. He wasn't
abusive, neglectful, yes, but never purposely cruel. I believe losing
my mother totally shattered him." Dylan reached for her again, but
Finley waved her off. "Please don't.

"My mother left when I was twelve—announced she didn't
love my father anymore—and walked out. I blamed myself, and
my dad must've too because he never looked at me the same again.
Guess I reminded him of her. I can see that—dirty blond hair, blue
eyes, and the high cheekbones. Not much I could do about that
though." She nervously fingered the hair cut out around her ears.
"They seemed happy before that, but maybe I just didn't notice until
things got bad. It's taken years for me to realize I did nothing wrong.
I was just a kid."

Finley looked ahead, tears reflected in her eyes from oncoming
traffic, and Dylan wanted to comfort her but resisted. "I can't
imagine growing up without a mom."

"I had to learn how while living the nightmare with my dad.
He started drinking before work. When I got home from school, he
was already in his recliner with a few drinks on board. He talked
about how much he loved my mother, how happy they had been,
and how much love hurt after she left. I'd listen, make dinner, clean
the house, and sit nearby doing homework until he passed out for
the night. The only part of his misery I missed was the gallons of

alcohol he poured down his throat." She swiped at her eyes and wiped her hand down her jeans. "But I learned a lot after she left. How to cook simple meals, clean house, do laundry, and lie to my dad's boss while he lay unconscious in his recliner."

"You were his caregiver."

"Until cirrhosis put him in the hospital and then hospice. Not much I could do after that." Finley pressed her hand against her chest as if it ached to tell her story. "So, you see, we really couldn't be more different. You had a perfect family and childhood. I envy that closeness."

"We were far from perfect, Fin." This time when Dylan cupped her hand and brought it to rest on her lap, Finley didn't resist. "Our lives changed the night the police chaplain and my dad's commanding officer told us he'd been killed by an armed burglar. It seemed life *had* been perfect until that moment. Papa was my champion, protector, and confidante. We talked about everything. G-ma and Mama were devastated but held it together for us, but his death affected each of the kids differently. Simon became the de facto man of the house too early, Ben turned into a wild thing and acted out, Jazz withdrew, and I…"

Finley looked over at her and squeezed her hand. "You what?"

"Grieved in silence, suppressed my anger, and decided to become a doctor to help people who'd suffered as my family had."

"*And* decided never to date cops and feel that loss again?"

Dylan caught her breath, surprised how easily Finley made the connection. "Yes." Something inside her softened at the way Finley stared at her and gently squeezed her hand. She understood how Dylan felt.

"I came to a similar place. If I don't care deeply, I can't be hurt like my dad was."

"Now I get your rep," Dylan said. "You're a poser." The pieces of Finley Masters were forming a different picture, one that Dylan liked very much.

"It serves me well."

But it didn't tell the whole story. Dylan nodded and choked back a sob. Without their shields of independence and camouflage, she and Finley were wounded souls who'd been hurt in different ways but come to the same conclusion—love wasn't worth the pain. Maybe they could comfort each other in another less damaging way.

"Hey, this is supposed to be a happy outing." Finley brought Dylan's hand to her mouth and pressed a gentle kiss into her palm before releasing. "Tell me about *Hamilton*."

The sensation of Finley's lips on her hand spiraled through Dylan like a backdraft spreading with the introduction of oxygen. For the first time in her life, she ached to be touched and kissed until everything else disappeared. She gulped for air and forced her attention back to Finley's question. "*Hamilton*. Yes. You seriously don't know anything about the play?"

Finley shook her head.

"It's about an immigrant from the West Indies who basically becomes George Washington's go-to guy and the first secretary of the treasury. Blah, blah, right? But the music, the music is to die for. It's a combination of hip-hop, jazz, blues, rap, R&B, and Broadway. And if that doesn't get you going, there's the history aspect. Aaron Burr, Thomas Jefferson, King George. And the family angle, which appeals to me as much as the music."

"You really are a fan."

"A fan? I'm a devotee."

"Good, because we're here. I hope you're ready to enjoy yourself, Ms. Carlyle."

"I am indeed, Ms. Masters." Finley started to get out, but Dylan caught her arm. "And thank you for telling me about your family. I know it wasn't easy."

"I was surprised how easy it seemed with you, but don't tell anyone. I have a rep." She winked at Dylan, grabbed her coat from the back, and came around to open the door.

When Dylan took Finley's hand and slid from the Jeep, she fake-stumbled against Finley and held just long enough to feel the press of their bodies and the perfect fit of breasts and thighs. "Thank you."

"My…my pleasure."

Dylan walked arm-in-arm with Finley toward the Durham Performing Arts Center entrance and thought this woman could definitely be a pleasure. No harm in casual sex with a self-professed playgirl who wasn't interested in long-term either. Sexual attraction wasn't love. She edged closer to Finley and again heat swelled between them. Yes, this could work, but it was time to stop kidding herself that one and done was even a possibility.

CHAPTER FOURTEEN

Finley placed her hand in the small of Dylan's back and guided her gently toward the entrance to the Durham Performing Arts Center, surprised when Dylan leaned into her touch. Unless her imagination was playing tricks, something had shifted between them on the drive. Maybe talking about her family had turned the tide. She sensed an opening, a possibility that hadn't existed before, but Dylan was no ordinary woman, so Finley's usual game wasn't likely to work. Was she even playing the game anymore, or was she being played?

She ushered Dylan through the front door enjoying the view as she entered. Her little black dress showed off curves Finley had only imagined beneath her scrubs. It was short but not slutty short, a tasteful get-a-glimpse-of-quad length, and Finley couldn't stop looking at her. A red jacket and matching calf-length boots added the right amount of spark. Dylan's brunette hair fell loosely around her shoulders and stopped at the scooped neckline of her dress that revealed a hint of her full breasts. Everything about Dylan Carlyle turned Finley on and scared her more than a little.

"Want a drink?" Finley asked.

"Lead the way. I'm in your hands," Dylan said, following her toward the lounge.

If only. But if Dylan truly placed herself in Finley's hands, she had a feeling she'd be more cautious and protective, possibly even gentler than she normally was with women. Nah, who was she kidding. She'd ravish the hell out of her until she couldn't walk. At least that's what her body wanted right now. "What would you like?" Finley asked.

"Chardonnay."

Finley ordered the wine, a beer for herself, and handed the glass to Dylan. "Every man in the room is looking at you…and envying me."

Dylan grinned. "But I'm the lucky one. Every woman's eyes are on you."

Finley raised her glass to hide her embarrassment. "Here's to an exciting evening."

Dylan quirked a brow and responded. "Yes, to excitement."

Finley's sip of beer warmed in her mouth as she swallowed. Was Dylan flirting or was it just wishful thinking on Finley's part? The twinkle in Dylan's brown eyes said the former, and Finley couldn't resist testing her theory. "Are you flirting with me, Doctor?"

Without a flicker of indecisiveness, Dylan said, "Definitely. Does that freak you out?"

"Considering our short but rocky past, just a little, but I'm recovering." She was way beyond recovered. Her mind flashed images of peeling Dylan out of that dress, and her body responded with heat and a hungry ache.

"Good." Dylan toasted her glass to Finley's again and stepped so close that Finley felt the warmth of her body against her chest. "Then here's to flirting…with possibilities." She took another sip. "This is good wine, but another glass could put me in the danger zone."

Finley placed her finger under the foot of Dylan's wine glass and playfully tipped it forward. "Bottom's up. I'm a danger junkie."

"I've heard that about you." Dylan slid a finger between the buttons of Finley's shirt and dragged her fingernail across her abs. "You're tight."

Finley sucked in a breath. "Damn, if you keep that up, we won't see the play. I'll find a place with more privacy and a locking door."

Dylan flicked the underside of Finley's breast before withdrawing her finger. "Guess I'll leave you with that, for now, because I really want to see this play." She finished her wine and placed the glass on a nearby table. "Let's find our seats."

Finley drained her stein and happily followed like a devoted puppy. "Yes, ma'am." She tucked her hand under Dylan's jacket and guided her slowly down the aisle, lifting her head higher with every admiring glance Dylan received.

They settled in the fourth row, and Dylan leaned over and whispered, "These are fantastic seats. Remind me to thank you properly later."

Finley's center tightened as Dylan's hot breath brushed across her ear and down the side of her neck. She cupped Dylan's hand and brought it to rest on her thigh, as close to her crotch as she dared in public. "I'll definitely remind you."

The curtain rose and the audience erupted in applause. "Here we go," Dylan screeched, gripping Finley's hand so tight she winced.

From the first note of the first song to the last, Dylan quivered with excitement beside her, often mouthing the words or quietly singing along. Finley couldn't stop watching her. She'd never seen Dylan so unguarded, engaged, or so happy. And she'd provided her this experience. By the end of the show, almost three hours later, Dylan's head rested against her shoulder.

When the final curtain call ended, and everyone filed out, Dylan remained in her seat, leaning into Finley's side, her arm wrapped across her waist. "This has been the most amazing night. The play was everything I imagined and more. I'm happy, invigorated, and exhausted. How is that even possible?"

"I have to admit, it was a powerful show," Finley said. "And you really got into it."

"I certainly did, but as much as I enjoy reveling in the afterglow, we should probably go."

Finley kissed the top of Dylan's head, inhaled the scent of her flowery shampoo, and slowly rose. Would she ever be this close to Dylan again, this connected to her? The playful mood of earlier seemed to have been replaced by something deeper, but what did it mean?

"Pit stop before the drive home?" Dylan asked.

"Sure."

Dylan grabbed Finley's hand and dragged her to the deserted ladies' room and into a stall. She eased her against the wall. "May I kiss you, Finley Masters?"

"Is that a trick question?"

Dylan stood on her tiptoes and licked Finley's bottom lip. The delicate action felt like a second request, one Finley was eager to answer. Dylan's kiss was so light that Finley ached for more pressure but didn't push.

"Thank you for tonight," Dylan said.

When they kissed again, Dylan was more assertive, lips pressing harder, tongue demanding. Finley's knees weakened, and she encircled Dylan's waist to pull her closer, but she backed away.

"Out. Get your own stall," Dylan said.

"Tease." Dylan slammed the door closed, and Finley placed her hands against the cold metal. She wasn't ready to stop kissing Dylan. She backed away slowly, staring at the door and the red leather boots underneath. A feeling shot through her that she didn't immediately recognize. *Fear.* She was never afraid—not at home with her morose father or at work facing dangerous criminals—but Dylan threatened a place her bravado couldn't protect. Her heart.

❖

Dylan's skin tingled as she walked toward the Jeep, a combination of excitement from seeing *Hamilton* and danger from kissing Finley. Twice. But she couldn't stop. Their intimate conversation on the drive over, Finley's chivalry all evening, the closeness of her body, along with the climax of the show stoked Dylan's desire. And damn it, she'd wanted to kiss her.

Finley opened the passenger door and waited while she settled. "Are you okay? You haven't said much since...the restroom."

"I'm good. Thanks." Was she really? Harmless flirting with a woman like Finley was one thing, but kissing her was another. Playing with fire came to mind. Before the show, she'd decided she could have casual sex with Finley, but after kissing her, she wasn't sure. She couldn't even stop at one kiss. Better to err on the side of caution. "Just tired, I guess."

"Most of the traffic has cleared, so I'll have you home in record time. Relax." Finley closed the door and made her way to the driver's side.

But Dylan couldn't relax. The firm texture of Finley's lips, the minty taste of her breath, and the tenderness of her kiss—something Dylan hadn't expected—spun like a record on a turntable in her mind. She grew warm again and lowered the window to let in the cool air.

"Sure you're all right?" Finley asked.

"Yeah." She squirmed in her seat and turned toward Finley. Time to distract. Things were getting out of hand quickly. "So...can I ask a question?"

Finley nodded and started to reach for her hand but stopped as if she sensed Dylan needed space.

"It's something I've wondered about for years, but no one seems to know the answer."

"Now I'm intrigued. Hope I can succeed where others failed." Finley gave her a quick smile while maneuvering through traffic on the highway. "Be brave. I'll protect you."

"Why are cops so dead set on being macho, fearless jerks?"

"Wow. So not what I expected. And I thought we'd gotten past that."

"Not likely." She hoped Finley wouldn't see through her effort to put some distance between them. Her sexually playful mood was slowly being replaced by anxiety as desire took over. "Well?" Finley's mouth tightened, her eyes darkened, and Dylan thought she wasn't going to answer.

"Cops feel fear like everybody else but are trained not to show it. We don't have all the answers but are taught to pretend we do. I can only speak for myself, but I live with fear on the job daily. Sometimes it's so thick I can taste it. I'm afraid I'll be killed or kill someone else, afraid of acting or not and the consequences of my choices. I worry about some dirt bag going free because of a technicality in my arrest, mishandling of evidence, or wording in my case report. The threats are often invisible, draining and frying my adrenal glands over and over throughout a shift. I think any cop who isn't a little bit afraid is crazy or just reckless."

"I've heard you *are* reckless." Finley's response was deeper and more insightful than Dylan expected, and she softened her tone to honor that. "I appreciate your honesty. Sounds like you've thought about fear a lot."

"I'd be shortsighted not to think about something that is such a major part of my work life, but I don't consider myself reckless on the job. I just have to be willing to step in when others won't. On the personal side, yes, I can be spontaneous and a bit reckless at times."

"What's your biggest fear, Fin?"

Finley increased her speed and passed several cars before answering. "I'm most afraid of not being good enough, of failing, and somebody I care about being hurt or killed." Her grip on the steering wheel tightened.

"Like Hank."

"Yeah, like Hank or Robin…or someone else. You could've easily been shot that day." Finley glanced at her, and Dylan saw her jaw tighten.

"Pull over."

"What?"

"Pull the car over," Dylan said again.

Finley steered to the side of the road, stopped, and turned on the emergency flashers. "What's going on?"

Dylan leaned over the console, pulled Finley close, and tried to kiss her. She'd been wrong about Finley. She was a sensitive but damaged woman beneath all the bravado, and Dylan wanted her so badly she couldn't wait to kiss her again. Distance and caution be damned.

"Dylan…what…are you doing?" Finley pulled away.

"What you said was so touching, and I want you so much right now. I mean a lot."

"What?" Finley was pressed against the driver's door as far away as possible.

Dylan stared in Finley's eyes, unable to understand her resistance. "Are you seriously not going to kiss me?"

Finley licked her lips. "On the side of the road? Yes, I mean, no, I'm not. I haven't made out in a vehicle since I was a teenager, and it doesn't suit a woman like you, Dylan. Besides, we're only ten minutes from your place."

"Not my place." Dylan settled back in her seat and straightened her dress, second-guessing her decision after Finley's reaction.

"Are you sure about this?"

"No, but if I think about it too much, I'll change my mind. Can we just go with it?"

"I'm not sure about my place," Finley said. "I've never...I mean, I don't usually—"

"Then just drop me at home. Your car shouldn't be in my driveway tomorrow morning when my family wakes up."

"My place it is." Finley gunned the gas and spun into the travel lane. She slid her hand up Dylan's thigh and stopped at the hem of her dress. "You have about eight minutes to change your mind."

Should she? Having sex with Finley would place her on a long list of similar conquests. But there was so much chemistry between them, and no one was more qualified as fling material than Finley Masters. The tenderness she'd seen in Finley tonight could just be part of her game, but Dylan didn't care. Decision made. Again.

Before she second-guessed herself yet again, she changed the subject. "So, how do cops deal with all the stress and fear of the job? I've never broached the question in my family because I didn't want to know the answer."

"Depends on the person. Lock it away, compartmentalize, deny, get a hobby, take drugs, drink, pray, fight, fuck—whatever gets you through. Some are lucky enough to have friends, family, or partners who know how to deal with the special brand of cop crazy."

"Mama used to say Papa never really took off his uniform because it was always there like a permanent tattoo or brand. I was never sure what that meant." Dylan glanced at Finley, her stare straight ahead, and her expression serious.

"The things you see and do on the job seep into your pores like a toxic gas. You can't rinse or scrub them away. Your partner and family expect you to come home from work, hang up the uniform, and be an open, loving, communicative person, like nothing's happened. It doesn't work that way. A lot of cops end up chasing the thrills of work off the job, through other vices, which doesn't help family life either." She cocked her head to one side. "That could be why I'm impulsive and reckless in my personal life sometimes."

"So...your coping mechanism is sex?" Dylan asked.

"Yeah, I guess you could say that."

Dylan stroked Finley's thigh. "Then I consider it my civic duty to help you cope tonight, Officer Masters." But her motives were far from selfless. She'd thought about her conversations with Holly and Bennett and about what she wanted in the future. She *had* put her personal life on hold—avoided feeling and buried her chances at love—while grieving her father, but he would never want her to sacrifice her happiness. Now she was finally able to admit she wanted more.

CHAPTER FIFTEEN

Finley parked in her driveway and hurried to the passenger side of the Jeep, her mind spinning. Was the house presentable? Were the sheets on the bed reasonably clean? Did she have anything to drink? Her body ached with arousal, and if Dylan changed her mind, which she might, Finley would be in a bad way and none of the trivial things would matter. Aside from the logistical considerations, Dylan was the boss's sister and way out of her league. *And* Dylan wasn't her usual fling material, but she'd asked for this, to Finley's surprise. The other alarming part, Finley didn't have women in her house. Ever. She opened the car door and offered her hand. "Are you sure about this?"

"Please stop asking me that." Dylan grinned and gave her a quick kiss on the cheek. "Let's go before I change my mind."

Finley unlocked the front door and waved Dylan inside. "Excuse the musty smell. I'm not here much and wasn't expecting company or I'd have cleaned." She flicked on a floor lamp.

Dylan quirked her mouth into a disbelieving grin. "*You* would've cleaned?"

"Or I'd have had it done."

"It's a Southern woman's curse to clean when company's coming, right?" Dylan asked.

"Or in my case, for periodic checks by social services." Finley cringed at the memory of scrubbing the kitchen floor on all fours while her booze-soaked father supervised from his recliner throne.

"I think your place is perfect and surprisingly beautiful. I love the Craftsman style. Your decorator has great taste. The house is more compact and intimate than my family's home, and I like that."

Finley grinned. "Thanks. Do you want the nickel tour?"

"Maybe another time?" Dylan yanked the hem of her dress like a schoolgirl wishing for more fabric, and Finley's hunger turned to protectiveness.

"Dylan, we don't have to do this…or anything really. I can take you home."

"Thank you for that." Dylan hugged her and rested her cheek against Finley's chest. "I want to have sex with you…but a part of me wants to keep this gentler side of you as long as I can." She paused and heaved a heavy sigh. "And…I've never had a one-night stand…or even casual sex, but I think I've just been afraid of getting involved and being hurt."

Finley's heart thrummed hard at the admission. Dylan probably got hit on daily, but she'd chosen Finley for her first hookup. Her responsibility gene flared again. She eased out of Dylan's hug and looked down at her. "Think I better take you home. I don't want either of us to do something we'll regret. I respect you too much for that."

Dylan flicked a button on Finley's shirt. "You'd regret having sex with me?"

"My body definitely wouldn't, but my mind is another matter. And I'm more worried about you right now."

Dylan tucked her fingers behind Finley's belt and pulled her closer. "Now you're just making me want you more. That's so sweet. Please stop trying to talk me out of this and help me. Bedroom?"

No one could accuse Finley of not trying to change Dylan's mind, but good intentions only went so far and she was only human. "Last door on the right."

Dylan led the way down the hall and guided Finley to the edge of her bed. "I apologize in advance for the lack of foreplay, but we've been teasing each other all night." Dylan grabbed the lapels of Finley's jacket, but she stopped her.

"Dylan, I want to be clear about what this—"

"This is two consenting adults having sex with no strings. I'm clear. It's out of character for me, but I saw a side of you tonight that I really like, and I want to hold that image while we...do this. Okay?"

Finley nodded. Dylan peeled Finley's jacket off and started to unbutton her shirt, but Finley grabbed her hands. "I don't usually—"

"Shush," Dylan said. "Let's drop that right here with this awesome jacket. I promise not to hurt you, Officer." She stood on tiptoes and kissed Finley and then nibbled her way to the hollow of her neck and the top button of her shirt. "Relax." Dylan held her gaze as she worked her shirt open, teasing her bottom lip between her teeth.

Finley ached at Dylan's playful concentration and determination to take charge. Women usually expected her to lead, so this might be fun...to a point. Dylan stripped Finley's shirt off her shoulders, followed quickly by her sports bra. Then she waited until Finley nodded to continue. Dylan unzipped her jeans and shucked them to the floor, and Finley shivered when the cooler air of the room hit her heated body. "Wait."

"Second thoughts? Are you uncomfortable? Feeling used?" Dylan cupped her hand over Finley's abdomen and waited.

"Used? No way."

Dylan inched her fingers toward the waistband of Finley's tight briefs. "May I?" She glanced up.

Finley grabbed Dylan's wrist but didn't pull her hand away. "I...can't...I don't...let other women take control."

"I thought we agreed to leave that. Let go, Fin. Just tell me if I do something you don't like." She kissed Finley's bare chest and blew her hot breath across her breasts. "Besides, I'm not other women."

"Damn." She released her grip and her body tightened as Dylan slid her hand lower into her briefs and through the slick heat between her legs.

"See," Dylan said, "you need this too."

When Dylan teased Finley's clit, sparks shot through her, and she felt like she was falling. Her breathing hitched and she grabbed

Dylan's ass to steady herself. She made women weak and needy not the other way around, but right now she'd do anything Dylan wanted.

Dylan pressed her fingers into Finley. "I want you so much, Fin." She slid her finger back and forth.

She should object, get things under control. "Me too." Her legs wobbled as she tried to meet Dylan's thrusts. "I want to touch you, Dylan."

"Later."

"Dylan, I can't."

"Of course, you can. Relax and enjoy."

Finley's labored breaths were like a chugging train in her ears, and the pounding between her legs kept time. "Need to sit down."

"Your injured shins?"

Finley shook her head. "Wobbly knees."

Dylan slowly eased her backward onto the bed and settled along her side. "I want you to come for me." She sucked Finley's breast into her mouth, and Finley felt the connection at her core.

Dylan's teeth and lips on her breast were blunted razors sending shocks of painful pleasure to her clit in uncoordinated blasts with her finger strokes. She wasn't used to so much attention and struggled not to come too soon. Dylan's touch was sure, but Finley needed a synchronized rhythm. She cupped Dylan's hand and tried to control the speed to match the efforts of her mouth, but Dylan kept the conflicting paces. Her resistance irritated and aroused Finley at the same time. "Damn it, Dylan."

Dylan sucked her breast and rocked into her crotch with the heel of her hand. "You are so hot, Fin. I want to watch you come. You're ready."

Finley tried to slow or stop the aggravating pace but just grew hotter and more aroused. "Ohhh, fuck!" While her mind concentrated on guiding Dylan, her body was letting go, exploding around her. "Yessss." As Finley started coming, Dylan finally pumped and sucked in perfect sync. Too much. Too good. She couldn't stop her orgasm, control it, or deny the feeling of surrender for the first time. The thought was freeing and sobering. She gasped and pulled for breath. "Holy crap, Dylan."

"Don't talk." Dylan peeled Finley's briefs off and then did the same with her own. She hiked her dress up and straddled Finley's center, rubbing against her. "Take me, Fin."

Dylan's heat spilled over Finley, and she grabbed her hips, riding up against her, pressing and grinding together, wanting Dylan to feel what she had. "Oh, yes. Come on, baby."

"Look at me, Fin."

Finley opened her eyes—another thing she didn't do with her casuals—and stared up at the most beautiful woman she'd ever seen. Dylan writhed atop her, hair wild, cheeks flushed, breasts bouncing, and hips seesawing back and forth bringing more pleasure than Finley had ever experienced. "Don't stop. Please, Dylan." When Dylan cried out and collapsed across her chest, Finley came with her. She'd violated so many of her rules tonight, but at this moment, she didn't care about any of them.

❖

Dylan opened her eyes with a start in the strange bedroom and scanned her surroundings. Silhouette window shades diffused light and provided privacy, tasteful bedding, neither too frilly nor too stark, and modern, functional furniture—everything suited Finley's style. Dylan rolled onto her side, her body aching with the sensitivity of overuse, and studied Finley. She'd done things to Dylan no one ever had, or they'd done them poorly, but fairy tales ended. *Hamilton* and sex with Finley were both one-offs. Cop equaled fun and nothing more. She ignored the niggling doubt in her mind that stopped short of calling bullshit.

She eased off the bed and glanced over her shoulder. Finley lay on her back, arms and legs spread, her breathing even and heavy. Dylan took a mental picture of the peaceful pose and resisted the temptation to wake her for another round. Finley was everything and nothing Dylan expected—gentler, more experimental, and totally obliging, even letting Dylan take charge.

One and done? Not likely. She plucked her clothes from the floor on the way to the living room and opened the Uber app on her phone. Sneaking out wasn't her style, but neither was a one-night stand. Since she and Finley had agreed on the terms going in, this seemed like the best option. No scene, discussion, or awkward good-byes. But she wanted to stay and wake Finley with gentle kisses, tease her into another round of sex, and share breakfast with her like a normal couple. She shook her head. Not part of the agreement, but it was still what she wanted.

Dylan dressed and glanced around the open-plan space, appreciating the cozy furniture and soothing earth tone color scheme. This would make a nice, comfortable home for a family. How did Finley live in a place with so many unpleasant memories while trying to sell it? If what she'd said last night was true, she didn't spend much time here at all, not even with lovers.

Dylan scribbled a quick note on the pad on the kitchen island and then hurried to the waiting Uber. She settled in the back seat, clicked to iTunes, and pressed Abba's "Waterloo." The music surged through the earbuds, and she felt buoyant and free, until a pang of guilt crept in. Had she used Finley? Should she go back and make sure Finley was okay? No. Casual was her jam, and she'd been all in. Dylan checked the time. Five thirty. Her family would be awake soon and looking for her. If she was lucky, no one would notice her predawn return.

Ten minutes later, she slowly opened her front door, expecting at least Bennett to be waiting. She breathed a thankful sigh into the quiet, empty space and peeled her clothes off on the way to the bathroom. A hot shower and time to relive the ecstasy of last night, file it away, and prepare for the real world were exactly what she needed.

But her body thrummed with tactile sensations. The shower spray struck tender skin and sparked memories of Finley touching, teasing, and tugging her to orgasm after orgasm. The smell of their mingled sex drifted to her nostrils in the steam. Nothing about their night had been ordinary, expected, or off-limits. And *that* was the reason she couldn't get it out of her head. That and the fact it couldn't happen again.

She squirted shampoo in her palm, rubbed it vigorously through her hair, and rinsed. One night of decadence with Finley and no more. Dylan gently spread the shower gel over her body, determined not to think about Finley's hands in place of her own. She leaned under the spray for a final cool rinse, turned off the shower, and pulled on her terrycloth robe. *But* sex with Finley had been totally freeing and satisfying. Was that what one-night stands usually felt like, or had Finley created a hunger only she could satisfy? "Do not go there. It's over. Mission accomplished. Dylan out."

While she towel dried her hair and finger combed it in the mirror, she caught a whiff of fresh, strong coffee. Bennett would've told the family about Dylan's date last night over dinner, and they'd be like wild horses ready to crash her door for details. Time to face the real world.

Bennett and Jazz sat at her kitchen counter sipping coffee and chatting quietly. "Good morning, sisters. To what do I owe the honor of this early visit and fresh coffee?" She pulled her I-love-my-doctor mug, a birthday gift from Ryan and Riley, from the cabinet and filled it, taking her time with the sweetener and cream.

"Just wanted to say good morning," Bennett said, holding Dylan's little black dress up with one finger. "Shouldn't leave your clothes on the floor if you're being sneaky."

"Give me that." She snatched the dress and tossed it toward the bedroom. "I wasn't sneaking. Last time I checked, I live here alone, though you guys apparently didn't get the memo." She took a sip of coffee to cover a blush when she noticed her boots and jacket still in the middle of the living room floor.

"So…good evening?" Jazz asked, sucking on her lip to hide a grin.

"*Hamilton* was outstanding. I've never seen anything so uplifting and expertly done."

"And was *Hamilton* the only thing uplifting and expertly done last night?" Bennett laughed, and Jazz joined in.

"Shut up, both of you. What happened or didn't happen after the play is none of your business. Are you two so bored being married and engaged that you're perving on my sex life?"

Jazz pointed her index finger. "So, you're admitting sex was involved?"

Dylan shook her head. "The only thing I admit is I had a great time. Period."

"And came home just before daylight...in an Uber I'm guessing," Bennett said.

"Oh, my God, you guys. How can you even know that unless you were staking out my place or...G-ma?"

"Bingo," Jazz said. "She was so excited that you had a date, I think she was up most of the night, hoping to grill you herself."

"There's no escaping the police inquisition." Dylan refilled her coffee cup to keep from looking at her sisters and to regain control of her growing irritation. They were concerned about her, probably more so because she'd been out with playgirl Finley Masters, but Dylan made her own choices and accepted the consequences. She turned to face them again.

"Seriously? I appreciate your concern, but I've got this. Sometimes I wonder if I should've moved across town or out of state maybe instead of across the yard."

Bennett came around to her side of the island, took Dylan's coffee mug and placed it on the counter, and hugged her. "We know you're a strong, capable Carlyle woman, but you have to accept that we'll never stop caring and worrying about you, just like the other members of our family. We love you, Sis."

Jazz joined them and hugged Dylan from the other side. "What Ben said. Sorry if we overstepped. You just haven't stayed out all night in...a long time."

"Yeah," Bennett said. "I hope you enjoyed yourself." She rocked her hips back and forth.

Dylan pushed away and playfully tossed a pot holder at Bennett's head. "Get out, you heathens. I have to work in a couple of hours and I might need a nap." She wiggled her eyebrows suggestively. That was all they were getting. She couldn't discuss Finley with her sisters when she didn't understand her continued craving, much less her emotions.

CHAPTER SIXTEEN

Finley woke thinking about sex with Dylan and became aroused again but kept her breathing steady and her body still. This was the awkward part. She rehearsed her normal morning-after speech, but balked at delivering it to Dylan. Last night, Finley had done everything she never did with other women and nothing she usually did. Dylan had flipped the script, orchestrated their encounter, and left Finley's head spinning and her body aching.

She reached across the bed for Dylan to either set the record straight or have sex again but found only cold sheets. Her arousal vanished. She checked the floor around the bed—her strap-on and discarded clothes—but nothing of Dylan's. Her gut tightened with disappointment and she sat straight up. Did other women feel this way when she left in the middle of the night or early morning without even a good-bye? And why did it matter that Dylan had?

They'd agreed on the guidelines and enjoyed each other all night. So, what was different? She couldn't claim being used since her motto had always been any sex is good sex. And sex with Dylan had been beyond good. She put on sweats and a T-shirt and headed to the kitchen for coffee. Before she made it to the pot, she noticed the note on her kitchen island.

Finley, thanks for everything. Last night was great. I'd appreciate your discretion. See you around. D

"See you around?" Isn't that what she always said to women? Dylan had mastered the fling rules on her first try, and that didn't set well with Finley. Was this payback for years of casual sex with women she never really connected with? She and Dylan had an emotional evening, talked about their families and fears, and shared some pretty fantastic sex…in *this* house. Nothing more. Nothing to reminisce about or dwell on.

She finished her coffee, showered, and dressed, refusing to unpack the evening any further. Every time her thoughts wandered to Dylan or the pleasurable soreness in her body, she changed the subject. She picked up her cell on the way out the front door and dialed Hank.

"Hey, buddy, are you up for a visitor?"

"Hell yeah. I need a break from Xbox zombies. And bring biscuits."

When Finley pulled in front of Hank's house, two marked cars were leaving. She waved and rang the doorbell, glad the guys were still dropping by, looking after Hank and his family.

"Come in," Becky called from inside. "It's open."

Finley stopped in front of the stairs leading to the second floor where Robin was perched to dive into her arms. She handed two bags to Becky with a smile. "Go for it, champ."

"Superman," he yelled and vaulted toward her.

Becky's welcoming grin turned to a look of panic while her son hovered between the security of the stairs and Finley's grasp. "Jeez, you're going to be the death of me." She pointed toward the sunroom at the back of the house that had been converted into Hank's bedroom. She leaned closer and whispered, "He's pretty grouchy today. Probably too much mac and cheese, fried chicken, and being cooped up."

Finley nodded toward the bags Becky held. "One of those is for you and Robin."

"You shouldn't have, but I love you for it." She ripped the bag open on the counter and waved Robin over. "Chocolate-glazed donut or bear claw, kiddo?"

"Donut."

Becky gave her a kiss on the cheek and handed over the biscuit bag. "As soon as we get rid of some of this food, I'll cook a proper meal and have you over."

"Sounds good." Finley waited until Becky and Robin settled at the kitchen banquette before going into the sunroom. "Hey, how's it hanging?"

"Fucking A, Fin. I'm going crazy here. A man can only take so much gaming, hovering by the missus, and pitying visits from the guys. Not to mention bland, homemade casseroles. Don't get me wrong, I appreciate everybody's concern, but you know me."

"Yeah. You want to get back in the thick of it."

"Roger that." He snatched the biscuit bag from her. "Give me those doughy, greasy gut grenades." He bit into one while she made a coffee from the small Keurig beside his recliner.

The scent of bacon and egg nagged at her because she hadn't eaten since lunch yesterday, but her stomach was as jumbled as her feelings, and the thought of food made her queasy. "I see you have all the comforts at your fingertips." She toasted her cup against his and dropped into a wicker chair overlooking the expansive backyard.

"The doctor says I can walk with crutches because there was no neurological damage. I'll be out for a while longer, then on limited duty four to six weeks. No regular patrol for three months. Becky makes sure I follow the rules. I love the hell out of her and I'm grateful to still be here, but I can't wait to be on desk duty at the station, see some of the guys, and talk about something other than zombie hunters and menus."

Finley tried to imagine being so badly injured that she couldn't work and staying in her house while she recuperated. She shifted in her chair, a sick feeling settling in her gut. Bad memories never expired. "I feel you."

Hank finished the first biscuit and reached for another. "So, what's going on with you?"

She sipped her coffee, stalling for time. They talked about all her conquests, but Dylan felt different, and Finley still hadn't figured out why or how. "Nothing really."

Hank cocked his head to one side. "Seriously?" He lowered his voice. "No strange lately?" Becky would finish him off if she heard him talking about women like that.

"Nope, nothing strange." She glanced toward the basketball court at the far end of the yard. "I'll come over and shoot some hoops with Robin when I'm off to keep him sharp."

"He'd like that. Now back to you. Who is she?" Hank just wanted her to be happy and to him that meant finding a nice girl and setting up house, but she'd never believed in the happily ever after scenario. He waited until Finley looked at him. "Somebody you finally care about? Just tell me it's not Dylan Carlyle. I warned you about her."

The question shot through Finley like a surge of electricity. *Did she care about Dylan?* Everything seemed off today. She couldn't concentrate or get Dylan off her mind, but that didn't necessarily mean anything. Sex had just been new and different with her. Hank was waiting and she wouldn't lie to him. "Can we move on?"

Hank chuckled. "Sure. You obviously don't want to talk about her. Her being Dylan."

"If you don't stop, I'm leaving." Finley sounded too defensive, but thankfully, Hank didn't push. She wanted time to figure out what had happened to her last night and what, if anything, she needed to do about it. In the meantime, she had the shooting to think about. "Any news about your case?"

"The sarge called this morning. CSI processed the bullet the doctor dug out of my leg, a .357, which is what Jeremy was using. They don't think Josh Spencer fired the shotgun. CSI didn't find any spent shotgun shells at the scene, and the shells in the weapon hadn't been fired. I'm thinking he didn't shoot at all."

"Interesting," Finley said. "He was the one mouthing off about his daughter. So, asshole Jeremy shot at people just to support his brother?"

"And for the fun of it. He's a druggie and more violent than Josh. Several assaults, robberies, and one attempted murder on his record. Anything new on where Jeremy is?"

"He slipped our net the other day. The CCTV footage from the shooting and our chase skipped a lot of time because of patchy coverage on the east side. Josh is still in a coma, but I'll get a call when he wakes up. He might agree to help with the right incentive," Finley said.

"Cap let you work the case?"

"Not officially, but you know I'm not letting this go."

"I counted on it, partner." Hank nodded his appreciation.

"Anything else you need before I go? I'm working a few extra hours this afternoon so one of the first shift guys can take off for his kid's birthday party."

"I'm good, but thanks, pal."

She stood to leave.

"Keep me in the loop."

"You know I will." She placed her coffee cup on the table, and her cell pinged with a text. *Josh Spencer is awake. Get here fast.* Finley didn't recognize the number, but the capital *D* at the end was all she needed. "This could be it, bro. Our suspect is awake, finally. I'll let you know how it goes."

She raced to the hospital, breaking more than a few traffic laws en route. When she stepped off the elevator on the ICU floor, Dylan was waiting, and the sight of her brought Finley to a full stop. "I... you...thanks for this." She babbled like a kid with her first crush.

"You're welcome." Dylan lightly touched Finley's arm and met her gaze, the intensity of their connection reminding Finley of so many things they could've said last night but didn't need to. "Remember, keep it short. He's still groggy and not making sense. You might not get much."

Finley nodded, started to go, but wanted to say something else. "About last nig—"

"Nothing to say. Go. Now." Dylan shoved her toward Spencer's room.

Finley walked slowly, unsure how she felt about being dismissed so easily. Was Dylan really okay with their evening? If so, why wasn't *she*? Dylan was giving her exactly what she'd asked for—no strings or expectations. She closed the door to Spencer's room behind her and eased the privacy curtain back. "Good morning, Mr. Spencer, I'm Finley Masters."

Spencer rolled his head slowly toward her, his eyes droopy and unfocused. "Cop?"

"Yes. I want to talk to you about the incident at Fairview Station."

He shook his head and grimaced. "Lawyer."

"I'm not asking about the actual shooting. Nothing incriminating or I'd be advising you of your rights."

"Then what do you want?"

"To find Jeremy. Where would he go in town? Who would help him?"

Spencer smacked his mouth and nodded at the cup on his bedside table. "Water."

Finley tamped down her revulsion at helping one of the men who'd shot her partner, threatened other friends and coworkers, and traumatized two children for life. She picked up the cup, held the straw to his lips, and waited while he drank.

"I just wanted to see my daughter."

She didn't bother telling him that shooting up a police substation was not the way to go about getting visitation. "Maybe I can help with that, if you're willing to cooperate. The longer Jeremy is on the run, the greater chance he'll be hurt or worse."

"I can't snitch my brother out. Besides, he's probably already back in Atlanta."

Finley shook her head. "He's still here, man. Help me find him and maybe I can help you see Shea. Otherwise, she'll forget she has a father while you rot in prison for a very long time."

Josh shifted in the bed and winced again. "He had a girlfriend on Clifton Road a while back. Gloria Bunker. Only place I can think of besides family." He waved her away. "All I know. And don't tell him I ratted."

Finley dialed Fairview Station as she pushed the door open and rushed toward the exit. "Finley Masters for Captain Carlyle. Hurry."

Dylan caught up to her at the elevator. "Did he tell you anything useful?"

"Yeah. Thanks again. I've got to go."

"Be careful. Please," Dylan said, "and—"

Finley held up a finger when the boss came on the line. "Captain, I've got a possible location for our second shooter. I need tactical assistance with a search ASAP. I'm five minutes from the station. Thank you, ma'am."

Finley turned back toward Dylan, but she was gone. Probably best. She'd already said there was nothing to talk about. Just keeping it real. Exactly Finley's style. So why did leaving without acknowledging what they'd shared feel wrong?

❖

As soon as Finley's back was turned, Dylan sprinted to the exit door on the ICU floor and bolted down the stairs. Holly's summons to the ER couldn't have come at a better time. She slowed as she reached the first floor, the thought of Finley in harm's way like a cold lump of concrete weighing her down. Even walking was harder. This was why she didn't date cops. Damn it, what had she been thinking? She opened the door and headed straight for Holly's desk. "What's up?"

"Possible fractured radius of a four-year-old in three. X-rays in progress, and I've texted the on-call social worker to take a look."

Dylan pulled up the chart and studied it to keep Holly from noticing her glum expression or reading something into her touchy mood.

"What's wrong?"

So much for her avoidance tactics. "Nothing. I'm good."

"Don't bullshit me, Dylan. You haven't said more than a few words that weren't work related since we came on duty. Then you disappeared for almost half an hour. Is it about your date?"

Dylan flailed her hands in the air and immediately dropped them. She never did that. "How many times do I have to tell you—"

"It wasn't a date," they said together.

"Whatever you say. I'm here when you want to talk," Holly said and turned her attention back to her tablet.

"I'll be in exam three." Dylan parted the privacy curtain and nodded to a young woman sitting beside a child on the gurney. "Hi,

I'm Dr. Carlyle." She shook hands with the mother and grinned at the young boy. "How are you feeling, sport?" He didn't meet her gaze, a sign she'd seen before in abused children. Most were inquisitive, asking questions and inspecting anything within arm's reach.

"Okay. I guess," the boy answered.

"I'm Dylan. What's your name?"

"Tommy."

"Okay, Tommy. We took a picture of your arm. Look. It's pretty cool." She slid the X-ray onto the light box and pointed. "These are the bones in your arm." She used her pen to indicate an area on the radius. "See that?" The child nodded, and she continued. "That little line means something is wrong with your arm. I bet it hurts a little. Am I right?"

Tommy nodded again.

"Can you tell me how you hurt your arm?"

He shrugged, his face a blank mask. Children often got that helpless, hopeless expression when their lives made no sense. How could they explain *that* to anyone?

His mother brushed his dark hair off his forehead. "He likes to roughhouse with Ned."

Bells sounded in Dylan's head as she studied the X-ray and listened to the mother's explanation. Hair on the back of her neck bristled, and she shivered. She wasn't buying the roughhousing story. The break was spiral shaped, more indicative of a twisting motion, not something caused by a simple fall. She checked the child's history, and cleared her throat to keep from calling the mother a liar. "And who is Ned?" she asked.

"My boyfriend for about nine months. They really get along. Ned babysits sometimes while I work. When I got home, Tommy was favoring his arm. Ned said they played touch football in the front yard, and Tommy must've fallen wrong. He's going to be okay, right?"

Before Dylan could answer, Emory interrupted. "Dr. Carlyle, a minute please."

"Sure. I'll be right back with you," Dylan said to the mother and then followed Emory into a consulting room across the hall. "I'm glad to see you. I'm getting a bad vibe here."

"You should be." Emory opened her tablet and tapped a few times, then swiveled it so Dylan could see. "Tommy has been in two other times in the past six months."

"Did you talk with the mother before?"

Emory nodded. "I don't think she's the problem."

"The new boyfriend?"

"Yeah. I've broached the subject with her, but she won't believe Ned hurt the boy. Maybe now she'll listen. When you finish your exam, I'll talk to her with an officer. She needs to understand this is an unsafe environment for the child and if it continues, she'll lose custody."

"The police may file charges this time since we have a pattern." Dylan started toward the door, but Emory touched her arm. "Jazz said she and Ben stopped by your place this morning."

"For God's sake." Dylan's temper rose at her sisters' meddling and spreading her business.

"And I apologize. I talked to her about giving you space. I also reminded her why you wanted the carriage house in the first place." Emory brushed a strand of her auburn hair behind her ear. "They think they're helping."

Dylan blew out a long breath. It wasn't Emory's fault the Carlyle clan involved themselves in every aspect of each other's lives. "Sorry I jumped down your throat. They're overbearing sometimes, but I know they love me." She hugged Emory and felt her warmth and caring. "Maybe you can hold a session on boundaries at brunch one Sunday."

Emory snorted. "When Jazz and I celebrate our tenth anniversary, possibly."

Would Dylan ever find someone who fit her as completely as Kerstin complemented Ben and Emory suited Jazz? Maybe Finley, in time? Then she caught herself. She had a child's welfare in her hands. No time for worrying about a one-night stand that was going nowhere. "I'll catch up with you later. And thanks, Em."

By the time Dylan finished Tommy's medical exam and turned the results over to Emory, she was starving. She'd dashed out of Finley's place before dawn, only had coffee at home, and skipped her first break. She caught Holly's eye and nodded toward the elevator to let her know she'd meet her in the cafeteria.

A few minutes later, Holly settled across from her at their usual table by the windows overlooking the courtyard and twirled her baked spaghetti with a fork.

"We had sex." Dylan said, her voice almost a whisper.

Holly stopped twirling and stared. "Oh."

"No idea what I was thinking. Well, I wasn't thinking, not logically. You and Ben said I should open up, branch out, live a little. And Finley and I talked all the way to Durham. I mean *really* talked. She's not like her reputation, or what I imagined. She's deeper. Like you said, a soft underbelly. I saw her as more than a cop for the first time." She clamped her hands over her mouth. "I sound like a bad romance novel. The more she talked, the more I liked her. By the time we got back to her place, I was so turned on I couldn't imagine *not* having sex with her." Heat flooded Dylan's body and she reached for her iced tea. "What have I done?"

Holly smothered a grin. "And…"

"Oh, Holly, it was unbelievable. It wasn't just sex. It was sex max. I've never been so…but none of that matters." She waved her hand through the air as if she could erase everything they'd enjoyed and the lingering effects. "Besides, she was probably just getting on my good side so I'd let her know when the shooting suspect woke up. She got what she wanted this morning, and he apparently gave her a lead. Now she's off to find his accomplice. She'll boost her career, make detective, and I'll be a footnote."

"Do you really believe that?"

"It doesn't matter what I believe. We agreed to one night. Now life returns to normal."

Holly reached across the table and cupped Dylan's hand. "But that's not really you, is it?"

Dylan didn't answer. Couldn't answer honestly, so she said nothing.

"Talk to your family."

"About having sex with a near-stranger? Are you mad?"

"About life with a cop. Norma, Gayle, Kerstin, and even Emory can provide perspective, soften this hard line you've drawn between you and Finley based on her profession."

"There's nothing to talk about, Holly." Discussing the challenges of life with a police officer hadn't occurred to her because she was never going to be in that position. But what if she was already heading in that direction? Finley's easy dismissal as she rushed toward her next chase made that seem unlikely. They'd enjoyed each other in the bubble of a magical evening, but the bubble burst at daybreak.

CHAPTER SEVENTEEN

In the squad lineup room, Finley, the detectives working the shooting case, and the tactical squad waited for Captain Carlyle and Lieutenant Perry's briefing. To keep from pacing, Finley studied the wanted posters tacked around the room, but it didn't ease her anxiety about the upcoming operation. When the bosses entered, the energy in the room shifted, and Finley straightened, preparing for her part in the updates.

"Okay, guys," Captain Carlyle said, "Officer Masters has a possible location of our second shooter, Jeremy Spencer. Finley, fill us in."

Most of the officers in the room were more senior than her, and Finley's mouth dried as she scanned their expectant faces. She licked her lips and began. "Josh Spencer, the hospitalized shooter, said his brother, Jeremy, had a girlfriend who lived in the apartments on Clifton Road off Merritt Drive. Her name is Gloria Bunker, and she doesn't have a record. I've included a photo, her address, and the layout of the complex in the handout. The apartment manager says Gloria still lives there, but she doesn't know Jeremy and hasn't seen him. But he could still be there. That's all I have. I'll let the tactical sergeant make assignments." She sat down and glanced up at Bennett who gave her a quick nod.

"Good job getting this info and the background for us, Fin," Jazz said.

The tactical sergeant assigned the teams of officers strategically around Gloria's apartment building. "Let's try for a consent search first. If Gloria doesn't have a record, she might be more willing to let us look. And if not, we'll explain the seriousness of harboring a fugitive. If we have to, we'll lock the place down and serve the warrant."

"All right, guys," Bennett said. "Officer Masters will handle the approach since she spoke with Josh. Let's roll, and be careful." Bennett started toward the door with Jazz and called back over her shoulder. "Fin, you're with us."

Finley slid into the back seat of Captain Carlyle's vehicle while Jazz took shotgun. Nobody spoke for several minutes, and the ride felt a bit like waiting for a condemned man to die. Did they know she and Dylan had spent the night together? She certainly wasn't about to bring it up. Either of these formidable women could ruin her career with one word or negative recommendation.

She looked out the window, unable to make idle conversation because only one thing was on her mind, and she couldn't talk about *that*. The thought of Dylan made her ache and want all over again. She clamped her legs together as heat gathered in her center. Last night had been amazing, unforgettable—Dylan's soft skin, the sound of her moans, her responsiveness—and, and damn it, Finley wanted to do it again. Soon.

"Yo, Masters." Bennett said. "Focus."

"Ma'am?"

"I asked how you got to Spencer so quickly after he woke up."

"Dy—" She almost ratted Dylan out, which would've been bad for both of them. "I got a call from the hospital."

"Inside information. Way to use your contacts. Anybody we know?" Bennett looked at her in the rearview mirror, and Finley could've sworn she knew about her and Dylan.

Before she could answer, Jazz said, "Leave the woman alone, Ben. She got what we needed. That's the important thing."

Finley thought Bennett mumbled, *"And what she needed too,"* but couldn't be sure.

Bennett stopped in a circle of apartments next to Gloria's, and they waited until the other officers surrounded the beige target building. When the tactical sergeant gave the okay for them to approach the door, Bennett waved for Finley to lead the way.

Finley took the concrete stairs two at a time, positioned herself beside the door with another officer behind her, and waited until Jazz and her backup flanked her on the other side. She breathed deeply and then knocked twice, using casual thumps instead of her usual police pounding. Gloria might be more agreeable to consent if Finley didn't piss her off first.

When the door opened, a petite, gray-haired woman of about forty greeted them with a look of surprise. "Yes, Officers?" She glanced back inside.

"Ma'am, are you Gloria Bunker?" Finley asked. When the woman nodded, Finley signaled to Captain Carlyle who stood farther down the stairs, indicating the suspect was probably inside. Finley returned her attention to Gloria. "Ms. Bunker, do you know this man?" She held a photo of Jeremy Spencer up, and Gloria's eyes grew even larger.

"Umm...maybe. Why?"

"He's wanted in connection with a shooting that occurred at Fairview Station. Maybe you heard about it on the news." She nodded. "I have information that he's here, and we need to search your apartment." Finley edged her foot over the threshold so Gloria couldn't slam the door.

"Well..." She looked over her shoulder again, obviously stalling.

"Ms. Bunker, if Jeremy is here, and you don't let us search, you can be charged with harboring a fugitive, which is a very serious crime. You don't have a record yet. Are you willing to risk your job and apartment for a man you barely know?" Finley let the question sink in.

Gloria seemed to consider the situation, glanced back a third time, and finally stepped aside. "Go ahead, but he's not here."

Finley and Jazz fanned out to cover the left side of the apartment, the second team went right, and Bennett stood guard at the front door with Gloria. Finley crouched and covered one half of each room, and Jazz the other. They moved in sync like they'd served together before, each anticipating the other's movements. The teams shouted the all-clear until each room had been swept. Jeremy wasn't in the apartment. The officers regrouped in the center of the space.

"I told you he wasn't here," Gloria said.

"But he's been here recently." Finley pointed to two drink glasses sweating circles of condensation on the coffee table and Newport menthol cigarette butts with chewed ends in the ashtray. "Looks like you stalled just long enough for him to get away."

"Officer, I really had no idea what he'd done or I would've called. I swear."

Finley scuffed her boot in the carpet, unable to look at the other officers or her bosses, feeling like she'd let everyone down, again. She'd listened to Gloria's excuses too long, and Jeremy had gotten away. Glancing down at the floor, she noticed light flecks on the toe of her shoe. She stooped and wiped at the substance, rubbing it between her fingers. The sharp edges scratched her skin and made her itch. Insulation. She looked up, and the cover of the attic crawl space was cockeyed. "There."

One of the officers dragged a chair into the center of the hallway, and she made a stirrup with her hands and hoisted him up before following quickly behind. "He's definitely been up here," he called back to her. "The insulation is disturbed leading straight ahead."

The space was covered with dust making it hard to breathe, and Finley gagged at the smell of rotting flesh, a large rat caught in a trap. Finley crouched and duck-walked along the supporting beams behind the other officer while reporting to the guys on the ground. "We're traveling east from our location. It looks like we're passing supporting walls, possibly into other apartments." They continued forward. "Now another one. Have the officers outside expand the perimeter and stand by."

The officer in front of her pointed down into another apartment and reached for his walkie. When he turned, he lost his footing and stepped between the rafters. "Fuck." His face twisted into a shocked mask.

Finley grabbed for him as he started falling. She went down hard across three rafters—one hit her chest, one her ribs, and the last one she tucked her feet behind to anchor her—but she held onto the officer's arms. "I've got you, pal."

"Jesus H. Christ. Don't let go until I see what's under me."

"I'm really glad you're not a weightlifter, but hurry." She hurt everywhere, and her shoulders were shifting, threatening to dislocate. "Now would be good."

"I think I'm okay. Let go."

She released her grip, heard him drop to the floor, and dangled her arms over the opening for several seconds before attempting to move. Voices grew louder below her. "Are you okay?"

"Might've sprained my ankle, but the suspect is in the wind. I'll advise the others."

Damn it. She'd wasted too much time before entering the apartment—just long enough for Jeremy to hoist himself into the attic and scurry to safety. She coiled herself up from the opening and eased back across the rafters to the original apartment. As she lowered herself to the floor, she caught a glimpse of the captain and lieutenant huddled near the front door.

"I'm sorry, ma'am."

"It's not your fault," Bennett said, glancing toward her vehicle. "This guy is making us look like a bunch of amateurs. The tactical sergeant and his squad are going to check the area before clearing. Make sure our injured officer gets his ankle checked. You'll have to hitch a ride. Jazz and I are leaving."

"Yes, ma'am, but—"

"We have to go *now*. It's family." Bennett sprinted toward her car.

Jazz started to follow but turned and said, "Find us in the ER."

❖

Dylan cranked up the volume on her iPhone to block her thoughts while she changed clothes in the locker room. The aggressive, percussive beats and eerie electronic sound of Jack Trammell's "Dark Effect" matched her mood perfectly. She ached for Finley one minute, and never wanted to see her again the next. Their involvement promised only regret and pain. The physical release and short-lived pleasure weren't worth sacrificing her beliefs and interrupting a path that worked for her.

"*Dr. Carlyle to ER stat.*"

Dylan paused with her green scrub pants halfway up her legs. She hadn't checked in yet, and only a few people knew her schedule. An unsettling feeling snaked up her back, and she finished dressing quickly. She grabbed her tablet, and her phone pinged simultaneously with a text from Holly. *ER. Stat.*

Something was definitely wrong. She slammed her locker shut and sprinted to the elevator. When the door opened on the ER floor, Holly rushed to her, eyes wide. Usually nothing fazed Holly. "What?"

"It's going to be okay." Holly pulled her into a hug. "Really."

"Holly, what's wrong?" She glanced over Holly's shoulder at her entire family huddled near a consulting room and Finley standing off to the side. Their somber faces and stooped shoulders broadcasted bad news. She spun out of Holly's grasp and ran. "Who?" She struggled for breath, but her chest was too tight.

Mama reached her first. "Baby, it's going to be all right."

"Okay…what is?" Tears welled in her eyes and she fought them back, reverting to work mode. She didn't panic in emergencies, especially when family was involved.

Bennett flanked her on the opposite side and guided her toward the room where the others now waited. "Let's have some privacy."

"Would you like a glass of water?" Stephanie asked.

Dylan waved her hands in front of her. "Stop coddling. What I'd like is for someone to tell me what's going on. You're in my bailiwick, so the chances are pretty good that I'm better equipped for whatever is happening than any of you." She met her mother's watery gaze. "So?"

"It's G-ma."

If G-ma were a typical seventy-eight-year-old, Dylan could rattle off any number of possible maladies, but she was healthy, never sick, never complained, never even caught a cold. "What?" She said the word so calmly that everyone stared. They were used to the slightly scattered baby-girl Dylan, not the focused hospital version.

Mama eased her into a chair and squatted in front of her. "We're not sure what happened. I found her collapsed at the bottom of the stairs this morning when I got up." She swallowed hard. "A lot... of blood."

Oh my God. Dylan pushed her first thought and the accompanying panic down. "Where is she now?"

"Holly took her back to one of the treatment rooms and called a doctor immediately," Mama said.

"Was she still breathing when you found her?" Dylan asked. "Did you have to resuscitate her? Any visible injuries?" She rattled off the questions automatically, trying to determine a diagnosis and what to do next. She refused to lapse into the personal yet. "Tell me."

"Breathing fine, bleeding from the head, and her right wrist was obviously broken," Mama said. "She knew where she was but was really groggy and didn't know exactly what happened. I called Ben first."

"And I called an ambulance, Jazz, and Simon. You'd already left for work," Bennett said. "And I didn't want to tell you while you were driving. So, I called Holly."

"Did she seem dizzy, have balance issues, or was she forgetful? How about respiration and blood pressure?"

Jazz shrugged. "From what I saw, she seemed pretty normal, but I'm not a doctor. Ben and I checked the house, thinking maybe she was attacked, but the place was secure."

"I should've gone over for breakfast or at least coffee. I would've found her sooner," Dylan stuck her hands in her pockets so the family wouldn't see them shaking. They needed her to be strong right now.

"Don't you dare," Mama said. "This isn't your fault, and you couldn't have done more than we did after the fact."

Dylan stared at her in disbelief. "Of course, I could've. I'm a doctor for God's sake, Mother. All of you stay here." She stood. Her mission was now G-ma's care. "I'll let you know something as soon as I do."

She didn't look back but stepped into the hallway and closed the door behind her. Her legs trembled, and she grabbed for something to hold on to. Finley raced to her side, but when Dylan leaned into her, Finley grunted in pain and they both backed against the wall for support.

"Are you okay?" Dylan asked.

"I'm good. Ben and Jazz got the call while we were searching for Jeremy. Are *you* okay?" She shook her head. "Stupid question. Sorry. If I can help, let me know."

Dylan met Finley's gaze, and her offer seemed sincere, her concern genuine. For a moment, Dylan needed not to be strong, to have someone see her pain and be there just for her. She allowed Finley to calm and ground her for a few precious seconds. Now she could do what needed to be done. "I have to go, but thank you for being here."

Finley nodded. "Go do your doctor thing. I'm not going anywhere."

Holly was waiting in front of the nurses' station with exactly what Dylan needed. Facts. "Treatment room one. Laceration to right forehead, nothing unusual about it, but we can't rule out possible hemorrhage, edema, or concussion, especially for a woman her age. No complaints of headache or change in vision, weakness, dizziness, or nausea, and her speech seems fine. I've ordered a CT scan. We've done X-rays of the simple fracture to her right wrist. No idea what caused the fall yet."

"Thank you, Holly." Dylan cupped her elbow, needing a little extra support, and followed toward the treatment area. She breathed in a deep gulp of air before pulling back the curtain. "Well, what do we—" When she saw her grandmother's pale face and silver hair covered with dried blood and her wrist grotesquely twisted, Dylan faltered and grabbed the gurney railing.

Holly whispered, "You've got this."

"Hi, honey. Isn't this a sight?" G-ma waved her left hand toward her face. She chuckled, and the sound brought Dylan back to her responsibilities. If anyone deserved the benefit of her training, it was her grandmother. She and G-pa had set aside college funds for their grandchildren before they had any, and G-ma had been Dylan's staunchest supporter when she chose a field other than law enforcement. It was payback time.

"Well, it's certainly different." She held G-ma's hand for a few seconds, reveling in the warmth and familiarity of her touch before pulling on a pair of gloves. She opened some alcohol wipes and dabbed at the dried blood around the injury. "Can you tell me what happened?"

"Darn if I know really. I was sitting at the kitchen counter waiting for my coffee to brew. When it finished, I was going back upstairs to enjoy it in a hot bath. I started to step up on the first stair and then bam. Nothing. The next thing I remember was waking up in a pool of blood, my wrist throbbing, and Gayle beside me on the floor."

"So, you passed out?" Dylan asked.

"Maybe I was magically transported out of my body or someone else took over for a while. Your guess is probably better than mine, at least it's an educated one."

"Do you remember anything else, G-ma?" Dylan asked.

"I lost a tooth from my bridge in the fall. One of those nice young EMT fellas got down on hands and knees and fingered through all that blood until he found the tooth and then put it in a plastic bag for me. Wasn't he sweet?"

"Very," Holly agreed.

"And then…" G-ma continued while Dylan checked her pupillary response, pulse, and the heart monitor. "At the ER, one of the nurses asked if I wanted her to take my bra off or cut it off. I checked if it was one of my good ones and told her to stand back and cut away."

Holly snickered. "The fall obviously didn't damage your sense of humor."

"The day I lose that, you might as well plant me six feet under, girly."

"Okay, let's get your forehead stitched." Dylan turned, and Holly had a suture tray ready. She smiled her appreciation and nodded at Holly's questioning look. "I'm good. Would you find someone to stabilize her wrist, please? The ortho doc won't do surgery until we know what caused the blackout." She looked down at G-ma. "You're going to feel a sting while I irrigate and numb the area."

"Do what you have to, honey. I'm in good hands. And we should probably let the rest of the clan know I'm not going to die... at least not right now."

Dylan flinched at the mention of dying and felt an overwhelming sense of grief. It had been the first thing that flashed through her mind—like the night Papa died. Thank God it wasn't G-ma's time yet. "As soon as I get you stitched up, I'll let them in. The kids don't need to see you in your current condition." She carefully pulled the skin together and closed the wound using a simple line of interrupted stitches, periodically checking that G-ma was okay.

"You've never been much of a seamstress, so will I have a ragged pirate scar across my forehead to brag about?"

"If I do my job right, you'll hardly notice. The laceration is pretty close to your hairline."

"Aww, that's too bad. The kids will be disappointed."

Dylan finished the final stitch and cut the suture. "There. Almost good as new. The stitches will dissolve in a few days." She wiped more cotton swabs across G-ma's face and got as much of the dried blood off as possible. "Ready for the horde?"

G-ma nodded but caught Dylan's hand. "Thank you, honey. You're an excellent doctor, and I love you. Can I ask one more favor."

"When have I ever denied you, G-ma?"

"I remember a few times I tried to set you up with some handsome young men—"

"Besides that," Dylan said.

G-ma paused, gave Dylan a steady stare, and said, "I want everyone to carry on with the fundraiser tomorrow night. Promise me."

"That won't be easy without you. You're the belle of the ball and our matriarch."

"It's true," G-ma grinned, "but the show must go on. We established the Carlyle Memorial Fund for police families who've lost loved ones in the line of duty. Their needs don't stop just because I fell over."

"It's probably too late to cancel anyway, but I'm not in the mood to act happy around a bunch of strangers, especially with you here," Dylan said.

"You can do this, honey. You do much harder things every day. Just remember, it's for people who really need our help."

Dylan buried her face in G-ma's shoulder, inhaling her familiar powdery scent, and let the tears come. "Sorry I didn't come by this morning."

"Oh, baby, you couldn't have done anything to stop the magical blackout if you'd been standing beside me. You've been wonderful, and I'm so proud of you. I get to wear some of my granddaughter's handiwork for a while. Thank you." She brushed Dylan's hair away from her face. "Now, dry your eyes and bring in the others. If I know my family, they're pestering every nurse and doctor who passes by."

"For sure. I'm going to set up a CT scan and another consult while the family showers you with love. We need to know why you blacked out."

CHAPTER EIGHTEEN

Morning slipped into late afternoon while Dylan checked G-ma's CT scan, monitored her heartbeat, and waited for consults with the cardiologist and neurologist about her condition. Now she and the electrophysiologist who specialized in heart rhythm issues were back in G-ma's room explaining their findings and care options to her and the family.

"So, young man, you're telling me I need a pacemaker?" G-ma asked.

The EP, at least Bennett's age with stark black hair and a slight Indian accent, nodded.

"My heart is mostly fine, but it's not getting some kind of signal on a regular basis and makes me pass out?"

"It's called a vasovagal or neurocardiogenic syncope. Your body reacts to certain triggers, and your heart rate and blood pressure drop suddenly, which leads to reduced blood flow to your brain, causing you to briefly lose consciousness."

"And these triggers are why I've always hated the sight of blood and feel sweaty and queasy when I get shots?"

The EP nodded again. "Normally, it's not a serious problem, but we've also seen irregularity in your heart rhythm, two to four seconds without a beat, which further supports the pacemaker recommendation."

"And if I don't want metal in my chest?"

The doctor glanced at Dylan and took another path. "This decision will have a serious impact on your life. Without a pacemaker to stabilize your heart, we can't do surgery to set your wrist. No surgeon will chance having a cardiac event while you're under anesthesia. And you'll never be able to drive a car again. What happens if you pass out at the wheel?"

G-ma looked around at her family and then met the doctor's gaze. "Well, guess I'm getting a pacemaker then."

"Yeah, I guess," Mama said, breathing a sigh of relief. "Nothing keeps Norma Carlyle from burning up the streets of Greensboro in her little purple Toyota."

After the EP left, Dylan gathered the family closer. "I think you made the right decision, G-ma. I'll go check on the surgeon's availability. I know just the man for the job." She turned toward the door, but Mama stopped her.

"Dylan, that can wait. You've been going wide open since this morning. Take a break, get something to eat, or at least a cup of coffee. I'm sending everyone else home in shifts to do the same."

"In a bit." She hugged her mother, and the comfort of her arms made Dylan suddenly tired and needy, but this wasn't the time to break down.

"And," Bennett added, "maybe you could find Finley. She's been here all day too. I'm sure she'd appreciate an update."

"I told her she could join us," Mama said, "but she insisted on giving us privacy."

Emory slid her arm around Dylan's waist. "She has some kind of family wound. I see it in her eyes, and we're probably a bit much for her all at one time. Talk to her."

Finley wasn't here because she didn't feel comfortable with Dylan's family or possibly in any family situation, as she'd seen at brunch. Could Finley adapt to her family's intimacy and oversharing like Kerstin and Emory had? And why would she? They'd been out and had sex once. Nothing more. The thought left her sad and even more drained. It seemed like ages since she'd stumbled into Finley's arms in the hallway this morning and felt her strength and courage. She needed that again, but they didn't have that kind of relationship.

She gave everyone a hug and tracked Holly down in the supply room. "Have you seen Finley?"

"She asked if there was an outdoor space nearby, and I sent her to the healing garden about half an hour ago."

"Why was she here anyway?" Dylan asked.

"She kept another officer from falling through a ceiling and hyperextended her shoulders, no muscle or ligament injury though. She'll be sore as hell for a few days."

"Thanks. I'll catch you later."

"Why don't you head home?" Holly asked. "Working a full day is stressful enough, but you've been pulling double duty with your family. Besides, you started before your shift."

"I want to make sure G-ma is on the surgical schedule for her pacemaker."

Holly hugged her and then held her at arm's length to make eye contact. "I'll take care of that. In other news, are you still having the fundraiser tomorrow?"

"G-ma demands it. I'll see you there."

"Bringing a date?" Holly asked.

Dylan nodded, not really feeling the party vibe. "I invited Wendy Kramer a few months ago. We're each other's faux dates any time we don't want to be pawed all evening. I hope she hasn't found a new girlfriend yet. You?"

"Great, you're taking the hot cardiologist and I'm stuck with my gay BFF."

"At least we can be miserable together. Thanks for today, Holly. Think I'll take your advice and head home." Dylan texted Bennett so the family wouldn't worry, purchased a coffee, and went in search of Finley.

She found her stretched out on a concrete bench, staring up at an oak tree, arms resting over her stomach, and her legs dangling. She still wore her police pants, shoes, and a black long-sleeved T-shirt but not the rest of her cop paraphernalia. Dylan had an unexplainable feeling she'd known Finley much longer than a week. Maybe their connection seemed so quick and intense because of the emotional events that kept bringing them together—the shooting, *Hamilton*, their intimate conversation, sex, and now G-ma's fall.

"Why don't you join me, Dylan?" Finley asked without turning her head.

"How did you know it was me?"

Finley gingerly rose, crossing her arms over her chest, and scooted over to give Dylan more room. "We spent about twelve hours together yesterday-ish. I smelled you."

Finley's comment sounded like a cross between a bad romance novel and a science fiction tale with extraordinary creatures. Dylan chuckled, and it felt so good to release some tension after the day she'd had that she laughed aloud. "So, I smell like..." she glanced around to make sure no one was within hearing distance. "...sex?"

Finley ducked her head like she was embarrassed by her words. "Not exactly sex. You have a very distinctive fragrance mingled with a hint of jasmine perfume. I like it, a lot." She nudged Dylan's foot with hers. "I was just thinking about you."

Dylan settled next to her and sipped her coffee, her gaze never leaving Finley's. "Why?"

"Honestly?" There was a pause as Finley seemed to consider what else she wanted to say. "I think I miss you."

Finley's voice was soft, her words heartfelt, and Dylan felt their effects bore straight to her heart. She automatically shifted closer. "You miss me?"

Finley nodded. "And I'm worried about you."

"It's not your job to worry about me, Fin, but I appreciate it. I think. As long as you're not trying to manage me. I get enough of that at home."

Finley feigned shock. "I'd never." She reached for Dylan's hand and brought it to rest in her lap. "I'd just like...to help. How is G-ma?"

"Stable but she's spending a few days here until her wrist is set and a pacemaker inserted." She filled Finley in on the details.

"Hey, want to get out of here? You could probably use a distraction."

The thought of leaving, actually running from this place right now, felt perfect. "I'd like that. What did you have in mind?"

"Pick up some takeout and crash somewhere. My place, if you want. Yours if you need to stay close to your family."

Finley's kindness continued to surprise Dylan, and she considered the options. "Not mine. Give me a few minutes to check on G-ma one last time and change out of these scrubs?"

"I'll swing by Outback and see you at my place in an hour?" Finley stood, offered her hand, remembered her hyperextended shoulders and withdrew. When Dylan stood, Finley threaded their fingers together.

"Thank you." Finley slid her thumb across the back of Dylan's hand, and she felt the connection surge through her. What was it about Finley that intrigued and aroused her so thoroughly with a simple touch or kind gesture? Probably hormones. Add to it the exhaustion of today and no wonder she was like the raw end of a live wire. She just needed some downtime.

❖

Finley cupped her hands, enjoying the residual warmth from their touch as Dylan walked back toward the hospital. Dylan not only intrigued her, she made Finley want to be a better person. She'd even invited Dylan to her house, again. Maybe the simple fact that Dylan didn't seem to need her was compelling. But how much of that independence was a show for her family, a challenge to the baby-girl box of protectiveness they'd established around her? Finley had sensed an underlying need that Dylan didn't show anyone else and that need kept drawing her back. *Don't overthink.* She hurried to her car.

Before she could collect the food and get home, the sky opened up with a steady downpour, and the wind plunged the temperature to a biting chill. She rushed into the house, dropped the food on the counter, and took a quick shower. When she came out, Dylan was shucking her coat by the front door. "Perfect timing, Doctor."

Dylan shook her body like a dog coming in from the rain. "It's brutal out there."

"Why don't I start a fire?"

"I'd love that. My only regret from the last visit was I didn't get to enjoy that huge fireplace. Do you think it's too hot?"

Finley pointed to her temple. "I have a perfect solution." She crossed to the front windows and raised the two that overlooked the porch. A cool breeze swept in along with the pattering of rain on the tin roof.

"I love that sound." She closed her eyes and listened for several seconds and then sighed contentedly. "Would you like me to dish up the food while you start a fire?"

Finley nodded.

Dylan opened several cabinets before asking, "Plates?"

Finley stood for a few seconds mesmerized by the sight of Dylan Carlyle playing hostess in her kitchen. *Her kitchen.* She hadn't thought of this place as hers in years, but somehow with Dylan here, the house took on a comfortable, homey feel. The perpetually chilly nooks and crannies brimmed with warmth and possibility.

"A-hum. Plates?"

"Oh, sorry. We'll just need a couple of spoons and lots of napkins. I purposely got things we could eat from the cartons with our fingers." She stopped short of saying so they could lick the crumbs from each other's fingers, snuggle in front of the fire under a blanket, and not leave for hours.

"I like the way you think, Masters…some of the time." Dylan collected the utensils and rejoined Finley in the living area.

"What do you mean some of the time?" Finley closed the fireplace screen and then opened a container of slaw and stuck two spoons in while Dylan unwrapped the ribs.

"You were in the ER again today. Some heroic stunt to save another officer."

Finley settled on the sofa, waited for Dylan to join her, and placed a blanket over their legs before answering. "What? You don't like superheroes? In case you hadn't noticed, they're trending right now." Dylan stiffened beside her and stared at the fire. "Dylan?"

"We've covered this ground. I don't like people I care abo— know putting themselves in harm's way. You have a job to do, I get that, but you could be more careful. Your hospital records indicate you're either accident prone or reckless."

"You read my medical history?"

"Of course. I checked your shin injuries, remember? Any competent doctor consults a patient's history before treatment."

"What am I supposed to do, Dylan? Let someone get hurt when I might be able to help? That's not me. Could you stand by and let an injured person suffer and not offer aid?" Finley reached for Dylan's hand, but she hugged the blanket tighter around her. "And FYI, I don't take stupid risks and I'm not reckless. I just have a sense about trouble and know when to step in. And I have amazing cat-like reflexes." Finley clawed the air and hissed. "Okay?"

Dylan released a heavy sigh and her shoulders sagged. "I'm sorry, Fin." She leaned her head back against the sofa and closed her eyes. "I'm just tired. It's been a tough day, and seeing G-ma hurt has made me more hypersensitive than usual. I have no right voicing an opinion about your life or how you choose to live it, on or off the job."

Dylan's resigned comment bothered Finley. She never thought she'd feel this way, but she wanted Dylan to care about her—and it scared her—but she brushed her fear aside and reached for Dylan again. She needed to feel safe and cared for after her traumatic day, and Finley could set aside her discomfort to help. She gently guided Dylan closer and tucked the blanket around them. "I hereby give you the right to say anything you want about my life."

"Be careful, Masters. I might have quite a lot to say." Dylan snuggled against Finley's chest and breathed deeply. "This feels nice. Thank you."

Finley grunted.

"What's wrong?"

"My Wonder Woman stunt. I'll probably have some righteous bruises across my chest and abdomen. I'm pretty sore."

"No extracurricular activity for you tonight then," Dylan joked.

Their food turned cold, forgotten on the table, while rain drummed rhythmically on the roof, and Finley bundled Dylan tightly. "Relax. I've got you." She kissed Dylan's forehead and scooted down on the sofa beside her. Dylan met her gaze, and Finley wanted to kiss her so badly she ached, but sensed it wasn't the right time. "Can I ask a question?"

"Uh-huh."

"Why did you leave without waking me the last time you were here?" The question had tumbled around in her head ever since, followed closely by another—why did it matter? She and Dylan had both chosen to avoid being hurt by keeping their distance. Wasn't that reason enough?

"We agreed no strings. It was easier. And I was afraid the awkward morning-after vibe would spoil our wonderful night." Dylan's voice had become soft, almost a whisper.

"And if I wanted to renegotiate?" She held her breath. What was she saying? She definitely wanted to have sex with Dylan again, but renegotiating her no-strings policy wasn't something she'd consciously considered. The question just came out.

Maybe they could date, get to know each other, like a normal couple. Dylan made her feel things, want things she never had, emotionally dangerous things. "Dylan?" Finley looked down at Dylan. Her eyes were closed and her breathing was deep and steady. Finley kissed her forehead again and pulled her closer. "I've got you." *But who's got me?*

CHAPTER NINETEEN

F inley woke slowly, stretched her back, and almost rolled off the side of the sofa but pressed her hand against the floor to stop her fall. The sharp pain across her shoulders reminded her of her heroics the day before. She reached for Dylan but found empty space. Again. What was it about waking up with her that Dylan couldn't handle? And why did it bother Finley so much? She stood and folded the blanket over the back of the sofa. Dylan didn't date cops, and Finley couldn't do families or intimacy, so remaining focused on their differences worked best.

She clicked the coffee maker on and automatically checked her phone. She'd missed texts from Anita and Hank and brought his up first.

Jeremy Spencer took the guys on another wild goose chase last night. Will we ever get this fucker?

Finley dialed his number. "What happened?"

"One of the tact guys spotted Spencer around the apartment complex you searched yesterday. He probably hid until everyone left, boosted a car, and tried to get away. It was a short chase, but he dodged us again. And still no fucking CCTV footage worth a damn."

"He's making us look like the Keystone Cops, and it pisses me off," Finley said. "His brother is still in the hospital. Maybe he's waiting until Josh is released to try to spring him from custody. But don't worry, Hank, we'll get him. And when we do I'll make him pay."

"Don't say that shit, Fin. I taught you better. Just bring their asses to trial. I want to stare them both in the face when I testify."

"You got it. How are you feeling?"

"I'm getting a little better with the crutches. I'll catch you later. Becky is giving me a sponge bath. Fun times. Oh, why don't you come by after lunch. Robin and the Carlyle kids are going to play ball."

"I'll be there." They hung up, and Finley chuckled at the image of her six-foot coach being manhandled by his five three wife. She flipped to Anita's message next.

What are you wearing 2nite? Need to coordinate.

Tonight? She poured the strong coffee into her mug, settled at the kitchen counter, and checked the calendar on her phone. The Carlyle fundraiser. Damn it. She'd agreed to go with Anita months ago, probably at a weak point in the heat of passion. She'd promised and couldn't back out now. She tapped. *Tux. Pick you up at 7?*

Can't wait. Let's make a night of it. Anita's code for sex later.

Finley didn't respond. The heat of Dylan's body pressed against hers on the narrow sofa, and the way they'd shifted and remained together during the night made her want only one woman. It was a dance they'd never rehearsed but performed instinctively. She wanted Dylan, and more than sexually. That was the part that worried her. What could she offer in return?

She started to dial the station to check on the manhunt, but this was her day off. Time to relax. Could she forget about work, even for a few hours? She'd done so nicely with Dylan here, but without her, the house again felt cold and hollow, and she grew restless.

Finley finished her first cup of coffee, poured another, and carried it to her bedroom. She rummaged to the back of her walk-in closet where she'd stowed her tuxedo. The last time she'd worn anything vaguely formal was at her father's funeral—a black suit and tie and white shirt that her father always said made her look like a waiter.

She unzipped the clothes bag and slid the tux and two vests onto the bed. Her usual combo was black slacks, jacket, and tie with the gray vest and a white shirt. She glanced at the red vest. What would Dylan be wearing? What did it matter? She was going with Anita. Would Dylan have a date? *Did* Dylan date? All Finley knew was she didn't date cops. Her stomach lurched, and she sat on the side of the bed. *Oh fuck.* She was in so much trouble.

To stay busy and not think about this evening, Finley ran the dust mop over the floors, just in case Dylan came back or Sharon needed to show the place again. She focused on the afternoon at Hank's, playing with children who still believed anything was possible. If Dylan was there maybe they'd have an opportunity to talk about last night. She'd asked to renegotiate their arrangement, but Dylan hadn't heard her. Maybe she should leave well enough alone.

She changed into a worn pair of sweats and her most comfortable tennis shoes and made the short drive to Hank's, her heart rate rising with each block. One black SUV with the thin blue line decal in the back window was parked in front of the house. Before she made it up the steps, Robin crashed through the front door and headed toward her at full speed.

"You're here."

"Of course, I'm here, but don't jump today." She pointed at her still-tender shoulders. "Work injury." She tickled him under the arms, which made him squirm and try to break free.

"So, how many people are playing?"

When Finley stopped tickling him, Robin counted on his fingers. "Ryan, Riley, and a new girl named Shea, who's pretty cool too. And dad's bosses, and the doctor lady from the hospital."

Finley swallowed hard. She wanted to put on her game face before seeing Dylan again, especially in front of her sisters. "Dylan?"

"I guess. She's too short for basketball, but we'll be nice and let her play."

She rubbed his head as they entered the house. "Good man."

Finley kissed Becky on the cheek on their way through the kitchen toward the backyard. "How's our guy today?"

"In his element. He's playing umpire."

Finley laughed. "I think it's called a referee in basketball."

Becky waved her off. "Whatever. It's a ball thing."

Robin ran to the backyard yelling, "Fin's here. We can start now."

Finley honed in on Dylan the second she stepped outside. She wore a pair of bright pink tights and an equally snug top with a neckline that revealed just enough cleavage to be distracting. Finley licked her lips. How in the hell could she concentrate on basketball?

"Hey, guys," she said, shaking hands with Bennett and Jazz and nodding to the kids. She shuffled in front of Dylan like a new student on the playground, unable to meet her gaze. "Hi."

"Hi, yourself. Sure you're up for this, after your fall?"

"I'm nicely bruised, but exercise will help with the soreness. Just no body blocking," Finley replied. "And no more of these, if you please." She pointed to the scar on her chin.

"I wondered how you got that sexy little addition. Very nice." Dylan grinned and wiggled her eyebrows. "Prepare for a thumping, Masters."

"Says the five-foot-nothing woman," Finley teased her.

"Yeah, but I have a secret weapon." Dylan waved at her outfit. "Just for you." She winked and moved closer. "Try to keep your eye on the ball, Masters."

"If you two stop sparring, we'll begin. We only have a two-hour window," Hank said. "Becky and I divided everybody up into fairly equal teams. "Ryan, Shea, Bennett, and Finley are on one team, and Riley, Robin, Jazz, and Dylan on the other. Becks will do the ball toss, and I'll referee from the sidelines on my magic sticks." He tapped the crutches under his arms. "Any objections speak now."

When nobody responded, Becky stepped to the center of the court between equally matched Bennett and Jazz. "Try not to crush me." She made the toss and ran for her life.

Bennett tipped the ball toward Finley, and she passed it to Ryan who was already under their basket. He tossed it up, and Bennett assisted for the dunk and the first points of the game.

"Great job, Ryan!" Finley high-fived him and handed the ball to Dylan.

"Beginner's luck," Dylan said. She in-bounded the ball to Robin, and he dribbled down the court, passing back and forth with Riley who matched his stride step for step. Dylan stopped in front of Finley and wiggled her shoulders. When Finley glanced at her chest, Dylan reached out and tipped her chin up. "The ball's not in there." She swept past Finley, who was still stunned at the reprimand, and caught a pass from Jazz to execute a neat layup.

"Hey," Bennett said, "no fair distracting our players with your...assets."

"It's not my fault she can't multitask."

Finley wanted to dig a hole in the concrete pad and crawl in, but Bennett shrugged. "Valid point."

Shea took the ball out and threw it in to Bennett, who passed it back. Shea was quick and wove an intricate pattern around the adults, and then handed off to Finley for the basket.

Jazz in-bounded to Riley, who dribbled down the court with Finley in pursuit. Dylan slipped into position and planted her feet. Riley grinned, recognizing the pick Dylan set, and altered her course slightly so that Finley, who was focused on pressuring Riley, slammed into Dylan. Time froze and heat pulsed between them as they lay in a tangle of arms and legs.

Dylan's grin was wide. "Couldn't wait to get me prone again?"

Finley jumped to her feet, hoping Dylan's sisters hadn't heard the whispered taunt. She looked over to Hank. "Foul, ref."

"Looked like her feet were planted in plenty of time, Fin," Hank said. "The foul is on you."

Finley shook her head, but offered her hand to help Dylan up, wincing only slightly from the strain on her shoulder. Her body still burned from the contact with Dylan, and Finley could not tear her gaze from Dylan's backside as she trotted away to rejoin her team.

Hank ordered the ball in-bounded from the sideline to restart play. Riley passed the ball in to Jazz, and Finley, still dazed, was slow to react when Riley sprinted toward the basket. Jazz passed the ball to Robin, who passed it back to Riley, who scored a neat layup.

"Great assist, Robin," Bennett said as Robin and Riley shared a celebratory chest bump.

"No fair." But Finley was loving every minute of the game—being physically active, playing with Dylan, laughing, and watching her move. She hadn't seen this lighthearted side before, but she liked how uninhibited and free Dylan seemed.

All the adults played at a level that involved the kids and allowed them to score most of the baskets. Finley played basketball in high school and college, and it felt good to help kids learn and enjoy the game. They played hard and fast, stopping only briefly for water breaks, until Hank gave the three-minute warning.

Ryan took the ball out for their team, passed in to Bennett, and she made a long pass down court to Finley for an easy two points.

"And that's how it's done," Finley said.

"Well, watch this, sport." Dylan dribbled down court with Finley keeping pace, reaching in and trying to dislodge the ball.

Every time she touched Dylan, even inadvertently, she felt a spark and her body misfired. She stumbled over her own feet, couldn't reach the ball, and finally just grabbed Dylan.

Hank blew the whistle. "Holding."

"Yeah. My bad." Finley clenched her fists at her sides. Kids were present, along with Dylan's older sisters. This was neither the time nor the place to let her feelings show.

Dylan threw the ball to Robin for the shot and stopped beside Finley. "Can't keep your hands off me, can you?"

"So it seems," Finley admitted.

Dylan grinned and walked off the court. "Time's up. The Carlyles have to make a command appearance at the hospital for G-ma's inspection before this evening's event."

"That means we end with a tie," Hank said. "Guess we'll have a rematch."

The kids erupted in cheers and sprinted toward the house.

Jazz hung back with Finley when she reached into the cooler for a bottle of water, and the rest of the group followed the children inside. "Be careful of your next move with my sister." Her tone was soft, non-threatening, but very matter-of-fact. "I don't want her hurt."

Finley stopped and met Jazz's stare. She'd expected Bennett to warn her off because Jazz was so quiet and non-confrontational. But Jazz's comments hit the target like an expert marksman and demanded honesty. "I feel like I'm the one in danger."

"Possibly. She's never been interested in a cop, and I don't know how she'll handle it or if she'll even let herself go there...for anything but fun."

Finley nodded, her heart feeling like someone held it in a vise. "Thanks for the warning."

CHAPTER TWENTY

When Finley picked Anita up that evening at seven, she was a total wreck. She faced armed suspects with more focus and courage. She'd enjoyed this afternoon with Dylan, but they hadn't talked. Probably best, considering Jazz's advice.

"Hey, babe," Anita said, climbing in the Jeep beside her. "I've missed you." She leaned over the console and pulled Finley into a kiss. "Yum. Good as ever."

Anita's proximity made her anxious, but she vowed to be courteous. Anita wasn't to blame for Finley questioning her beliefs and acting totally out of character. "Nice. Green looks good on you. So, are we going to a dinner, dance, or what? It's my first time."

"Mostly dancing and mingling. A three-month online auction led up to this event. The winners will be announced tonight. It's a huge fundraiser, and the Blandwood Mansion Carriage House is the perfect venue for just about anything."

Finley seized the topic and ran with it. Conversation was not their forte. She was usually too busy helping Anita undress to actually talk. "Yeah, I toured the mansion in high school. I liked the Tuscan style, the central tower, stucco walls, and the symmetry of the two end pieces."

Anita laughed. "The end pieces? They're called dependencies or wings, and they house the historic Governor John Motley Morehead law offices on one side and a kitchen on the other."

"But the carriage house is awesome too," Finley said. "Octagonal shaped. Pretty progressive for the period."

She stroked Finley's thigh. "Why are we talking about architecture? And when did I fall from hot to nice? What's wrong?"

"Maybe I'm a little nervous. This is a huge deal for my boss's family. Guess I want to make a good impression. Plus, formal and crowds really aren't my thing."

"Stick with me. I'm a frequent flyer." Finley gave her a quizzical glance, and she added, "Always looking for Ms. Right who runs in the best social circles."

Another reason she and Anita could never be serious. "May be your lucky night, and don't let me cramp your style."

Anita eyed her. "You said formal events aren't really your thing, Finley. I won't run off with someone else and leave you on your own."

"No, really. There will be plenty of people I know from work to hang out with. Don't worry about me if you find somebody really interesting. I'm cool with it."

Finley parked on a side street and escorted Anita to the queue at the carriage house's French door. As they stood in line, Finley glanced up at the cupola with its louvered openings and glazed windows that allowed both air flow and light and reminded her of a small lighthouse. The building's buff-colored cladding topped by white lattice strips around the curves gave it a beachy feel. She'd pay to be at a beach right now or anywhere but here.

"Earth to Finley." Anita nodded in front of them. "Your boss, twelve o'clock."

Gayle and Bennett Carlyle stood on either side of the arched entry welcoming each guest, flanked by Jazz and Kerstin respectively. Finley craned her neck to look for Dylan but didn't see her. Good, a few minutes to settle her nerves before going inside. She addressed Gayle first. "I hope G-ma is doing better today."

"Yes, we went by the hospital to get her approval on our outfits for the evening. It made her feel included. She's progressing well, according to our resident physician. Thank you for asking, Finley, and thanks for coming."

She introduced Anita, and the Carlyles greeted them warmly, but Bennett glared at her before they walked away. Another warning from a protective sister? She wrote it off to paranoia and concentrated on her surroundings. The spacious room felt cramped with people standing shoulder-to-shoulder, and Finley moved to the outer perimeter so she could breathe. The tile floor combined light and darker inlaid pieces in the shape of an octagon to match the building, and Finley distracted herself by counting the darker squares over and over.

"You okay?" Anita asked, and Finley nodded. "Why don't I get us a drink. Beer?"

She nodded again and watched Anita weave her way through the throngs of people like she belonged here. She really was a beautiful woman, so why wasn't that enough anymore? Finley glanced up and the answer was staring back at her.

"Finley. I didn't know you'd be here," Dylan said, slowly scanning Finley twice.

"Yeah, first time. I…promised…months ago." She sounded like an idiot and just stared at the red dress hugging Dylan's body and the glimpses of skin it revealed at her thigh and down her back as she moved.

"Well, thanks for your support. It takes a village." She waved toward her blond companion. "This is Wendy Kramer. Wendy, Finley Masters, an officer at Bennett's substation."

Finley offered her hand. "You a doctor too?"

"Pediatric surgeon," Wendy said smoothly, her stare confident, smile genuine. Doctors were touchy about their specialties, like police officers were about rank and detective status, but Wendy made the distinction unemotionally without the air of supremacy some physicians had.

"Right." Finley liked Wendy until she took in her smoking hot figure sheathed in a black formal dress that was the perfect contrast to Dylan's red one. Hank would've said these two were a straight man's wet dream. The thought just made her queasy, a feeling that deepened when Wendy encircled Dylan's waist and asked, "Vodka tonic or wine?" The question reeked of familiarity, and Finley had to get away.

"Wendy?" Anita approached the group, pushed Finley's beer at her, and grabbed Wendy's hand. "I haven't seen you in ages. You look…" Anita gave Wendy a visual that rivaled an X-ray checking for breaks, "…delicious."

Wendy blushed and nodded toward Dylan. "That's what my date said too. Thanks."

"Oh, sorry, Dr. Carlyle, I was just appreciating your choice of partner."

Finley forced her arm around Anita's waist. "I'm going to check out the displays. You can come or—"

"Don't mean to barge in, but maybe Anita could show me the way to the bar," Wendy said, "while you look around."

Finley walked away without answering and headed to the table displaying the plaques honoring all the officers who'd died in the line of duty. Each showed a picture of the officer and the dates he began work and his end of watch. Finley gave every man a few seconds of silent respect. When she reached Garrett and Bryce Carlyle's plaques, she stopped. She couldn't imagine losing one relative to violence, much less two. What did Dylan feel when she looked at these or saw her siblings in uniform? No wonder she didn't want to date cops. She felt a soft touch on her back, knew it was Dylan by the way her body warmed, but didn't turn.

"It's a little overwhelming to see them all at once, isn't it?" Dylan asked.

"Yeah."

"I should probably know this, but where are these kept when they're not here or on display for National Police Officers Week? G-Pa's and Papa's hang on the walls in the Fairview Station community room."

"One hundred Police Plaza downtown," Finley said. She kept her answer short. She was being distant, but seeing Dylan with Wendy had thrown her for a loop.

"Are you all right, Fin?"

"Yeah, just not much for crowds." She didn't add, *or seeing you in the arms of another woman.*

Dylan brushed her hand up and down Finley's back and said, "I wanted to thank you for this afternoon. The kids had a great time, I had fun, and I think it helped Hank too." When Finley didn't respond, she added, "Okay, then, I'll leave you to it."

Finley wanted to ask Dylan to stay by her side all evening and then share the night with her, but her courage vanished when she saw Anita and Wendy making their way toward them.

"I got you a vodka tonic. It seems like that kind of night," Wendy said, offering Dylan the drink.

"You know me too well." Dylan took a long drink and looped her arm through Wendy's.

"Guess we'll see you both later," Anita said. "And save me a dance, Wendy."

Finley guided Anita toward the patio, determined to have a good time in spite of the sick feeling in her stomach from seeing Dylan with another woman.

❖

Dylan watched Finley walk away with her arm around Anita and remembered the first time they'd met—Finley servicing Anita in the on-call room. She gripped her clutch and tried to suppress an unfamiliar and unwanted jealousy that broadsided her. She couldn't be jealous of Finley because that meant she had deeper feelings for her, wanted more than their casual sexual arrangement. *That* kind of thinking could lead to breaking her no cops rule, and she couldn't live with the constant fear.

Wendy's hand on her bare back returned her to the moment. "Want to tell me what's going on with you and tall, blond, and handsome?"

"Nothing." She squeezed the lime on the side of her glass into her drink and licked the tart juice from her fingers. Wendy rolled her eyes. She wasn't buying that answer any more than Dylan was. "We hooked up once. No big deal." But the pleasure she felt being with Finley—enjoying *Hamilton*, playing basketball, talking in the healing garden, having sex, actually anytime—hinted at deeper feelings.

"Nothing? Really? The warning look she gave me when I touched you said different. And the smoldering stare you threw at her says you really like her."

Dylan took another sip of her drink. "She's not what I expected, but she's a cop and—"

"I know, your number one rule. Maybe it's time to consider the possibility that your rule is now ruling your life and not in a good way."

"And I thought your specialty was surgery not psychiatry." Dylan bumped shoulders with Wendy. "What about you and Nurse Anita? She seemed pretty keen to get you alone."

"We've talked, but it hasn't actually progressed any further. When I heard she was seeing someone, I backed off. I had no idea who it was until tonight."

"I don't think they're serious." But how could she know? Had Finley said they weren't exclusive when Dylan caught them together? Was it wishful thinking? "Maybe tonight's your opportunity to find out."

"And leave the path to Finley open?" Wendy toasted her glass to Dylan's. "I like the way you think. Operation Separation is hereby initiated. I'll ask Anita to dance, and you find Finley in the garden."

"But...I need to mingle and—"

"Don't you dare say you don't want her as far away from Anita as possible."

The thought of Anita's, or any other woman's, hands on Finley brought Dylan's drink clawing up her throat, but she wasn't ready to admit that aloud.

"I want them separated as soon as possible and I didn't even realize it until tonight." Wendy gave Dylan her puppy-dog eyes. "Please? Help a sister out."

Dylan finished her drink. "Fine. For you. But give me time to work the room or my family won't be happy."

"I'm quite sure I can occupy Anita for more than one dance." Wendy kissed her on the cheek, downed her martini, and headed for the garden.

Dylan worked her way around the crowded room, thanking folks for attending the event and for their financial support of the Carlyle Foundation. When she glanced at her watch, almost two hours had passed, and Wendy and Anita were still on the dance floor, but she didn't see Finley. Did she want to be with Finley? Had her feelings grown in spite of her efforts to maintain distance?

Wendy guided Anita into an alcove and gave her a quick kiss, and Dylan breathed easier. Definitely what she wanted with Finley. She was about to search for Finley, but her mother caught her arm and pulled her toward the front of the room. Time for the family's public appreciation speech and the announcement of auction winners.

Bennett brought the music to a halt, silenced the room, and handed a microphone to Mama, who greeted and thanked the crowd for their attendance and contributions. Dylan counted the minutes, anxious to go find Finley before she got bored or a better offer and left.

Dylan waited until all the winners were announced before she ordered another drink and a beer for Finley and stepped out onto the patio, but Finley wasn't there. She checked the grounds nearby and around the corners near the street and finally spotted Finley at the gardens near Blandwood Mansion.

Dylan avoided the moonlight and stuck to the shadows, her heels sinking into the plush grass as she edged closer to catch a glimpse of Finley unawares. She was staring at the sky, fists clenched at her sides, a contrast to the playful, relaxed Finley on the basketball court earlier. What was she thinking? Was she upset that Anita and Wendy were dancing? Was she annoyed that Dylan hadn't asked her to the event?

"Fin, are you okay?" Finley didn't move, and Dylan wasn't sure if she'd heard her, so she asked again, "Are you all right, Fin?"

Finley's hands relaxed at her sides and she blew out a long breath. "I thought I imagined your voice. Yeah, I'm fine."

"I brought refreshments." She handed the beer to Finley and came closer. "Is it okay that I'm here? If you'd prefer to be alone, I'll go."

"It's fine." Finley continued to stare at the sky.

They stood in silence for a while, both enjoying the light of the full moon and the beat of music from the gala. Dylan felt like she was intruding on a private moment and turned to leave.

"Don't go. I'm glad you're here. It's like you materialized from my thoughts."

"So, you were thinking about me, again, Masters?"

"Who is Wendy?"

Finley's reserved behavior suddenly made sense. She was struggling with the green-eyed monster too, and Dylan knew instinctively not to kid her about it. "We serve as each other's faux dates for events if we don't have a real one and don't want to be hit on all night. Nothing for you to worry about." She paused, considered her question, and asked, "And Anita?"

"Like I said earlier, a promise I made months before I met you." Finley turned and looked at her for the first time. "Did we just cross the line into exclusivity?"

Dylan chuckled and tucked her arm through Finley's. "Something certainly shifted." The possibility surged through Dylan leaving her excited and weak. Exclusivity was the last thing she'd expected from Finley Masters, ever. "For God's sake don't tell anyone or they'll have us committed."

"Agreed." Finley took their drinks and set them down on the raised border surrounding a grouping of roses. "I'd really like to kiss you, if that's okay."

Not at all what Dylan expected, but Finley surprised her a lot. She could say no, walk away, and not look back because kissing without sex implied a level of affection she wasn't ready to admit she felt. But they had just tacitly declared exclusivity. *And* she didn't want to walk away.

Finley stepped closer, so close that if Dylan breathed deeply, their breasts would touch, and she wanted that touch. Seeing Finley so handsome and vulnerable in the moonlight and willing to ask for what she wanted had opened something inside Dylan. "Kiss me."

Finley slid an arm around Dylan's waist and brought them together. With her other hand, she caressed Dylan's face with a feather touch and traced her fingers across her forehead, down her cheek, and then cupped her chin. "You are so beautiful. I can't even…" She leaned in and outlined Dylan's lips with the tip of her tongue before kissing her lightly. She pulled back, as if giving Dylan a chance to reconsider.

But Dylan threaded her hand through Finley's hair and brought them back together. The next kiss was hot, deep, and hungry. Their tongues probed and played in each other's mouths, bringing Dylan up on her toes and tighter against Finley's body. "So…good."

"Dylan…I…"

"Shush," Dylan breathed. "Just keep kissing me, Fin. Don't stop."

Dylan lost herself in the intensity of their kisses and the melding of their bodies. Time stalled, and the surroundings vanished until all that remained was the moonlight enveloping them like a protective glow. Nothing could tear them apart or hurt them here. They were safe.

"Ah-hum." Wendy cleared her throat, and Finley reluctantly stepped away from Dylan.

"Yes?" Dylan asked without breaking eye contact with Finley.

"Anita is ready to go. In the South, you leave the party with the one you came with, so I wanted to make sure I didn't commit a social faux pas or create an enemy by escorting her home, but it looks like I'm safe."

Finley started toward the Carriage House. "I should probably say good-bye."

Wendy stepped into her path. "She's good. Trust me." She nodded back toward Dylan. "Carry on. I'll catch you later, Dylan."

"Thanks." Dylan waited until Wendy was out of sight and opened her arms to Finley. "Shall we carry on?"

"I'd prefer to take you home with me if you're okay with that."

"Sounds perfect." She texted Mama to let her know she was getting a ride home. Mama texted back. *Bring her to brunch tomorrow.* Her mother didn't miss much. Dylan hooked her thumb into Finley's back belt loop as they walked toward the Jeep.

"Will you do me one favor?" Finley asked.

"Yes." Dylan was surprised by how quickly she answered without reservations.

"Promise not to leave again without waking me up."

"That depends."

"On what?"

"How late you keep me up. I have early shift in the morning, but I promise to try. You sleep like the dead." Was there a deeper meaning behind Finley's request, behind her agreement? Were they both saying the same thing—that they wanted to spend more time together, get to know each other, and see where it led? Dylan took a deep breath. She was wishing exactly that.

CHAPTER TWENTY-ONE

The short ride to Finley's house seemed to take forever. Sexual tension pulsed between them, and Dylan slid her hand along the firm muscle of Finley's thigh as she drove, unable to keep from touching her. "I've never been quite so handsy with anyone before."

Finley grinned at her. "And surprisingly, I don't mind."

"You don't like being touched? We've already established you like being in charge."

"No one has ever touched me the way you do, and yeah, I like it a lot."

"And how is that?" Dylan asked, practically purring as she caressed higher.

"Like you're pouring yourself into every touch." Finley stopped the car in her driveway but didn't look at her, almost as if she'd gone shy.

"It's how you make me feel," Dylan said. She leaned over to kiss Finley, but she got out of the Jeep instead and came around to Dylan's door.

"We should probably take this inside. I don't feel like giving the neighborhood a show."

Finley clasped Dylan's hand and escorted her to the front door where a folded piece of paper was wedged between the screen and wooden doors. She pulled it loose, unlocked the door, and waved Dylan inside.

"Are you being evicted?" Dylan chuckled.

Finley unfolded the paper and gave it a quick read. "Not yet, but my Realtor has an offer on the house. I wonder why she didn't text me?"

"You're really selling?" Dylan dropped her clutch and coat on a side chair and turned to face Finley.

"Probably. The only pleasant memories here have been with you and…excuse me. I need to get out of this monkey suit ASAP."

"Yes, please. It reeks of Anita's questionable perfume."

"Jealous much?"

"No more than you, Officer Masters."

"Then you should be boiling. I almost told Surgeon Wendy to keep her hands to herself but refrained for the sake of your family."

Dylan gave Finley a gentle push toward the bedroom. "And I'm grateful."

Finley tried to capture her hand, but Dylan danced away. "Would you like something more comfortable? I probably have an old pair of sweats that would work."

Without answering, Dylan followed her to the bedroom. She wanted Finley right now but she also wanted to stretch their evening out as long as possible. Her body screamed for release, while her mind clung to the intimate connection they'd established in the garden. They had agreed on exclusivity, but was it purely sexual or did it mean more? She wanted it to.

Finley retrieved a pair of sweats from the closet and placed them on the foot of the bed. "Try these." Dylan stopped in the doorway and watched Finley shuck off her coat and slide her tie from her neck. With a flick of her wrist, she snapped the tie toward her. "Are you coming in?"

She shook her head and waved her hand. "I'm going to watch you change clothes. Please continue." Something about Finley brought out a brazenness Dylan hadn't experienced with other women. She'd taken charge of their first sexual encounter, and now she wanted an equal playing field. She'd never totally surrendered to anyone, any more than she imagined Finley ever completely gave up control, but Dylan wanted to test both their boundaries.

"O—kay." Finley pulled off her red vest next and placed it on the bed on top of her coat. She bent forward, untied the black Oxfords, and slipped out of them.

Dylan's mouth watered at Finley in bare feet with her open collar revealing a glimpse of skin, but otherwise fully clothed. Her shirt and slacks highlighted the musculature of her body, and Dylan ached to touch her.

"You're enjoying yourself, aren't you?" Finley asked as she slowly unbuttoned her shirt.

"So much."

As the last button came loose, Finley gripped the sides and peeled them back but stopped short of removing the shirt completely. She grinned and reached for the zipper of her slacks.

"Oh my," Dylan breathed. Finley's exposed chest made her knees tremble. Finley was gorgeous naked, but seeing her partially undressed, untouched, and unapologetic revved Dylan up even more.

Finley shimmied out of her tuxedo pants and stood in only a pair of black low-rise briefs and her open shirt. Watching Finley move, actually everything about her, turned Dylan on. She'd have to touch her soon and no longer kidded herself that she could keep from it.

Finley carefully folded the pants over a hanger, added the vest and coat, and hung them in the closet before turning back to Dylan. "If you want to see more, you have to shed something. I feel like I'm losing at strip poker."

"Trust me, you're not losing." Dylan finally moved to Finley, ran her hands inside her shirt and down her sides to the top of her briefs, and pulled their hips together. "You're far from losing." She leaned in and kissed the hollow at Finley's neck before turning around. "Help me out of this?" Finley's warm hands on her bare shoulders brought Dylan up on tiptoes. "Why does your touch feel so damn good? Every. Single. Time."

"Because I have special talents." Finley was so close that her breath raised goose bumps on Dylan's skin. Finley slid the spaghetti straps off Dylan's arms and eased the fabric down her body, following each fold until the dress pooled on the floor at Dylan's feet. Her touch was gentle, unlike her assertive moves on the basketball court earlier, and Dylan craved both equally.

Finley carefully placed Dylan's dress over the back of a chair before kneeling in front of her and lifting her right high-heeled foot onto her leg. "May I?"

"I'd be happy if you stayed right there for a few seconds," Dylan said.

"You like me on my knees?"

"I like your hands on my leg."

"Whatever you want." Finley chuckled and looked down at the straps of Dylan's shoe. "How did you get into these things, and more importantly, how do I get you out of them?"

Dylan rested a hand on Finley's broad shoulders, stirring as the muscle tensed under her touch, and pointed. "There's a buckle at the back. Release it and the rest unwinds easily."

Finley followed her instructions, tossed the shoe to one side, and slid her hands up Dylan's leg. "You're so soft and hot and you're making it hard for me to be a good host. I wanted to redress you, offer you a drink, and make a nice fire before I devoured you."

Dylan gasped as Finley inched her hand slowly to the inside of her thigh. Her left leg wobbled, and she tightened her grip on Finley's shirt, bunching the fabric in her fists. "We…might not… make it."

Finley glanced up with a mischievous grin. "To which part?"

"Any of it." She sucked in a breath when Finley stroked her soaked bikinis. "Oh, God."

"You can't wait until I perform my hosting duties?"

"Finley."

"Yes, Dylan."

"Stop teasing and finish undressing me stat. I'm not a patient woman when I'm in pain." She clawed Finley's shirt off her shoulders and tossed it on the floor, desperate to touch skin.

"You like me on my knees, and I like you begging." Finley slid her hand down Dylan's leg to her foot, placed it gingerly on the floor, reached for the other, and unlaced the straps.

"Fin, please. You can do anything you want, just do it quickly." Her insides coiled into knots and released every time Finley touched her and then withdrew. She'd never been so wild for a woman's touch.

"Not a chance." Finley rose, draping Dylan over her shoulder.

"Careful. You're injured," Dylan said. Finley hardly seemed to struggle under the added weight, and Dylan loved the view down Finley's sleek back to her tight ass. When they reached the side of the bed, Finley grabbed the bedspread with her free hand and yanked it and the pillows to the floor with one pull before lowering Dylan onto the sheet.

Finley's gaze held hers as she shimmied out of her briefs and stood naked in front of her, exposed and waiting. The gesture ripped at Dylan's heart. "I want to make love to you in my bed, slowly. If you have any reservations, please…tell me now."

Finley's voice quivered at the end. Had she also registered the reference to making love instead of having sex? Or was she simply feeling as needy as Dylan? Finley's courage didn't end at work, but now was not the time to question what it meant. "No reservations."

Finley eased onto the bed, removed Dylan's black bikinis and lacy bra, and then sat back on her feet. "You are so beautiful."

"And how many women have you said that to, Officer Masters?"

"Some, but never one in this bed."

Dylan raised up on her elbows. "You've had sex here before."

"Only with you. I never associated this place with any kind of happiness until you came along. You're different, Dylan. Something about you calls to me, and it's not just your body, which is superb. I can't explain it. I'm no good with words."

"Your words are perfect." Dylan stroked Finley's face, kissed her lightly, and lay back again. No one had ever looked at her the way Finley did—worshiping—teasing her cheeks and lips, caressing her breasts, skimming over her torso, lusting for her sex, and refusing to rush. She felt shy under the intensity of Finley's gaze, but it was an invisible touch that brought heat and desire and she couldn't look away.

Finley wrapped Dylan's legs around her waist, pulling her closer between Dylan's thighs. She draped her body over Dylan's and caressed her cheek, stared into her eyes, and said, "I'm going to kiss you now, Dylan."

Their lips met lightly at first, almost tentatively, but almost immediately, the gentle press of Finley's mouth turned hungry, and Dylan answered with equal vigor. She couldn't get enough of the hot moisture of Finley's mouth, her sweet taste, or the probing of her tongue. She opened and responded greedily, pulling for breath but unwilling to stop. "Yes, Fin."

Finley nibbled her way down Dylan's neck to her breasts, cupping one in each hand. "Perfect. They were made for me." She licked each nipple, and Dylan felt them swell, pucker, and ache. "I love how your eyes grow wide and your pupils dilate when I touch you. And my God, how you smell when you're turned on."

Finley's words fed Dylan's desire, and she needed more contact. She gripped Finley's hips and tried to rub against her. "Do you always talk this much during sex?"

"Not usually. Guess you bring out something in me." Finley backed her hips away from Dylan. "Slow down."

"I can't. The sex talk is working…and you're on top of me." She squeezed Finley's ass. "I need you."

"And how would you like me?" Finley kissed beneath Dylan's breasts and continued down her body to the crest of her pubic mound.

Dylan bucked at the sight of Finley so close to her aching center. "I like your strap-on. You *really* know how to use it."

"Maybe, if you're really good, I'll finish you with that, but first things first. I promised a slow burn, and that's exactly what we're having, Ms. Carlyle."

"You're killing me, Fin."

Finley rose on her knees and slowly circled Dylan's clit with her index finger, and Dylan arched to meet her. "Ohhh, yes. I like that too." Her touch was magic. Dylan wouldn't last long.

"Your whole body just turned pink." Finley eased a finger toward her opening but suddenly returned her attention to the clit. "You must've liked that a lot."

"Yessss," Dylan hissed and reached to keep Finley's hand in place, but she pulled back.

"Patience."

"I lost it...about two strokes ago. Please, Fin." She licked her dry lips and swallowed against the heat burning her body, but the only moisture she felt was between her legs. She stared into Finley's blue eyes and saw her passion reflected there. She wanted this as much as Dylan, but she wanted it to be perfect, and Dylan just wanted it now. "Touch me, damn it."

Finley slowly eased a finger inside her and continued to circle her clit with her thumb. "Like this?"

"*Just* like that." Dylan rose to accommodate her, and Finley slid a pillow under her hips. "A little faster." She captured Finley's wrist and increased the pace, demonstrating exactly what she wanted.

"I love watching you, Dylan." Finley matched her pace for several seconds, but when Dylan released her wrist, Finley slowed again. "I want to make this last all night."

"And I want to come. We can take it slow later," Dylan pleaded, her voice sounded needy but she didn't care. Right now, all she felt was need and the pleasurable way Finley touched her, bringing them together again and again.

Without answering, Finley pumped faster, her gaze never leaving Dylan's. "Whatever you want." She kept the pace until Dylan clutched the bedsheet on either side of her.

"Yessss. I'm getting close." But Finley pulled out suddenly. "Noooo. Don't stop." Before Dylan could catch her breath and figure out what was happening, Finley slid into her with the strap-on, and Dylan cried out in ecstasy. "Ohhhhh, yes. Faster." She clenched her eyes shut and stars burst behind her eyelids. Finley filled her and teased her clit in perfect sync while Dylan clawed at her back and thighs. She heard herself scream but couldn't stop. She tensed as shivers exploded inside her and then collapsed as the energy drained from her in wave after wave of orgasm.

A few strokes later, Finley finished, withdrew and tossed the strap-on to the side before staring down at her. "Are you okay?"

"Great but don't...talk." Dylan pulled for breath, enjoying the aftershocks of her climax and the expert way Finley had teased and tormented her in perfect proportions.

Finley stretched out beside Dylan and hugged her tightly. "I love you, Dylan."

Dylan stilled as Finley's words scorched through her sowing hope and fear. She never imagined Finley Masters would say the L word first or at all. Their short journey had been swift and intense, and she'd known early that her feelings for Finley were special. She loved Finley too but couldn't admit it. She wouldn't spend her life waiting for another visit from the police chaplain. She pretended she hadn't heard, giving Finley a chance to recant. "What did you say?"

"I'm in love with you."

The second time produced the same result. She leaned back to look Finley in the eyes and saw sincerity along with a touch of nervousness. "Dude, you can't just say that after sex. The 'I Love You' statement deserves its own space, not wedged between orgasms." She tried for levity, but Finley didn't even grin.

"You probably don't feel the same, and I apologize for blurting. It just came out."

"It's called post-orgasmic euphoria, and I promise not to hold you to it." Dylan tried for humor again though her gut screamed for honesty.

"I don't think so. Being with Anita tonight and seeing you with Wendy made me realize I don't want to be with anyone else and I don't want you to be either. Selfish I know. Probably too soon, but I feel what I feel. No one is more surprised than I am."

Watching Anita touch Finley tonight hadn't made Dylan's highlight reel either. She'd questioned then if her feelings for Finley went deeper than just a sex partner. The answer seemed obvious now, but she struggled to say the words.

"I think we have something different, Dylan, and I'd like to find out if it's real." She stroked Dylan's cheek and brought her head back to her chest. "You don't have to say anything, and if you want to leave, I'll understand."

Dylan curled against Finley again and pressed her ear to Finley's chest. Her heart beat rapidly and her breaths came quickly. She was just as nervous and confused as Dylan, but she'd had the courage to admit her feelings. Dylan couldn't reciprocate. The last thing she wanted was to hurt Finley, but the long-term consequences of saying those three words terrified her.

"Do you want to leave?" Finley asked.

Dylan stroked Finley's face and rested her hand between her breasts. "No, you gorgeous woman, I don't want to leave. I want to rewind before things got heavy and enjoy you for the rest of the night. Can we do that or have I spoiled it?" It broke her heart not to return the gift Finley had given her, though she felt the same. The words just wouldn't come.

"Sure," Finley said, but her tone lacked conviction. "After all, I'm famous for my sexual prowess and stamina. I can't risk my reputation by refusing a willing woman, can I?"

Dylan flinched at Finley's return to her cavalier, cocky persona but recognized it as a defense against the pain she'd inflicted. She clung to Finley, sexual desire giving way to the need for closeness and intimacy, both of which she'd just destroyed. "I'm sorry, Fin."

CHAPTER TWENTY-TWO

Dylan stood beside Finley's bed and watched her sleep. She was gorgeous, vital, and exciting when awake, and a portrait of vulnerability and innocence when sleeping. She was everything Dylan wanted and one very important thing she didn't. Why couldn't she tell Finley that she loved her last night? Every time they'd made love again, she'd wanted to yell the words, but her fear was stronger.

"Sorry I couldn't keep my promise, love," she whispered.

She dressed in the sweats Finley had left for her and tucked her crumpled dress under her arm, pulling up the Uber app as she walked toward the living room. While she waited, she scribbled Finley another note. Leaving her like this felt familiar, but today it also felt wrong.

When the Uber driver dropped her off at the employee entrance of the hospital, she checked her watch. She had enough time to check on G-ma before her shift started, so she sprinted to the locker room to change into her scrubs. If she could concentrate on work today, it would be a miracle. Finley's words replayed on a constant loop, and every time Dylan felt their authenticity and her own cowardice.

She eased G-ma's room door open quietly in case she was still sleeping, but saw her sitting up in bed with her breakfast tray in front of her. "You're up early."

"Makes two of us. How are you, honey?"

"That's supposed to be my question." She pulled up G-ma's chart and read the night nurse's notes. "This says you're bothering the nurses too much and should be released soon."

"Thank the good Lord for that. I considered a jailbreak. Come here." G-ma pushed the overbed tray aside and opened her arms, her right sporting a bright purple cast to match her car. "Tell me about the fundraiser."

"It went really well, but you were terribly missed. Several people asked about you. I think we held up the tradition." Dylan hugged G-ma and lost herself in the unconditional love she always felt in her arms. Tears burned her eyes, and she blinked them back. G-ma was recovering from surgery and didn't need to be burdened with her problems.

"What's wrong, honey?" The room door opened and a nurse started to come in. "Not now." The nurse faltered, and G-ma shooed her. "I mean it. Go away. Immediately."

Dylan laughed. "Seriously? No wonder they want to get rid of you. Have you been this uncooperative since you got here?"

"Never mind about that. I know my girls, and you're struggling." She patted a spot beside her like she'd done in her old four-poster bed when Dylan was a child. "Hop up here and unload. And like a newspaper friend of mine says, don't bury the lede."

There was no arguing with G-ma when she set her mind to something, especially if it involved her family. Dylan settled on the side of the bed and started to talk, but the words caught in her throat and the tears returned.

"Oh, honey, whatever it is, it's going to be fine. Trust your old granny."

Dylan wiped her tears on her shirtsleeve and let loose. "Finley told me she loves me." She met G-ma's gaze, hoping for an intervention, but she wasn't getting off that easily.

"And?"

"I didn't say it back." She glanced around the room and finally focused on the window overlooking the parking lot.

"Because you don't love her." It wasn't a question.

"*No.*" The strength and volume of her response surprised Dylan. "I mean I do love her, or I'm pretty sure I do." G-ma grinned, and Dylan play punched her leg. "Nice trick to make me admit my feelings."

"So, you do love her. What's the problem?" G-ma covered Dylan's hand where it rested on the bed and gave it an encouraging squeeze.

"You know why, G-ma. I can't even put my father's badge on display in my home because it's too painful to look at. I don't know how you and Mama lived with the fear of losing your husbands every day they went to work. Kerstin and Emory seem to manage the uncertainty too, but I'm not that strong."

"Dylan, look at me." She stared into G-ma's brown eyes that somehow managed to see into her depths. "You love women. You chose a career different from the rest of your family. You heal injuries and sickness and fight off death. You tell family and friends their loved ones have passed. All that takes courage, so don't tell me you're not strong enough to love someone."

"But I don't risk my life, and I'm not sure I can love someone who does."

"Who's to say which gift is greater, giving a life or saving one? In the end, it's probably just semantics. Doctors and police officers understand the challenge of doing their jobs." She leaned forward and kissed Dylan's forehead. "You already love Finley. You only need to ask yourself two questions. Would you love her any more if she wasn't a police officer? And will you be happier with her or without her?"

"You're wrong this time, G-ma. There's another question. Can I live with the uncertainty and fear of losing her forever?"

"There are no guarantees, honey. Any of us could go at any time, totally unrelated to our jobs or how careful we are." She gestured to her head. "This fall could've been the end of me. We don't get to choose, but you know that."

Dylan nodded but couldn't form words. The thought of losing anyone else she loved was too much to imagine.

"Your grandfather and father would be heartbroken that you're letting their deaths limit your life. Love Finley and enjoy every day you do have with her. I'd give anything to be with Garrett again for one more day or even an hour. Love is worth the risk, honey."

Dylan rested her head in G-ma's lap. "I'll think about what you said."

"Don't let that brilliant mind of yours lead you in matters of the heart. You'll live to regret those decisions." She stroked Dylan's hair and nodded toward the door. "Guess I better let Nurse Ratched in before she calls security and has me restrained."

"Good idea. I need to get to work. I love you, G-ma."

"Will you be back for brunch? The family is smuggling in all my favorites."

"It depends on how busy the ER gets this morning." Dylan waved good-bye and stopped at the nurses' station. "I hope she hasn't been too much trouble."

The nurse who'd tried to get into the room answered, "She's a genuine joy who likes to pretend she's in charge."

"Don't we all? Thank you." Dylan caught the down elevator with G-ma's advice still swirling in her mind. Could she just love Finley without always expecting the worst? Could she watch her strap on a gun every day, never knowing if she would return home? But G-ma's last question haunted her most. *Will you be happier with her or without her?*

❖

Finley didn't hear Dylan breathing steadily or feel her warmth next to her in bed. She was gone again, in spite of the promise to wake her before leaving. But this morning, the emptiness felt more permanent, and it was her fault. She'd spoken those three words that either made life seem fantastic or turned everything into an awkward mess. She'd done the latter.

When Dylan hadn't responded in kind, Finley felt her heart might explode and she'd fought back tears. She'd promised herself no one would ever get close enough to devastate her the way her father had been. Sleeping around served her well, insulating her from relationships and involvement, until Dylan Carlyle gave her a dose of her own medicine.

She rolled over and inhaled Dylan's fragrance on the sheets, and another stab of pain doubled her over. Unable to bear the memories of their night, she jumped up like she'd been launched out of bed. She needed to work. In the field, she anticipated danger and prepared for it, but at home, memories appeared like traps laid in the darkness and she had no defense.

As she dressed, three questions hounded her. Was she really in love with Dylan? Or had she blurted the sentiment in a post-orgasmic haze as Dylan suggested? Was she sorry she'd said the words? Yes, probably, and no. She was in love. Nothing else explained why she thought of Dylan constantly, didn't want to be with anyone else, and couldn't imagine a future without her. Which meant she was totally fucked because Dylan didn't feel the same.

Finley grabbed her jeans jacket and went to the kitchen for coffee, but spotted Dylan's note on the bar. She stared at it, trying to summon her courage, before picking it up. Her breath hitched when she saw the red kiss at the bottom of the page.

Fin,

Sorry I broke my promise. We played hard and long, and you were sleeping so peacefully I couldn't wake you. I hope you're okay. Last night was fantastic. You constantly amaze me! If you're not busy for lunch, join me and the family in G-ma's room at the hospital. We're smuggling in some goodies. Would love to see you. And I promise we'll talk about everything later.

D

Finley reread the note twice before folding it and slipping it in her back pocket. She wouldn't be able to hide her feelings from Dylan's family, but she didn't run scared. She'd face whatever Dylan had to say with the courage required of any dangerous situation. Besides, she still needed to go to the hospital. Josh Spencer had woken from his coma three days ago and would probably be released to jail soon. If one last conversation before he ended up behind bars could help her locate Jeremy, she'd take the shot.

Finley drove to the hospital and took the stairs up. Josh's room was only one floor below G-ma's, so a quick stop on her way out would be easy. She breathed deeply and tried to regulate her heartbeat as she approached G-ma's door. Seeing Dylan again so soon might break her. The uncertainty between them, and the weight of her emotions ping-ponged inside until she felt weak and steadied herself with a hand against the wall. If this was what her father felt, she understood why he'd rather drink himself to death. She'd prefer a bullet to get it over with quickly.

"Take a deep breath. Facing the Carlyles isn't always like facing a firing squad." Bennett placed a hand on Finley's shoulder. "Are you all right? You look a little pale."

If Bennett knew how apropos her firing squad analogy was, she'd probably get a kick out of it, but Finley wasn't in a laughing mood. "Just thinking I should've brought something."

"I can't imagine what else we could possibly need. The room is overflowing as it is, and I just invited the entire floor to whatever's left." She nudged Finley toward the door. "Let's go."

Finley nodded and followed Bennett in. The usually sparse room was transformed by dishes of food on overbed trays, extra chairs, and Carlyles. She spotted Dylan immediately, standing on the opposite side of G-ma's bed eating green Jell-O. Their eyes met, and Finley couldn't help laughing. "Seriously? Green Jell-O?"

"That's what I said," G-ma answered. "Welcome, Finley. Give me a hug." She stretched her arms wide, and Finley obliged. G-ma hugged her and whispered, "Be patient with our girl. She'll come around." G-ma winked, and Finley felt the pressure in her chest ease. "Eat. We have to get rid of the evidence."

"As if the entire floor can't smell those ribs and that sweet potato casserole," Simon said.

Finley worked her way around the room greeting everyone, barely able to keep from running straight to Dylan. Her energy drew Finley like a magnetic beacon. If she needed confirmation that she was in love, the warmth and excitement she felt when Dylan was close provided it. "Hi."

"Hi, yourself," Dylan said. "I wasn't sure you'd come."

"I'm no coward." She placed her hand in the small of Dylan's back and leaned close enough to plant a quick kiss on her cheek.

"You certainly aren't." Dylan's chestnut-brown eyes turned dark chocolate as she looked at her, and heat crawled up Finley's neck.

"Stop looking at me like that," she whispered.

"I'd be happy to just eat you for lunch." Dylan dropped her arm behind Finley's back and cupped her ass. "Think we could sneak out unnoticed?"

"What did you have in mind?"

"On-call room?" Dylan asked with a mischievous wiggle of her eyebrows.

"Been there, done that, bad outcome."

Dylan squeezed her ass harder. "But I have a key."

"Care to share what you two are whispering about over there?" Mama asked. "On second thought, the look on your faces says I probably don't want to know."

Finley started to offer a defense, but Dylan's phone pinged with an unusual tone.

Dylan glanced at the screen, and her mischievous expression turned grim. "I have to go."

"Is everything all right?" Bennett asked.

"Evacuation, fourth floor. Armed gunman. We're in lockdown." Dylan stopped at the door. "Everybody stay here until I give you the all-clear." Bennett and Jazz moved toward her. "No," Dylan said holding her hand out. "This is my turf. Our security is trained for these type things."

"And we're not?" Jazz asked incredulously.

"I didn't mean it like that and you know it. I don't have time to argue. If you have to do something, coordinate with our security chief." She made eye contact with Finley. "Don't rush in like a bunch of cowboys. Please."

The door closed behind Dylan, and Finley started after her, but Bennett blocked her path. "She's right. We can't barge in without knowing hospital protocol. Jazz, contact the security chief, tell him our position, and offer our assistance. I'll inform Communications and the chief and get SRT rolling. Fin—"

"I have to protect Dylan. I love her." The words flowed without hesitation or editing.

Bennett stared at her for several seconds as if Finley's announcement stunned her. "And we don't?"

"Spencer is on that floor, and his brother is probably with him." Finley tried to go around Bennett, but she didn't budge. "Get out of my way, Ben. I don't want to hurt you."

"Do you want to hurt Dylan?"

Finley felt like she'd been gut punched. "What the hell are you talking about?"

"Dylan's first responsibility is evacuating the patients on the floor. She's smart enough not to go near that room, so she's in no immediate danger, unless you make her a target. Let her do her job with the evacuation, and we'll do ours containing and managing the threat. We have to do this by the numbers, Fin."

Finley released a long breath and sagged against the door. It went against everything inside her to let Dylan go out there unprotected, but Bennett had a point, and she was thinking more clearly than Finley right now. "Then give me something to do."

CHAPTER TWENTY-THREE

Dylan took the stairs two at a time and opened the door on the fourth floor to chaos. Nurses wheeled moaning patients toward the elevators, while aides herded ambulatory patients toward the stairway exits. She spotted Holly and ran toward her. "Why are you up here?"

"Just visiting when all hell broke loose."

"What's the situation and how can I help?" Dylan asked.

"Room 412, armed gunman. The shooter from Fairview Station and his brother, who was being released to jail today. One of them shot the officer on duty and dragged him into the room as a hostage. The officer got a shot off as well and may have injured the shooter. Unconfirmed. We've almost cleared the floor. Help me double-check the rooms. You take left. I've got right."

They started their search, and Dylan swept the rooms on her side except the one where the suspects were. She paused briefly outside the door, and heard someone groaning in pain. She continued to the end of the hall. "Clear," she called to Holly.

"Same." They met at the nurses' station again. "Security should be here by now, but considering what they're paid, I'm not sure I'd hurry either."

"My entire family is one floor up, so the cavalry will be here shortly."

"Now what?" Holly asked.

"We should leave, but someone in that room needs medical attention," Dylan said.

"Are you crazy? I'm not going anywhere near that room, and I'm very fond of you, so I'm not letting you go either. Besides, I'd have the entire Carlyle clan hunting me down if anything happened to you, not to mention my own guilt."

"There's a police officer in there too, Holly. I can't just walk away. And if the shooter is hurt, I might be able to establish rapport with him while I treat his injuries. If I can talk him out, it would beat the police storming the room or getting into a shoot-out." She met Holly's gaze, pleading for her support.

"This really isn't a good idea, Dylan."

"I could use you outside the door to hand me supplies." She gave Holly a quick hug. "I know I'm asking a lot. Please?"

"If you insist on doing this, of course. I'm not leaving you alone up here."

Dylan grabbed a trauma kit and tucked it under her arm. "Let's go." She had a flash of the station shooting and running through gunfire to help the injured. She brushed the thought aside and focused on what she had to do as she slid along the wall toward the door with Holly close behind. "I'm going to call your phone. Leave the line open so you can hear what's going on and what supplies I need." She tapped on the door.

"Get the fuck back or I'll blow you away," an angry voice called.

"I'm a doctor. Is anyone injured? I can help."

"How many cops out there?"

"None. I swear." Dylan held her breath. Her family was going to kill her for rushing into another dangerous situation, if one of these guys didn't do it first. But it was her job, just like it was theirs...and Finley's.

"Okay, just you," the guy answered. "Come in slow with your hands up."

Dylan eased the door open with her foot, her hands out in front of her, and almost gasped aloud when she looked around. The floor was covered in blood. A young police officer lay curled into the fetal position behind the door, and the shooter stood beside the patient's bed cradling his left arm with blood dripping from his fingers. "I have a trauma kit to treat the injuries." She stooped beside the officer and snapped on a pair of gloves.

"Me first, bitch."

"This man is unconscious. If he dies, that's murder. Let me at least check his vitals and send him to the ER. Your injury isn't life threatening."

The patient, who Dylan recognized as Josh Spencer, said, "Let her do it, Jeremy. Who needs a cop hostage when we've got a pretty doctor."

Jeremy nodded, and Dylan checked the officer. His pulse was thin and thready. GSW to the abdomen with no exit site. He'd already lost consciousness from blood loss, which combined with shock could kill him without immediate attention. "Holly?"

"Yeah."

"I'm going to slide the officer out to you. Get him to ER stat. I'll be fine until you get back."

"I won't leave you."

"He's going to die if he doesn't get treatment now." She slid the officer in his own blood feetfirst outside, and Holly took over. When the door closed and Dylan was alone with the suspects, she felt nauseous. What had she been thinking? She wasn't a hero. Her hands trembled but she took a deep breath, focused on what needed to be done, and moved toward the other injured man. "Now, Jeremy, is that right?" He nodded, and she stepped in front of him. "Have a seat and let me check your arm. I'm Dylan."

Jeremy sat in a chair facing the door beside his brother's bed with a gun resting on his thigh. "Don't try anything stupid or I *will* shoot you."

"Understood. Can you take your shirt off?" While Jeremy unbuttoned and removed his shirt, Dylan listened for any movement outside the room to indicate help was on the way but heard nothing. The entire floor was eerily quiet. She prayed her family and Finley were still safe one floor up and that the lunch they'd shared wouldn't be their last.

She should've told Finley she loved her last night. Facing the possibility of death brought everything into focus. Papa used to say the only time anyone could be courageous was when he was afraid, and she'd failed miserably with Finley. Hindsight sucked, especially when she might not get to correct her mistake. Finley would never know how much Dylan loved her.

Jeremy pressed the barrel of his gun against Dylan's temple. "Are you going to fix me up or what?"

"Y…yes, but that's not helping me concentrate."

"Jeremy, give the woman a chance," Josh said.

Dylan opened an alcohol swab and cleaned the site. The injury looked superficial, and she didn't detect any bone or muscle damage, but only an X-ray would be definitive. "You got lucky. The bullet went straight through. I'll clean and bandage the wound."

"And give me something for pain. It hurts like a motherfucker."

Dylan glanced at Josh while she cleaned and dressed Jeremy's wound. "So, what's the plan here, guys? You can't just hold a floor of the hospital hostage forever."

"I'm taking my brother out of here," Jeremy said.

"And how is that going to work? The place is probably swarming with cops by now."

Jeremy chuckled. "You were nice enough to provide us with a get-away-free card, unlike that cop who couldn't walk. Nobody is going to shoot us as long as we have you."

Dylan shivered. She hadn't thought her plan through, but being taken hostage wasn't part of it. "And what about your daughter, Josh?"

"What about Shea?" he asked.

"I saw her yesterday. We played basketball. She's a pretty good little athlete. I understand she runs track too."

Josh grinned. "Yeah, she gets her speed from me."

"Do you want her to grow up thinking her father's a murderer?" Josh's expression softened, but she felt Jeremy's arm tense as she secured his dressing with tape.

"Are the people she's living with good folks?" Josh asked.

"They are, and she likes them too," Dylan said, "but seeing you shot and shooting at other people has been hard on her."

"But I didn't shoot anybody," Josh said. "I didn't even fire my shotgun."

"Shut up, Josh. She's fucking with your head." Jeremy pointed the weapon at Dylan again. "Keep your mouth shut or I'll kill you right now."

No one spoke while Dylan picked up the wrappers she'd dropped on the floor and tossed them in the trash. She'd outlived her usefulness as a doctor, and now she was just a hostage. She wrapped her arms around her waist and looked from Josh to Jeremy. "So?"

Jeremy directed her against the wall opposite the bed and down on the floor.

"We can't do this, Jeremy," Josh said.

"What are you talking about? We hold all the cards, bro."

"We can't get out of here. She's right. The place is surrounded by now. I know I'm going to do time, but I want to see my daughter again someday."

"And what do I have to look forward to?" Jeremy asked.

❖

Finley paced the room next door to where the suspects held Dylan hostage, checking the monitor with each pass. The Special Response Team had run a snake scope through the air duct to give them eyes on the situation, but only Bennett could hear what was going on. She'd gotten Holly's cell and was listening through earphones and relaying to other officers on the scene.

"What happened to Dylan being smart enough not to go in the room?" she asked Bennett.

"She's a Carlyle, duty-bound and stubborn."

Every time Jeremy Spencer pointed his gun at Dylan, Finley lunged toward the door separating the two rooms. "If he does that shit one more time," she whispered, "I'm going to kill him with my bare hands. We have to get in there. Now." She'd never felt so useless or emotionally raw.

Bennett grabbed her shoulder. "Stop pacing. These walls are paper thin. Dylan is making progress with Josh. She might be able to talk them out."

"And if she can't?"

"The entire floor is locked down, and SRT is in position to take the shot if necessary. In the meantime, if you want to stay in this room, calm the fuck down. That's my sister in there."

Finley nodded. "And the woman I love. I just feel helpless."

"I'm with you, but we have to give her time. She knows what she's doing and the risks involved. She wouldn't have gone in there without a plan. Now sit, be quiet and patient."

Bennett keyed her mike and gave Jazz, who was in position with SRT in the parking deck nearby, a sitrep before returning her attention to the monitor.

Finley clasped her hands between her knees and thought about the things she wanted to do with Dylan, all the things she never imagined before they met—dating for real, living together, marriage eventually, and sharing a home. If she lost Dylan today, it would break her, as she'd seen her father broken, and rip the emotional heart out of the Carlyle family. If Dylan escaped unhurt, Finley vowed to give her all the time she needed to figure out her feelings. Any amount of uncertainty and waiting beat losing her completely.

The minutes dragged as she stared at the monitor and watched Dylan sitting on the floor, her back against the wall, and her lips moving silently as she tried to convince the Spencer brothers to surrender. All she saw was the woman she loved in danger. How long could this go on? Her adrenaline levels had ebbed and flowed since the lockdown started, and her muscles ached with the need to do something. The department's preference for negotiation over force took time, but Finley's primal, protectiveness demanded action.

"I've got movement in the room," Bennett whispered.

Finley was on her feet beside her in seconds. "What's happening?"

Bennett unplugged the earphones so Finley could hear the exchange between Dylan and the brothers.

"You're making the right decision, Jeremy. I'll ask that Josh be allowed to see Shea one last time, but you have to put down your weapon or the officers will consider you a threat."

"Yeah, yeah, I get it," Jeremy said. *"I'm only doing this so my baby brother can have a chance at a better life someday."* He lowered his head in resignation. *"And he really didn't shoot anybody that day. He had a shotgun. I had the .357. Maybe that'll help with his sentence."*

"It certainly won't hurt," Dylan said.

"What do I do now?" Jeremy asked.

"Leave your gun on the bed, raise your hands, and both of you follow me."

"They're coming out," Bennett said.

CHAPTER TWENTY-FOUR

F inley didn't wait to hear anything else. All her anxiety and frustration vanished with a jolt of adrenaline. She sprinted into the hallway, and as soon as Dylan exited the room, Finley stepped between her and the brothers and tackled Jeremy to the floor. She cocked her fist to hit him, but Dylan grabbed her arm.

"Don't."

"But he—"

"It's over, Fin."

Finley leaned close to Jeremy's face and whispered, "You're a very lucky man." She stood and gave him a quick kick in the ribs before handing him over to the patrol officers who'd secured the floor.

"Take them to Fairview Station," Bennett said. "The detective working the case will want to interview them both."

The adrenaline drained from Finley, and her knees wobbled as she grabbed Dylan and hugged her close. "Are you okay? Please tell me he didn't hurt you."

"I'm fine, and I'm very glad to see you."

Finley stroked Dylan's face. "I was afraid I'd never—"

"Shush, you're not getting rid of me that easily. You said you loved me, and I'm pretty sure that means you'll be seeing a lot of me." Dylan kissed her, and Finley felt the familiar heat flood her body and build between them.

"What are you saying?" Finley looked down to meet Dylan's eyes.

"I'm saying we need to talk as soon as this mess is cleared up." She stepped back and glanced around. "Has anyone seen Holly?"

Bennett hugged Dylan next and handed her a mobile. "Not recently. She loaned me her phone so we could hear what was going on in the room. I think she's still in the ER with the injured officer. I can find her if you'd like."

Dylan shook her head. "I should get back down there. I'm on duty."

Finley checked her watch. "Your shift ended an hour ago while you were negotiating with criminals. I can't believe you did that. We need to have a serious discussion about your job description. Can we get out of here now, please?"

"Not yet," Bennett said. "Dylan needs to give a statement at the station."

"Can't that wait? She's been through enough for one day. I'll make sure she's there first thing in the morning, boss."

"Both of you stop trying to manage me," Dylan said. "I'm going to the ER to check on the officer and Holly." She kissed Bennett on the cheek. "I'll be at Fairview Station in the morning…or sometime before noon." She grabbed Finley's hand and tugged. "And you're coming with me."

"Aye aye, ma'am," Finley said, grinning at Bennett over her shoulder and following Dylan onto the elevator. When the doors closed, she mashed the emergency stop button, pulled Dylan against her, and poured all her emotions into their kiss. When they finally broke, she said, "I love you more than my life, Dylan, so please don't ever scare me like that again."

Dylan hugged Finley tighter and met her gaze. "I'm so in love with you, Fin, but I was afraid to admit it."

"And now?"

"I've been too focused on losing you like I did my father, but after what I've just put you through by doing my job, I realize there are no guarantees in life. I want to enjoy whatever time we have together. It won't be easy for either of us because I'll nag you all the time about being safe, and you'll have to constantly reassure me that you're being careful." She rested her cheek against Finley's chest. "Want to give it a try?"

"More than anything," Finley answered.

"Good, because while I was a hostage in that room, I thought about all the things I wanted to do with you."

"Funny, I was doing the same thing next door. What do you want, Dylan?"

"I want a real date like our *Hamilton* night, complete with dinner and a movie, followed by sex, lots of it. I'd like to spend more time in your home, if that's not too difficult for you. It's cozy, intimate, and just large enough not to be claustrophobic and still gives us each some personal space."

"You really have thought about this, haven't you?"

Dylan nodded.

"Does that mean you'll actually be in bed with me when I wake up for once?"

"Definitely. I feel very comfortable there. It would make a great family home…eventually."

Finley kissed her lightly. "Family home, huh? What about Carlyleville in Fisher Park?"

"I've broken from family tradition before. Your place is perfect, less than ten minutes from the family but far enough for some separation. What do you think?"

"I think I better call my Realtor and turn down the offer she has." Finley kissed Dylan again, pressing her against the wall and fitting into the curves of her body to seal their agreement. When they started sinking to the floor, she finally stopped. "We better turn this elevator back on before the fire department comes to check it out."

Dylan's breathing was ragged and her eyes glassy. She licked her lips and reached for Finley again, tucking her leg between Finley's. "Can I have another one of those first?"

"One more like that and we'll be on the floor."

"That's the idea." She captured Finley's hand and slid it inside the elastic of her scrubs. "I'm not sure I can wait much longer. You know what adrenaline does to the body, Officer."

"No fair." Finley moaned and jerked her hand from Dylan's pants as the elevator door swished open. "Check in with Holly and meet me at the exit. Stat."

Dylan kissed her forefinger and touched it to the scar on Finley's chin. "Roger that."

EPILOGUE

A year later

Dylan brushed the front of her cream-colored wedding dress and glanced at Emory in the mirror as she swept an escaped sprig of hair back into place. "I really appreciate this, Em. Without you and Kerstin, I'd be a nervous wreck. You survived G-ma and Mama playing wedding planners, so there's hope for me."

"They just want everything to be perfect."

"I know and I love them for it, but I thought a ceremony at home would be easy, quiet, and quick, just the way Finley and I wanted it." Dylan nodded toward G-ma, Mama, Stephanie, and Kerstin staring at them lovingly. "They're looking at me like I'm something to eat. Please tell me they're not planning another surprise like that mortifying bridal shower last week."

"I think you're clear." Emory grinned. "Finley survived the bachelor party night before last, and no one got arrested."

"After I threatened Ben's life if she hired a stripper."

"Yeah," Emory said, "Kerstin and I supported your decision. Ben tried to pull the same trick for Jazz's party last year, but I put my foot down. Hell hath no fury like a redhead pissed."

"You fit into our enmeshed and dysfunctional family perfectly, Emory. I'm so glad Jazz found you and had the good sense to marry you."

"Amen," Mama said, moving her quartet closer. "And very soon, all my children will be happily married at last."

"Bring on the babies," G-ma added with a sweeping hand gesture that resembled a lasso move.

Dylan gave each of them a hug. "Thank you all for everything you've done to make this day possible. I love you and I'm going to miss you and the cottage." She looked around the almost empty space, most of her belongings now at Finley's. She pulled open a dresser drawer, removed a tissue wrapped item, and handed it to Mama. "I wanted Papa to be with us today, so I didn't pack this."

Mama unwrapped the Lucite encased badge and clutched it to her chest. "Oh, Dylan, this is precious. He'd be so proud and happy."

"Just make sure I get it back before we leave. It's going on our mantel." She kissed her mother and started toward the door. "And now I have to see Fin." She heard a chorus of objections but ignored them and cut across the backyard toward the big house holding the tail of her dress to keep it from dragging on the ground. A ring of flowers surrounded the seating area of cushioned chairs for fifty hand-chosen guests, and a small platform of pavers with an arched canopy marked the spot where she'd make Finley hers in less than an hour. Her heartbeat trebled.

"Where's Fin?" Dylan asked as she burst through the sunroom door. Simon, Bennett, Jazz, and a couple of police officers and firefighters were huddled together at the kitchen counter near several bottles of chilling champagne. The ring bearers, Riley and Ryan, gorgeous in matching white suits, were on the settee tossing the ring pillows back and forth like footballs.

"You can't see her before the ceremony. It's bad luck," Jazz said.

Dylan shook her head. "Seriously? That's old heterosexual bullshit. Where is she?"

Bennett pointed to the ceiling. "She and Hank, her best man, are in your old bedroom upstairs dealing with a case of nerves, I think."

Dylan scrunched her face. "It better just be nerves and not an escape attempt."

"She wouldn't dare," Bennett said, reaching for the weapon that usually rested at her side.

Dylan started up the stairs and called back. "Don't open that champagne until after the ceremony." She stopped at the bedroom door, listened to the quiet mumbling from inside, and then knocked. "Bride, incoming."

Hank opened the door. "She's all yours. If you ever need any tips on how to handle her, let me know. I've had a few years of experience."

"No fair ganging up on me," Finley said.

Hank kissed Dylan on the cheek and met her gaze for several seconds. "You two are great together. All the best."

She waited until Hank's steps sounded at the bottom of the stairs before going to the woman she loved. Finley stood at one of the windows overlooking the backyard in tuxedo pants and a white shirt with a cummerbund that matched Dylan's dress. Every time she saw Finley, her breath hitched and her temperature spiked. A few short months ago, marriage, especially to a cop, had seemed impossible, but love proved more powerful than she'd imagined. Now, life without Finley didn't make sense.

"Second thoughts, Detective?"

Finley turned toward her and froze. "My God, you get more beautiful every time I see you." She stepped closer, smiled her brilliant smile, and lightly kissed Dylan. "No second thoughts. You?"

"Not a single one. Are you sure about this, Fin?"

"Totally. I was thinking about my dad," Finley said. She reached inside the collar of her shirt and pulled out the thick silver chain with the dog-tag medallion. "He would've loved you."

Dylan cupped the locket in her palm and traced the intricate carving of a tree on the front with her finger. "Tree of life? Family tree?" When Finley shrugged, Dylan flipped it open to the laser photo of a man and woman staring tenderly at each other. "I think they loved each other very much."

"At one time." Finley broke eye contact and stared out the window again.

"That's not going to be us, Finley Masters. If I thought what I felt for you was temporary, I wouldn't be in this costume heading down the aisle in front of family and friends to pledge my undying love. This is for keeps. And if you don't feel the same, now is the time to bounce, not when I'm standing at the altar with a bouquet in my hands like a schmuck."

Finley turned suddenly and grabbed Dylan around the waist. "I've never been more certain of anything in my life. When Spencer was holding you hostage and I thought I could lose you forever, I finally understood the devastation my father felt. Even knowing how painful losing you could be, I still choose to love you. And I promise I'll always come back to you...or die trying."

Dylan stroked Finley's face. "The dying part doesn't work for me. Always coming back, totally. Agreed?"

"Agreed." Finley finally smiled again. "Can I kiss you now?"

"Yes, please." Dylan stretched on her toes, met Finley's lips, and immediately lost herself in the moment. She automatically guided them backward toward the bed.

"Oh, no, you don't," Finley said, pulling away. "We have a wedding to attend."

"There's no rule that says we can't have sex again before we're married." Dylan slid her hand down Finley's chest and cupped her crotch. "I *really* want you right now, Finley."

"Stop."

"Please," Dylan crooned. "Couldn't we just rub one out to take the edge off? It could be hours before we're alone again."

Finley pushed her hand away. "Dylan Carlyle, you're incorrigible."

"One of the many reasons you love me?"

"Absolutely. Now, let's get married." Finley threaded her fingers through Dylan's and led her toward the stairs. "We have two weeks off, and I plan for us to be naked the entire time."

Dylan clenched Finley's arm and stopped halfway down the staircase. "The house?"

"Officially transferred into both our names. I hope you'll like College Hills as much as I do now, and your family isn't too disappointed we won't be in Fisher Park."

"They're good with it, and I'm thrilled for a bit of distance since we'll probably be naked for the rest of our lives. Did you pick up provisions? Food? Wine? Beer?"

"Fully stocked. Relax. I've taken care of everything we need for our hibernation, but I promise you a proper honeymoon after the Spencer trial, somewhere exotic."

"Anywhere with you is exotic enough for me," Dylan said. She grabbed Finley's ass, squeezed, and continued down the stairs.

"Bride, front and center," Bennett called. "Let's get this show on the road."

When Dylan and Finley reached the bottom of the stairs, the Carlyle family gathered in a horseshoe formation, the other guests already seated in the garden. "Family." Dylan pulled Finley with her into the center, and everyone closed around them in a group hug.

"I like being part of your family," Finley said.

"Good thing." G-ma laughed. "Because you're about to be stuck with us for the rest of your life."

"Perfect," Finley said.

As Dylan was whisked into the living room by Mama, Stephanie, and Kerstin, she called back to Finley. "See you at the altar."

"Don't keep me waiting. I might have a heart attack."

Dylan blew her a kiss. "Fortunately, I'm a doctor."

About the Author

A thirty-year veteran of a midsized police department, VK Powell was a police officer by necessity and a writer by desire. Her career spanned numerous positions including beat officer, homicide detective, vice/narcotics lieutenant, captain, and assistant chief of police. Now retired, she devotes her time to writing, traveling, and volunteering.

VK can be reached on Facebook at @vk.powell.12 and Twitter @VKPowell.

Books Available from Bold Strokes Books

Date Night by Raven Sky. Quinn and Riley are celebrating their one-year anniversary. Such an important milestone is bound to result in some extraordinary sexual adventures, but precisely how extraordinary is up to you, dear reader. (978-1-63555-655-1)

Face Off by PJ Trebelhorn. Hockey player Savannah Wells rarely spends more than a night with any one woman, but when photographer Madison Scott buys the house next door, she's forced to rethink what she expects out of life. (978-1-63555-480-9)

Hot Ice by Aurora Rey, Elle Spencer, Erin Zak. Can falling in love melt the hearts of the iciest ice queens? Join Aurora Rey, Elle Spencer, and Erin Zak to find out! (978-1-63555-513-4)

Line of Duty by VK Powell. Dr. Dylan Carlyle's professional and personal life is turned upside down when a tragic event at Fairview Station pits her against ambitious, handsome police officer Finley Masters. (978-1-63555-486-1)

London Undone by Nan Higgins. London Craft reinvents her life after reading a childhood letter to her future self and in doing so finds the love she truly wants. (978-1-63555-562-2)

Lunar Eclipse by Gun Brooke. Moon De Cruz lives alone on an uninhabited planet after being shipwrecked in space. Her life changes forever when Captain Beaux Lestarion's arrival threatens the planet and Moon's freedom. (978-1-63555-460-1)

One Small Step by Michelle Binfield. Iris and Cam discover the meaning of taking chances and following your heart, even if it means getting hurt. (978-1-63555-596-7)

Shadows of a Dream by Nicole Disney. Rainn has the talent to take her rock band all the way, but falling in love is a powerful distraction, and her new girlfriend's meth addiction might just take them both down. (978-1-63555-598-1)

Someone to Love by Jenny Frame. When Davina Trent is given an unexpected family, can she let nanny Wendy Darling teach her to open her heart to the children and to Wendy? (978-1-63555-468-7)

Tinsel by Kris Bryant. Did a sweet kitten show up to help Jessica Raymond and Taylor Mitchell find each other? Or is the holiday spirit to blame for their special connection? (978-1-63555-641-4)

Uncharted by Robyn Nyx. As Rayne Marcellus and Chase Stinsen track the legendary Golden Trinity, they must learn to put their differences aside and depend on one another to survive. (978-1-63555-325-3)

Where We Are by Annie McDonald. Can two women discover a way to walk on the same path together and discover the gift of staying in one spot, in time, in space, and in love? (978-1-63555-581-3)

A Moment in Time by Lisa Moreau. A longstanding family feud separates two women who unexpectedly fall in love at an antique clock shop in a small Louisiana town. (978-1-63555-419-9)

Aspen in Moonlight by Kelly Wacker. When art historian Melissa Warren meets Sula Johansen, director of a local bear conservancy, she discovers that love can come in unexpected and unusual forms. (978-1-63555-470-0)

Back to September by Melissa Brayden. Small bookshop owner Hannah Shepard and famous romance novelist Parker Bristow maneuver the landscape of their two very different worlds to find out if love can win out in the end. (978-1-63555-576-9)

Changing Course by Brey Willows. When the woman of your dreams falls from the sky, you'd better be ready to catch her. (978-1-63555-335-2)

Cost of Honor by Radclyffe. First Daughter Blair Powell and Homeland Security Director Cameron Roberts face adversity when their enemies stop at nothing to prevent President Andrew Powell's reelection. (978-1-63555-582-0)

Fearless by Tina Michele. Determined to overcome her debilitating fear through exposure therapy, Laura Carter all but fails before she's even begun until dolphin trainer Jillian Marshall dedicates herself to helping Laura defeat the nightmares of her past. (978-1-63555-495-3)

Not Dead Enough by J.M. Redmann. A woman who may or may not be dead drags Micky Knight into a messy con game. (978-1-63555-543-1)

Not Since You by Fiona Riley. When Charlotte boards her honeymoon cruise single and comes face-to-face with Lexi, the high school love she left behind, she questions every decision she has ever made. (978-1-63555-474-8)

Not Your Average Love Spell by Barbara Ann Wright. Four women struggle with who to love and who to hate while fighting to rid a kingdom of an evil invading force. (978-1-63555-327-7)

Tennessee Whiskey by Donna K. Ford. Dane Foster wants to put her life on pause and ask for a redo, a chance for something that matters. Emma Reynolds is that chance. (978-1-63555-556-1)

30 Dates in 30 Days by Elle Spencer. A busy lawyer tries to find love the fast way—thirty dates in thirty days. (978-1-63555-498-4)

Finding Sky by Cass Sellars. Skylar Addison's search for a career intersects with her new boss's search for butterflies, but Skylar can't forgive Jess's intrusion into her life. (978-1-63555-521-9)

Hammers, Strings, and Beautiful Things by Morgan Lee Miller. While on tour with the biggest pop star in the world, rising musician Blair Bennett falls in love for the first time while coping with loss and depression. (978-1-63555-538-7)

Heart of a Killer by Yolanda Wallace. Contract killer Santana Masters's only interest is her next assignment—until a chance meeting with a beautiful stranger tempts her to change her ways. (978-1-63555-547-9)

Leading the Witness by Carsen Taite. When defense attorney Catherine Landauer reluctantly becomes the key witness in prosecutor Starr Rio's latest criminal trial, their hearts, careers, and lives may be at risk. (978-1-63555-512-7)

No Experience Required by Kimberly Cooper Griffin. Izzy Treadway has resigned herself to a life without romance because of her bipolar illness but wonders what she's gotten herself into when she agrees to write a book about love. (978-1-63555-561-5)

One Walk in Winter by Georgia Beers. Olivia Santini and Hayley Boyd Markham might be rivals at work, but they discover that lonely hearts often find company in the most unexpected of places. (978-1-63555-541-7)

The Inn at Netherfield Green by Aurora Rey. Advertising executive Lauren Montgomery and gin distiller Camden Crawley don't agree on anything except saving the Rose & Crown, the old English pub that's brought them together. (978-1-63555-445-8)

Top of Her Game by M. Ullrich. When it comes to life on the field and matters of the heart, losing isn't an option for pro athletes Kenzie Shaw and Sutton Flores. (978-1-63555-500-4)

Vanished by Eden Darry. A storm is coming, and Ellery and Loveday must find the chosen one or humanity won't survive it. (978-1-63555-437-3)

All She Wants by Larkin Rose. Marci Jones and Tessa Dalton get more than they bargained for when their plans for a one-night stand turn into an opportunity for love. (978-1-63555-476-2)

Beautiful Accidents by Erin Zak. Stevie Adams and Bernadette Thompson discover that sometimes the best things in life happen purely by accident. (978-1-63555-497-7)

Before Now by Joy Argento. Can Delany and Jade overcome the betrayal that spans the centuries to reignite a love that can't be broken? (978-1-63555-525-7)

Breathe by Cari Hunter. Paramedic Jemima Pardon's chronic bad luck seems to be improving when she meets police officer Rosie Jones. But they face a battle to survive before they can find love. (978-1-63555-523-3)

Double-Crossed by Ali Vali. Hired thief and killer Reed Gable finds something in her scope that will change her life forever when she gets a contract to end casino accountant Brinley Myers's life. (978-1-63555-302-4)

False Horizons by CJ Birch. Jordan and Ash struggle with different views on the alien agenda and must find their way back to each other before they're swallowed up by a centuries-old war. (978-1-63555-519-6)

Legacy by Charlotte Greene. When five women hike to a remote cabin deep inside a national park, unsettling events suggest that they should have stayed home. (978-1-63555-490-8)

Royal Street Reveillon by Greg Herren. Someone is killing the stars of a reality show, and it's up to Scotty Bradley and the boys to find out who. (978-1-63555-545-5)

Somewhere Along the Way by Kathleen Knowles. When Maxine Cooper moves to San Francisco during the summer of 1981, she learns that wherever you run, you cannot escape yourself. (978-1-63555-383-3)

Blood of the Pack by Jenny Frame. When Alpha of the Scottish pack Kenrick Wulver visits the Wolfgangs, she falls for Zaria Lupa, a wolf on the run. (978-1-63555-431-1)

Cause of Death by Sheri Lewis Wohl. Medical student Vi Akiak and K9 Search and Rescue officer Kate Renard must work together to find a killer before they end up the next targets. In the race for survival, they discover that love may be the biggest risk of all. (978-1-63555-441-0)

Chasing Sunset by Missouri Vaun. Hijinks and mishaps ensue as Iris and Finn set off on a road trip adventure, chasing the sunset, and falling in love along the way. (978-1-63555-454-0)

Double Down by MB Austin. When an unlikely friendship with Spanish pop star Erlea turns deeper, Celeste, in-house physician for the hotel hosting Erlea's show, has a choice to make—run or double down on love. (978-1-63555-423-6)

Party of Three by Sandy Lowe. Three friends are in for a wild night at billionaire heiress Eleanor McGregor's twenty-fifth birthday party. Love, lust, and doing the right thing, even when it hurts, turn the evening into one that will change their lives forever. (978-1-63555-246-1)

Sit. Stay. Love. by Karis Walsh. City girl Alana Brendt and country vet Tegan Evans both know they don't belong together. Only problem is, they're falling in love. (978-1-63555-439-7)

Where the Lies Hide by Renee Roman. As P.I. Camdyn Stark gets closer to solving the case, will her dark secrets and the lies she's buried jeopardize her future with the quietly beautiful Sarah Peters? (978-1-63555-371-0)